Buddha Baby

By Kim Wong Keltner

BUDDHA BABY
THE DIM SUM OF ALL THINGS

Buddha Baby

Kim Wong Keltner

AVON
TRADE

An Imprint of HarperCollinsPublishers

HarperCollins books may be purchased for educational, business, or sales promotional use. For information please write: Special Markets Department, HarperCollins Publishers Inc., 10 East 53rd Street, New York, NY 10022.

FIRST EDITION

Interior text designed by Elizabeth M. Glover

Library of Congress Cataloging-in-Publication Data

Keltner, Kim Wong.
    Buddha baby / by Kim Wong Keltner.—First ed.
        p.   cm.
ISBN-13: 978-0-06-075322-1
ISBN-10: 0-06-075322-6 (alk. paper)
1. Young women—Fiction.   2. Chinese American women—Fiction.
3. Chinese American families—Fiction.   4. Chinatown (San Francisco, Calif.)—
Fiction.   5. San Francisco (Calif.)—Fiction.   I. Title.

PS3611.E48B83   2005
813'.6—dc22   2005002203

05   06   07   08   09   WBC/RRD   10   9   8   7   6   5   4   3   2   1

Acknowledgments

Parents of the Year: Larry and Irene Wong, a.k.a. my parents, are better than chicken soup. They are turkey *jook* for my sleep-deprived soul. It would blow my cover as a cool person to enumerate all the things they do for me on a daily basis, so instead I'll just offer my eternal gratitude to them for never forcing me to go to summer camp.

Best Production Team: Many thanks to Erika Tsang, Pam Spengler-Jaffee, May Chen, and Jamie Beckmann at Harper-Collins. Their professionalism and sparkling personalities make me wish I shared an office with them, but then I suppose we'd be laughing all the time and not getting any work done.

Ace-in-the-hole: My agent, Agnes Birnbaum at Bleecker Street & Associates, is a class act. Having her in my corner helps me sleep at night.

Secret Weapon: Rolf Keltner is the one who bails me out when the sled flips over and the ice weasels are circling. Winner of the Strong Man Competition, he pulls me inside the Tauntaun to keep me warm long enough to get the shelter built.

Best Brothers: Rick and Mark, who've always shown me to keep my eye on the ball, and taught me how to kill someone with my bare hands should the need arise. Incidentally, Mark is a doctor, and assures everyone that no Asian males were harmed in the writing of this book.

Special thanks to: Jennifer Almodova, who deserves many pink cashmere sweaters; Barbra Lewis, who's always got my back; Mabel Maney, a great friend and swell American; and Jill Minkus, whose participation in Catholic hijinks is most definitely noted on the Permanent Record. Belated thanks also to Julie Felner for early copyediting on *The Dim Sum of All Things*.

Right about here is where the orchestra starts playing, but I also want to thank Letitia and Angie Wong for being the best sisters, my cousin, Garren Chew for being my Chinatown expert, Michelle Kim for her brains and beauty, Robert Martin for being my eyes on the street, and Dacher Keltner for inspiration.

And finally, of course, the Buddha statue goes to Lucy.

Buddha Baby

Lindsey Owyang was about to learn a thing or two about Chinese people, Catholic nuns, and taxidermy. She didn't know it yet, but this spring would be a season of unusually warm winds, blasts from the past, and stone-cold foxes. She was just a Chinese-American girl with two part-time jobs, a tendency to daydream, and a penchant for Hello Kitty toys, but as the days grew longer and the beach water slightly warmer, she would find herself prying nettles from her family tree and testing her mettle as she struggled to make her peace with Chinatown & country.

She had been born and bred in San Francisco, raised on Cocoa Puffs and Aaron Spelling productions. As a kid she never wore silk slippers or mandarin-collared pajamas, but rather was more often outfitted in checkerboard Vans and an "I'm With Stupid" T-shirt. Confucian proverbs eluded her, but she was well versed in the spunky aphorisms of great philosophers such as Fonzie and Fred Sanford, whose Nick-at-Nite reruns taught her handy phrases such as "Sit on it, Malph," and "Bring me some ripple, Dummy."

In high school she was more interested in *Tiger Beat* than

tiger balm, but her parents did occasionally attempt to blend Chinese and American cultures together by preparing meals such as *bok choy* with cut-up hot dogs, or macaroni salad with *pai don*, Chinese preserved eggs. When she played Monopoly, she passed Go as she ate *nian goh*, and cranking up the stereo after school, she danced to Bow Wow Wow while she munched on *cha siu bows*.

Her hair was straight and black, and she had a slight build with *chow mein*-noodly limbs. Pale and sun phobic, she was fairer than most white people, but her bridge-deficient nose and single-lidded eyes shaped like sideways teardrops proclaimed to the world that she was a descendant from the Middle Kingdom. China was a place she knew little about, but her face, her coloring, and her name led strangers to assume she knew more about her ancestors' country than she actually did. At any random moment, whether toiling as a retail drone, squeezing her butt into jeans at Old Navy, or ordering a venti mocha frappuccino at Starbucks she might be asked for detailed explanations about Ming emperors, imperial porcelain from Jingdezhen, or the secrets of Yo-Yo Ma's success.

Socially, she had spent her youth dodging the inconvenience of her Asianness, but in the last three of her twenty-eight years she was forced to wake up and smell the *bock-fa* oil. She faced her Chinese identity head-on, like a person in the center of a dodgeball game who eventually got smacked in the face with the big, red rubber ball that was her Chinese self. She was by no means absolutely comfortable with her ethnicity 24-7, but she was on her way. If you looked on a street map of San Francisco you could spot Lindsey where the avenue to nowhere met the cross street of somewhere. She wasn't a complete dope, nor was she burning a path to success like the next Connie Chung.

* * *

Cosmopolitan told her she should be a dynamic, career-climbing, late-for-Pilates, bright, young thing. However, on this particular Saturday night, Lindsey was a mattress-slouching, tube-sock-wearing lazy girl with rug burns.

She had lain down to take a short nap at four, but now it was almost six. Sitting up in bed, she rubbed a prickly swath on the back of one leg, the result of a pillow fight turned ouchy when she'd fallen off the mattress and skidded across the carpet. She pressed the small pink welt with her finger, then pulled the blankets up to get a bit warmer. Wearing only a negligee and a pair of white-and-gold tube socks, she looked like a cross between Jodie Foster in *Taxi Driver* and one of the Bad News Bears.

Except, of course, she was Chinese.

Across the hallway she could hear the sound of an electric razor and running water. She smiled to herself, knowing that the guy who loved her was just a few steps away.

His name was Michael Cartier and he was a white guy. She'd become smitten with him three years ago and interracial hijinks had ensued. But alas, a twist.

Michael had come into Lindsey's life during the *Age of Hoarders*. By her own definition, a *Hoarder of All Things Asian* was a nerdy white guy in beige clothing whose good-guy demeanor camouflaged an insatiable hunger for Asian flesh. Hoarders came in many guises, such as co-workers offering to explain 401k plans or mall trawlers loitering around the Asian food court, and Lindsey had been hyper-vigilant about avoiding them. She knew a Hoarder's appetite was not satisfied by take-out dishes of sweet 'n' sour pork, but rather, he was fixated on the idea of Asian girls themselves as tasty dishes on the city's take-out menu. Lindsey knew that behind a Hoarder's innocuous façade, all he had on his mind was an evening of sweet-and-sour porking.

And into this paranoid world of hers, Michael Cartier had traipsed. She had initially suspected he was a Hoarder, but was surprised to find that not only was he not a pervo-goat in sheep's clothing, but he was, in fact, a Secret Asian Man. He was, as it turned out, one quarter Chinese. His non-whiteness was not readily apparent to the naked eye, and he'd grown up culturally removed from his Asian heritage. But his slice of life was not made completely of Wonder Bread, she'd learned. Blending easily into the Caucasian population, in his thirty years he'd been called lots of names, but not the same ones as Lindsey: chump instead of *chink*, jerk rather than *Jap*, geek but not *gook*. Asians had called him *round-eye*, *straight nose*, *haole*, and *gwei-lo*.

In their two years together, Michael had held her hand as they swam against a tide of cultural differences. And like every couple, they had to work some shit out. At first she was reluctant to show him her world of Chinese customs, organ meats, and odiferous ointments. But as time passed, they stuck together and she discovered there was no mountain of chicken feet too high for them to climb.

Of course, there had been bumps in the road. He once pinned Chinese couplets to the wall with the characters upside down, and on her dad's birthday he served a short-noodled pasta instead of the kind that would have represented long life. In an attempt to speak Cantonese when ordering crab in a restaurant, he once used the wrong intonation for *hai* and ended up asking the waitress for the cracked "pussy" smothered in black bean sauce.

And Lindsey hadn't been perfect either. She was hyper-germ-phobic as only an Asian girl could be, and sometimes drove him nuts with her refusal to touch public doorknobs unless her hand was mummified in swaths of paper towels. In spite of herself, she was superstitious, and when they changed to a new phone number they had to pay extra because she insisted on plenty of eights and refused their neighborhood's exchange of 664 because her dad had told her that in Chinese that number sounded like "roll over and die."

In learning to accept Michael's background, Lindsey eventually got off her multi-culti high horse and opened her mind to the fact that "white" was not really an ethnicity but a general catchphrase that didn't begin to describe the various cultures as proud and distinct as her own. In honor of Michael's Irish side, she reluctantly yet gradually accepted the lowly potato as a culinary staple.

These details aside, she knew that all her Chinese New Year lucky envelopes had done their job. She had hit the loverboy jackpot. Michael wasn't one of those lousy, just-pretending-your-ass-ain't-fat, I'm-throwing-out-this-damn-Anthropologie-catalog kinda guys with a channel-changing finger glued to the TV remote control. Michael Cartier was a you-look-great-with-no-makeup, let-me-hold-your-hair-back-while-you're-sick, should-I-run-out-and-buy-more-toilet-paper kinda dreamboat.

Still lying in bed, Lindsey craned her neck and peered across the hall. She could see him now, innocently scrubbing a bicuspid. Scooting to the far edge of the bed for a closer view of him, she watched him with a blend of admiration and deep affection. But then her relative calm was disrupted when her pulse quickened. She suddenly felt a surge through her blood and sat bolt upright. An urge to protect Michael overcame her, and she was gripped with the feeling that she would instantly kill someone with her bare hands like a trained ninja if they ever tried to hurt him.

It happened sometimes, this protective feeling. She readily admitted it bordered on the psychotic. She loved Michael so intensely, nonsensically, and possessively that sometimes she felt murderous. Not that he was ever in danger, or even defenseless. Nor was she particularly skilled in martial arts. It's just that she loved him so much that she wanted to be the only person privy to his stupid jokes, Christopher Walken impersonations, and retro stash of Bjorn Borg era hosiery.

Yes, it was official. She was twitterpated.

She knew that sounded pathetic, sickeningly cutesy, and *Fatal Attraction*-esque. When she was single, if anyone had ever told her she would fall so hard for a guy that she'd be willing to wear his tube socks, she would have balked. But hey, here she was.

She felt her face get hot as her eyes brimmed suddenly with tears. Looking across the hall once again, she watched Michael as he finished up his various grooming rituals. Overcome by the enormity of their domestic happiness, her tear ducts and sinuses began to feel prickly, and without warning she began to weep. What followed were not big sobs, but almost worse— the kind of crying where there was no sound at all, just hot tears and swollen, puffy eyelids, the kind that would require ice packs and teabags to look like a normal person again.

Michael came in and found her scrunched in the bed's corner, mashing Kleenex into her eye sockets.

"What's wrong?" he said, pulling the blankets up over both of them and wrapping his arm around her.

She didn't know how to explain her feelings. Instead of trying, all she could think to say was, "I forgot to tape *Zoolander*."

He hugged her for a moment, then said, "C'mon, we don't want to be late for your grandmother's party."

About an hour later, Lindsey found herself sitting in her parents' living room, staring at the prominently displayed statue of Buddha atop the television set. No Chinese home was complete without a fat-bellied, porcelain Buddha with children clamoring over his legs and shoulders, clutching his sacred love handles. But wasn't he supposed to be an ascetic who survived on only one grain of rice per day? This porcelain figure looked less like a holy man and more like Re-Run from *What's Happening!* She imagined if there was a pull-cord on the back of the statue's head, rather than, "*Om Mani Padme Hum,*" he'd say, "W'as happenin', Raj!"

Then he'd breakdance.

Lindsey's older brother, Kevin, suddenly emerged from one of the bedrooms, came down the hall and wandered over. He looked at the figurine and said, "I hate Buddhas. They scare me." Meandering away, he left Lindsey alone in the living room.

As she waited for Michael to come up from the garage, where he was replacing a washer on a sink at the behest of her mother, she slouched in the La-Z-Boy recliner. Fully sunken into the fake leather, she wondered what to expect this evening, not having spent time with her Owyang side of the family in quite some time. Her dad, Earl, was retiring and quiet like her grandparents, Yeh Yeh and Yun Yun, but her Auntie Geraldine and Uncle Elmore could always be counted on for entertainment.

Tonight being the occasion of Yun Yun's eighty-eighth birthday party, there was sure to be a certain amount of drama as relatives she hadn't seen for years would be coming to pay respect, offer lucky money, and devour all their *arare* crackers. Also, Yun Yun could always be depended on to spice up any occasion with a handful of well-timed, persnickety barbs, and Lindsey wondered which innocent bystanders would be stung this evening.

The first guest to arrive was Auntie Geraldine. Notorious for stealing food at parties, she scanned the room as soon as Lindsey opened the door, as if deducing which handy-sized hors d'oeuvres might fit conveniently inside her Louis Vuitton purse.

When Lindsey was younger, her aunt had looked like a Chinese Elizabeth Taylor circa 1973, and she hadn't been as obvious in her thievery. At family get-togethers she wore chiffony dresses and head scarves and took home regular portions of leftovers like everyone else. When Lindsey's parents hosted summer barbecues and roast beef dinners during the holidays, Auntie Geraldine used to politely ask, "Are you sure you have enough?" before taking small portions on a Chinet paper plate covered in foil.

Then one Fourth of July a whole platter of fried chicken disappeared, and shortly thereafter, on Labor Day, a clove-spiked ham evaporated, leaving just an ironstone platter with a puddle of rapidly coagulating gravy. Lindsey had quietly noticed a trail of crushed pineapple bits that led from the tablecloth to Auntie Geraldine's Le Sportsac.

Over the ensuing years Auntie Geraldine became quite adept at creating diversions to hide her culinary stockpiling. She would breeze into parties covered in jade and gold baubles so exquisite that everyone was fooled by her dazzle camouflage. They oohed and aahed at her perfectly manicured fingernails, like Barbra Streisand's at the end of *The Mirror Has Two Faces*, and were further distracted by the pamphlets she distributed about the joys of selling Amway products. Shortly thereafter, slabs of roast beef would disappear and rivulets of brown mushroom sauce could be seen dripping from her bell-shaped sleeves.

Sometimes, when an evening was well under way, Auntie Geraldine would go a-missing. After having spent the evening sauntering back and forth between her Buick LeSabre and the party, incrementally stashing plates of filet mignon, turkey legs, and five-layer dip, she would save the most difficult items for last, perhaps trying to figure out how to safely and inconspicuously insert a five-layer cake under her muumuu. Lindsey watched everything from underneath the dining-room table.

The most daring of Auntie Geraldine's capers had been the Christmas when she crammed a pyramid of shish kebabs complete with skewers into her Mary Kay cosmetics travel case. She apparently thought no one was looking, and with her eyes twinkling with holiday mischief, was tiptoeing away like the Grinch stealing the Whoville Christmas tree when Lindsey suddenly woke up from a nap and asked,

"Where are you going with our dinner?"

With big eyes she waited for an explanation just like Cindy-Lou Who, or rather, Cindy-Liu Hu.

"Go back to sleep, dear," Auntie Geraldine said, and then stole into the December night.

With all the different things Auntie Geraldine had made disappear, Lindsey had figured the woman missed her calling as the best magician this side of David Copperfield. As she chuckled at the memories, she got up to replenish the celery sticks and Ranch dip. Restocking the baby carrots, she wondered why Uncle Ran, Auntie Geraldine's husband, wasn't here tonight. Since it had been years since she had last seen Uncle Ran at any family gathering, she figured that maybe he had developed agoraphobia, or maybe he was just buried in his living room under a mountain of hoarded party snacks.

Hmm. Uncle Ran was a recluse and Auntie Geraldine stole vats of Swedish meatballs. Lindsey wondered if all marriages dissolved beneath the weight of a couple's idiosyncrasies. Rumor was that when Uncle Ran and Auntie Geraldine first got together, they were great party hosts who danced the limbo and made killer mai tais. Then they got hitched, made the beast with two backs, and the next thing they knew there were a couple of *leen yoong bows* in the oven. Over the course of several years they went from serving Brazil nuts and rum in coconuts to buying Beechnut baby food and Nutter Butters. And now, they were just plain nuts. Was marriage really a journey that required an emergency stash of candied yams inside your dented sedan's glove compartment?

Just then, Lindsey heard a voice call out to her, "Don't be a jive turkey, give your uncle a hug!"

Uncle Elmore had arrived. He walked over and grabbed Lindsey's hand, then spun her around and dipped her. He hoisted her up, and she gagged in a cloud of Brut by Fabergé.

Uncle Elmore was so thoroughly absorbed in his disco persona from 1975 that even now, thirty years later, he still danced the Latin Hustle and bemoaned the disappearance of fern bars. His personality was a blend of Boz Scaggs's aging cool and Bruce Lee's mystique, with a drop of Maurice White from Earth, Wind and Fire added for good measure. Tonight Lindsey noticed his perfectly blow-dried hair and his poly-blend shirt, which was unbuttoned one notch lower than what was currently considered respectable. Completely tan since the seventies, this evening he was sporting the "Crockett-Tubbs" look from *Miami Vice*.

"Dy-no-mite!" he exclaimed, to Lindsey's amusement. He added, "I might be getting older, but my niece still knows I'm ba-aad!"

Uncle Elmore was bad, all right. He wasn't technically divorced from his wife, Dee, but he haunted places like T.G.I. Friday's and asked girls half his age what their astrological sign was. At weddings, he always got embarrassingly drunk and either splashed wine on somebody or tried to make out with them, even if they were his blood relative.

Uncle Elmore often boasted of being mistaken for various movie stars such as George Hamilton and John Travolta, regardless of the fact that they weren't even Chinese. Although he was obviously deluded and his moral fiber was clearly made of macramé, he was generally accepted by the family as just an odd bird who marched to a different beat, a beat that invariably had something to do with the Bump or the Funky Chicken.

He took a seat on the vinyl sofa and clicked through the channels with the remote control. To no one in particular, he said, "Why did they take *Magnum P.I.* off the air? That dude was ba-aad!" Then, to Lindsey he said, "Hey, bring me a Tsingtao, would ya?"

By then, her cousin Belinda had wandered in. "Sorry about dat dad of mines," she said. Although she was capable of speaking normal English, Belinda had absorbed the specific patois of the San Francisco public school system. Her sentences often included purposely mispronounced words delivered with haughty machisma sprinkled with I'm-not-black-but-I-magically-speak Ebonics.

Belinda was a tough little dyke. But much to her chagrin, Uncle Elmore constantly criticized her for not wearing more makeup and tube tops. Last Halloween she dressed as Rambo, which left Uncle Elmore with quite a conundrum. Naturally he thought Stallone was ba-aad in every celluloid incarnation, from *The Lords of Flatbush* to *Rocky V* to *Judge Dredd*, but he still would have preferred his teenage daughter dressed up as Crissy from *Three's Company*, teetering on cork-heeled Candies instead of wearing a camouflage-patterned muscle-T and hoisting a plastic Uzi against a well-placed, bulging tube sock.

"You girls hurry on up with those drinks, now," Uncle Elmore said, eliciting a scowl from Belinda. As he turned back to the television, she flipped him the finger.

Lindsey patted her cousin's bicep. "It's okay," she said, then went into the kitchen to fetch her uncle's drink.

About half an hour later Lindsey and Michael were helping her mom extract an obstinate Jell-O concoction from a Tupperware mold. Lindsey heard a commotion in the living room, which meant that Yun Yun must have arrived. After running out to greet her, Lindsey could tell that she just had her hair coiffed in Chinatown because it was sprayed like a big, black, shellacked ball of cotton candy, making her look like a cartoon astronaut wearing a bubble helmet.

Yun Yun's face had the soft and puckered quality of an apricot that had been left to ripen too long on a windowsill. As Lindsey leaned in to kiss her cheek, her grandmother swatted her away like a gnat.

With great fanfare Lindsey's dad went to the hall closet and brought out a fancy lei made of eighty-eight precisely folded dollar bills interspersed with red and gold paper. He gently placed the garland around Yun Yun's neck, careful not to muss her hair.

"Wow!" everyone said, gathering around.

"These dollar bills are too crisp," Yun Yun immediately complained. "They're jabbing me!"

Confounded, Lindsey furrowed her brow. Didn't Chinese people love crisp, brand new money, fresh from the bank? Of course! Everyone preferred that their money hadn't been previously passed from the Chinatown branch of Bank of America to the palms of *bock gweis* and then back again into *tong yun* hands. Crisp money was de rigueur when folded into red envelopes at New Year's, Red Egg and Ginger parties, and on birthdays. To complain about such a thing was nonsensical. And these bills on the lei were extra special. They came straight from the Bank of Canton and had been folded like origami at a special shop. The bills were so new that Lindsey could smell the ink from where she was standing. How ludicrous that her grandmother was complaining about money being too crisp.

Other aunts, uncles, cousins, and extended family eventually arrived, and as they all chatted away, Lindsey took particular notice of her grandfather, Yeh Yeh, who silently shuffled in and parked himself in the corner. Lindsey had once overheard her dad say Yeh Yeh looked great for his ninety years, and that he looked the same as he did as a young man. While this was true, it was only because Yeh Yeh had always looked old. Lindsey once saw a picture of him as a younger man, and even when he was forty he looked eighty. He always wore the same dusty overcoat and woolen cap, his downtrodden, unassuming demeanor remaining unchanged over the years. Tonight he quietly blended into the furniture, and sat fused to his chair like a shlumpy Rodin sculpture.

Lindsey also noticed that Auntie Geraldine's daughter, Sharon, had arrived with her husband, Hanley. After Lindsey took their coats they made their way to two folding chairs a safe distance from Uncle Elmore. The three sat in awkward silence for a while and watched *Saved By The Bell*. The canned laughter was interrupted only by the periodic sound of fingers sifting through Chex Party Mix.

Lindsey hovered between the kitchen and the hallway, secretly eyeing her cousin. Sharon was exactly what Lindsey never wanted to be: one of those Chinese girls who never spoke up, never offered an opinion, or complained about anything. When they were kids, both Lindsey and Sharon had dreamed of being writers and artists, but these days Sharon was an accountant for a mortgage firm. She'd always loved reading books like *Pride and Prejudice* and *Wuthering Heights*, and had planned to write her own Heathcliff-humping romance someday. Lindsey wondered what had squelched her cousin's creative inclinations. Had she been sucked into the invisible, Chinese math vortex? Lindsey imagined that such a thing existed, a cultural force that made most Chinese people more interested in making money than art. Or maybe Sharon was simply more practical than Lindsey, who at present was juggling two low-paying jobs, one as a step-and-fetch-it gopher at her former grammar school, and another as a museum gift-shop clerk.

After having quit *Vegan Warrior*, Lindsey had been out of work for two months before landing her job at St. Maude's. She'd taken the second job working evenings at the museum to pay off the credit cards she'd abused while unemployed. Even though he'd offered, she didn't want Michael to have to pay for everything, and plus, she was deluded just enough to think that her noncommittal career choices qualified her lifestyle as "artistic."

Knowingly swimming against the tide of Chinese expectation, Lindsey wanted a little more fun out of life than just practical dollars and sense. She knew that if she was ever to be considered a good Chinese person, she should be scrimping for a rainy day, but she frittered away her earnings on CDs, DVDs, three-dollar chai lattés, and sparkly Hello Kitty lip glosses that required constant replenishing due to the fact that she missplaced them at a rate of two per week. Somewhere deep in her psyche was the firm belief that 24-hour entertainment was her right as an American, and she had the debt to prove it.

She sometimes thought about how so many Chinese families had pulled themselves up from poverty by sheer ingenuity and thrift, building laundry, restaurant, or real-estate empires from practically nothing. They went from sweatshop workers to engineers and surgeons in one generation, but for Lindsey and third-generation spawn like her, their forefathers' struggles seemed like ancient history. To them, opportunity had nothing to do with political or religious freedom, but was more about downloading music to their iPods and potentially getting a chance to star on a reality TV show. They thought little of spending thirty-two dollars for four ounces of peppermint foot cream or $450 to see Madonna. A sweatshop to them meant Bikram yoga, and Chinese Laundry was a brand of shoes. Jimmy Choo was more of a household name than Hu Jintao, and "Asian Rut" was just a Morrissey song.

But still, something in Lindsey's bones told her she should be saving money. After all, Chinese people had an ancient tradition of financial know-how. Back when the Phoenicians were busy dyeing swaths of drapery purple, the Chinese had already invented the abacus. And while the Greeks were busy perfecting the gay bathhouse, the Chinese were pinching pennies instead of each other's bare, Adonis-like rumps.

Speaking of money, the few times Yun Yun had deigned to speak to Lindsey in recent months, it was simply to tell her, "Make money now, play later." Lindsey had nodded obediently, but in her heart she didn't think that having a little fun before the onset of cataracts, arthritis, and support hose was too much to ask. As she looked over at Yun Yun now, she saw that her grandmother was meticulously trimming Kleenex squares in half with a pocket-sized pair of scissors, then daintily refolding and stashing the tissues up her sleeve for later use.

It occurred to Lindsey that Yun Yun had probably never had a day of frivolity in her life. She wouldn't know fun if it hit her in the head like an airborne whoopee cushion. As Lindsey stared for a moment longer, she nearly felt sorry for her grandmother until she saw Yun Yun glance Sharon's way with a sneer. She muttered, "Useless, good for nothing!" Lindsey took in the whole scene, watching her cousin visibly shrink as if a small pillow in her soul had been deflated. Lindsey sighed. Yun Yun wasn't the kind of grandmother who inspired spontaneous hugs.

Truth be told, Lindsey and Yun Yun had never gotten along well. Her other grandma, Pau Pau, had been playful and indulgent when Lindsey was small, but Yun Yun had been exactly the opposite, cranky every Christmas, Arbor Day, Groundhog

Day, and holiday in between. Lindsey had tried to reach out to Yun Yun in the past, but had always struck out. Every time she asked her grandmother how she was, Yun Yun just stared at her blankly as if she hadn't heard anyone talking to her. Even though Yun Yun could speak passable English, she usually spoke Chinese around her grandchildren to passive-aggressively punish them all for not learning Chinese.

Yun Yun used to scold Lindsey's parents incessantly for her rowdy and unladylike behavior. From the adults' Chinese conversation, Lindsey always recognized a few choice words like "lazy," "misbehaved," and "no respect." Yun Yun was critical of practically everything about her—if her hair was messy, if she took second helpings of any meal, or if she showed her teeth when she laughed. All the while, Yun Yun would gesture and point at Lindsey as if she were a flea-bitten chihuahua in the corner. Lindsey came to think of her grandmother as the antithesis of everything she wanted to be, which back then happened to be a combination of Malibu Barbie and Evel Knievel.

These days, Yun Yun irritated Lindsey most by pretending that Michael didn't exist. She never said hello to him, even though she saw him at least once a month at family dinners. Nor did she ever thank him when he routinely re-treaded the back legs of her walker with fresh tennis balls. Yun Yun acted as if romance and its entanglements were a waste of time, and Lindsey had once even overheard her say to her dad, "Why get to know flavor of the month? He probably dump her next week."

Perhaps Yun Yun's own marriage had been arranged, or life hadn't worked out the way she wanted. Lindsey wasn't sure what her grandmother's problem was. All she knew was that it was difficult to be around such a bitter person, especially one who routinely spat at the television. Yun Yun was addicted to watching programs about bachelors and millionaires, but all the while she spewed comments like, "Stupid oaf, but lots money," or "Big tits leave no room for brain."

Lindsey speculated that her grandmother, like other viewers, enjoyed the vicarious thrill of watching bitchy phonies having the last shreds of their dignity ripped from them like a flimsy bikini. But Yun Yun acted like all love was doomed, and seemed particularly unable to accept that Lindsey had found happiness somewhere between a Guandong village matchmaker and *ElimiDATE*. This lack of matriarchal approval silently gnawed away at the tightrope wire upon which Lindsey's self-esteem was precariously balanced.

Speaking of relationships, Lindsey was now quietly observing Sharon and Hanley. Maybe Sharon thought her husband as dashing as Mr. Darcy, but to Lindsey, Hanley was a cross between Tony Soprano and a porcupine, sitting there with his prickly hair, Matrixed-out leather coat, and poofy white sneakers that looked like small minivans. She recalled how Sharon hated sports, but hadn't protested when Hanley took her to the Handball Hall of Fame in Tucson, Arizona, for their honeymoon. What would be next, Big 5 Sporting Goods at the local strip mall for their anniversary? Lindsey wondered if that's what marriage did to a person: made a girl happy to live in a ticky-tacky suburb where early-bird dinners at the Hungry Hunter and John Madden football commentaries passed for a night on the town.

More guests trickled in. As Lindsey shuffled around the room replenishing the hors d'oeuvres, she eavesdropped as her dad, Auntie Geraldine, and Uncle Elmore squabbled about whose turn it was to clean Yun Yun and Yeh Yeh's house.

"I have a bad back," Geraldine complained.

Elmore laughed in her face. "Then lose some weight!"

"How long has it been since either of you went over there?" Lindsey's dad asked.

There was a long pause as they looked at one another. Lindsey just happened to glance up from a tray of cocktail weenies when she overheard her dad say, "You two are good for nothing. Lindsey and I will take over this month and we'll see what we can do."

Elmore and Geraldine went their separate ways. Lindsey, already trying to formulate an excuse in her mind, caught up with her dad.

"I know, I know," he said before she could protest. He offered, "Tell you what, I'll give you a hundred bucks if you go over there this week, okay?"

Lindsey thought about her credit cards. "Okay," she said, then went off to find Michael.

An hour or so later they were all feasting on Mrs. Owyang's cornucopia of 1950s Betty Crocker delights such as chicken and cornflake hash and her famous Imitation Crabmeat Puffs. Everyone complimented Lindsey's mother on her cooking, except, of course, Yun Yun, who sprinkled the meal with contradictory complaints such as "too salty," "not enough *may tsing*," "not fluffy," and "too airy." People pretended not to hear Yun Yun's gripes, but at the far end of the table, Lindsey watched her grandmother intently.

Throughout dinner, Lindsey overheard the birthday girl fire a few shots at unsuspecting civilians. Addressing Kevin, Yun Yun said, "Why you have no girlfriend? I guess no girl want to go out such short man." A few moments later she said to Sharon, "Why you marry such *fay-jei*? Fat and lazy, just like you." To Lindsey's mother she said, "Turkey dry. You want me choke?"

To distract everyone from the awkward silence, Uncle Elmore signaled for Lindsey and Belinda to bring out the dessert. The two retreated to the kitchen where they found a sheet cake from Chinatown, the kind with the whipped butter-cream roses and translucent gel icing. They lit the candles with Belinda's Zippo, then carried out the unwieldy sheet cake, each grabbing a side as it sagged under its own weight. Everyone looked up and started to clap when they saw the candlelit confection, and began to sing "Happy Birthday."

Across the table, Yun Yun was unsmiling with a sour expression carved into her face as if she was actually pondering where all the terrible noise was coming from. A few stragglers, including Lindsey, joined in on the last lines, but by the end of the song Yun Yun seemed more pouty than delighted. In a halfhearted attempt, she succeeded in blowing out only three candles, while managing to evenly distribute a mist of spit all over the strawberry shortcake, simultaneously spraying melted candle wax across the entire surface of the cake.

Michael went into the kitchen to help Mrs. Owyang retrieve utensils, paper plates, and ice cream, while Lindsey used the edge of a plastic knife to scrape the wax and spittle off the cake's top layer. Slicing through the wobbly sponge filling, Lindsey looked up when Michael returned and asked him, "What ice cream flavors are there?"

"Hmm," he said, examining the tubs. "Tin Roof Sundae, and something called Hopscotch . . . which looks like a vanilla and orange sherbet checkerboard."

"I think my parents shop at the time-warp Safeway," she replied as she continued to portion out thirty squares of cake while Michael scooped. When they were done, Lindsey watched Yun Yun dab whipped cream onto her tongue with a plastic fork.

"Tastes bad," Yun Yun said.

"It's good!" said Lindsey's mom.

Yun Yun tossed away the plastic utensil and began an inspection of her presents.

"Who wrap this? So much tape . . . who want such thing with so much tape?"

When Lindsey was done serving the dessert, she put aside her strained feelings toward her grandmother and tried to think of something to honor the old woman on her special day. Lindsey said to her dad, "Hey, let's bring out old photos of Yun Yun when she was younger. Do we have any?"

Yun Yun often faked deafness for her own purposes, but this time her ears perked up across the room.

"*Chuy*! No pictures!"

She jabbed an arthritic finger in the air, startling Lindsey with her ferocity. Lindsey tried to think of something to say, but Yun Yun didn't give her a chance to speak.

"Always up to something," she said. "Why you try to ruin my birthday, I'll never know."

Wok This Way

Someone should have warned Lindsey that under no circumstances should a grown woman ever agree to work at her old grammar school. She'd spent kindergarten through eighth grade at St. Maude's, and why she should want to go back was anyone's guess. Maybe she felt compelled to perform penance for all her venial sins. Maybe she was downright insane. Maybe she really needed $15.50 an hour plus health benefits.

Arriving at St. Maude's through a side entrance, Lindsey could hear the raucous sounds of children playing tag in the building's far quadrant. As she walked through the cast-iron gate, a small Chinese girl in a plaid uniform ran past her and burst through the double doors that led to the yard, her high-pitched squeal quickly merging with the other children's voices, which carried the frantic pitch of small-brained animals who could almost smell June, freedom, and impossibly fun days filled with petty crime and candy.

Lindsey walked through the foyer and down the gunmetal gray corridor, and then stopped for a moment in front of a gold gilt frame that held her favorite painting of Mary. She gazed at the sapphire blue cape draped across the Virgin's weary, feminine shoulders, and remembered how Sister Constance had once stated with authority that blue was Mary's favorite color. Although such a statement was ultimately unprovable, Lindsey could see now that the old nun was onto something. Mary did look great in blue. Admiring the portrait of the saint, Lindsey noted that the Mother of God was definitely a "winter"—fabulous in jewel-toned clothing and potentially dismal in autumnal earth tones, which would have simply washed out that luminous, holy skin.

This painting of Mary had been good to Lindsey when she was a student. The saint had kept Lindsey's secrets and conveyed compassion in Lindsey's times of need. She may have been just a Chinese kid in Buster Browns and a ricebowl haircut, but disturbing signs of evil had lurked in her non-baptized, pagan baby heart.

The threat of mayhem, idolatry, and sloth had begun in kindergarten. On the first day of school, Sister Boniface, the classroom teacher, had searched all the Chinese kids' pockets for Buddhist trinkets such as beads, necklaces, prayer cards or anything else with the graven image of any non-Jesus entity. Not realizing that Buddhists were simply not as doodad-oriented as Catholics, the nun was disappointed when she found nothing but lint and plum wafer crumbs in their pockets. Determined to single out the unsaved, she suggested a quarantine for all the Chinese kids in the back corner of the classroom, but Sister Constance, the sixth-grade teacher and principal, countered that perhaps they should all be seated in the front row because their slanted eyes most likely made it difficult for them to see the chalkboard. Eventually, a think tank of nuns and priests decided to evenly distribute the Chinese kids among the Irish and Italian kids to better dilute their heathenness.

Thus thwarted, Sister Boniface didn't give up. She proceeded to single out the wee Chinese kindergarteners with threats of physical violence. For instance, any time a student whose last name began with an "O" and an apostrophe misbehaved, the nun was lenient. Furthermore, she ignored the shenanigans of any redhead. However, whenever any kid whose ancestors hailed from east of Palermo ever so much as uttered a peep out of turn, she let loose her inner rage-a-holic and threatened to "box their ears" or hang them upside down from the exposed ceiling pipes. When agitated, Sister Boniface's throat closed up and she sounded like the mayor of the Emerald City on helium. But instead of enthusiastically encouraging the children to follow a yellow brick road, she stared down at them, and slowly enunciated, "I . . . will . . . crush . . . you."

Rumor had it that Sister Boniface had come from Dublin after having planned all her life to join the Irish Republican Army. Instead, she decided to teach five-year-olds. Why was this diminutive nun at St. Maude's choking them by their collars and disciplining them with her Vulcan death grip instead of lobbing Molotov cocktails into Paddy's Pub?

Maybe it was because she was only four foot eight. She was barely taller than some of the children, and perhaps being that short made it tricky for her to balance a machine gun on her hip. So rather than planting bombs beneath Citroëns, Sister Boniface educated children with jaunty little tales of hell and its environs. She caused deep feelings of dread in Lindsey who, even at age five, was very worried because she had never been dunked in a pool of holy water as a baby. Nor was she one of the majority of kids undergoing training to receive First Communion. Having been uncleansed of her infant sins and now facing the certainty of a waferless life, Lindsey knew that the best she could hope for, destiny-wise, would be a place among the Ethiopian babies in what sounded like a very crowded purgatory. She secretly hoped her soul had a slim chance of recovery if the old Italian ladies in church lit enough votives. Through the prayers of the devout, perhaps a rising tide of pity would lift all sinners in their rickety-ass dinghies. But Lindsey didn't count on it. Deep down inside, she knew she was doomed.

Around midyear, after having just mastered the alphabet, Lindsey seriously began to suspect that she was the Antichrist. The previous Sunday afternoon, she had watched *Rosemary's Baby* on television and discovered that she and the fruit of Satan's loins shared the same birthday, June 28. Roman Polanski had a hidden message for her: she was the child of the devil, and her true mother was a jackal.

Her fate, hell, was the end of the line. Hell smelled like newly tarred roofs and charbroiled rats. Up in heaven there would be parties, but St. Joseph would be too busy refilling his champagne flute with Veuve Clicquot to offer Lindsey a drop of water on her bloated, canker-sore-ridden excuse for a tongue.

Being non-Catholic and Chinese, *and* born on the same date as Mia Farrow's devil-child, Lindsey knew deep down inside that no matter how many good deeds she performed, she would end up in the Amityville Red Room with history's villains: Judas Iscariot, Adolf Hitler, and Yosemite Sam. God was a take-no-prisoners kinda guy. After all, look at the way he put the smackdown on Adam and Eve for sampling a measly apple.

Either one or both of her parents were obviously in cahoots with Satan. So with nowhere else to turn, Lindsey prayed to Mary. She implored the Virgin Mother that no one would ask her birthdate, and she begged for a grace period so she could figure out what to do. How much time would she need? Well, at least a few months, or until her real parents, Gomez and Morticia Addams, came to fetch her in their tricked-out hearse.

She prayed for weeks, but several Sundays later, another afternoon movie scared the bejeezus out of her. This time it was *The Exorcist*. She wondered why her parents let her watch such a movie, but then figured they were tipping her off about her evil core. Before bedtime she began checking her abdomen for raised welts that spelled "Help me," and if she had to pee in the middle of the night, she turned on all the lights and avoided mirrors so as not to see her own reflection, which was sure to resemble a guacamole-encrusted Linda Blair.

Lindsey suspected she would only have a few short years before her number came up. She had heard that puberty was a time when bodies changed and mysterious things called "hormones" kicked in. No doubt that's when her true evil self would begin to show. It made sense. Birds molted and developed adult feathers. Deer dropped their antlers, caterpillars became butterflies, and Lindsey would sprout horns and a pointy goatee. She begged Mary to make everything okay.

Soon after, she saw *The Omen* and began to check her scalp daily for the telltale 666. For weeks she ran home from school and sat on the bathroom countertop with her stocking feet in the sink. Using her mother's handheld compact and the medicine cabinet mirror, she checked the back of her head, crown, and behind her ears for the mark of the beast. She also searched for the nubby horns she dreaded would protrude any day now, just like the back molars inside her mouth. She found nothing on her entire head except one single chin hair that convinced her that a goatee was beginning to sprout. To delay the inevitable, she plucked it with tweezers.

Back at school, Sister Constance made another confident proclamation about the preferences of Mary. She decreed that the Memorare and the Act of Contrition were the Virgin Mother's favorite prayers. Lindsey wondered if inside the convent there was a blue telephone that directly linked communications between the nuns and Mary. If the mayor of Gotham could give Batman a jingle any ol' time on the Bat Phone, was it really that far-fetched that there might be a Nun Phone with which Sister Constance could ring up the Mother of God at all hours and ask her personal trivia? When she wasn't pondering such possibilities, Lindsey devoted many diligent hours to the memorization and recitation of these two prayers, and whispered them to herself several times a day for weeks, months, and then years.

In addition, every morning Lindsey paused for a few moments in front of this same corridor painting, stopping to offer up a desperate plea for help to the Holy Mother. As time passed and her horns and goatee never did develop, she knew that someone had taken pity on her.

Good Ol' Mary. She was all about forgiveness, grace, and mercy. Or maybe she was just getting sick of seeing the same droopy Chinese kid every day. Either way, Lindsey was confident that Mary had her back. She, in turn, was eternally grateful.

Stepping away from the painting now, Lindsey made a little sign of the cross, which she hadn't done in years. She then hurried to the main office, removed her coat, and stuffed it into the staff closet. She smoothed down her appropriately drab attire: a below-the-knee wool skirt, argyle stockings, and black oxford shoes. With her ponytail and fresh-scrubbed complexion, all she needed now was a peplum blouse with a peter pan collar to look like an abnormally large kindergartner who had flunked about twenty grades.

She headed to the library for the Monday-morning staff meeting. Entering the spacious room, she squinted in the fluorescent light and selected an amaretto cookie from the tray of

Italian pastries. Nibbling over a napkin, she stood in the corner, afraid to mingle.

It was surreal enough to be standing once again in front of the bookcase where she had checked out many a Nancy Drew mystery. But it was even weirder to be surrounded by her childhood authority figures: Sister Boniface and Sister Constance were in the corner by the outdated globe; Mrs. Yee, the piano teacher, was teasing her wiglet with her long scarlet fingernails; Mrs. Mann, dean of the lower school, still looked exactly like a man; and Mrs. Grupico, the librarian-registrar, squatted like a bloated bullfrog behind her same old desk scarred by cigarillo burns.

As intimidating as they still were, Lindsey noticed they all looked much older. Most had silver or white hair now, except for Mrs. Yee, whose wig was as black as a doll's. Also, they all seemed to have shrunken and looked like they could use blood transfusions and chocolate sundaes to give 'em a little pep. They each moved in slow motion, and Lindsey longed for a can of WD-40, since she could practically hear their bones creaking.

So many years had passed since she was a student, she hoped they had all forgotten about the intercom incident. In eighth grade, Lindsey and a friend had gone to the office to make a student council announcement and had found the room empty. They pushed several buttons on the switchboard but couldn't figure out how to work it. As they waited for Mrs. Grupico to return and help them, they had joked around, unaware that they had inadvertently turned on the P.A. system and the entire school could hear their conversation over the intercom.

"Don't you wish Patrick Swayze was your boyfriend?" her friend asked.

"Are you kidding?" Lindsey screeched. "Is the Pope Catholic?"

A second later she added, "Does a bear shit in the woods?"

The girls erupted in peals of laughter, and a moment later when they caught their breath, Lindsey delivered a final punchline, "DOES THE POPE SHIT IN THE WOODS?"

As their howls of merriment were broadcast in the teacher's lounge, throughout the halls, and in every classroom, Sister Boniface came charging through the office door and tried to grab their collars. The other girl, closer to the door, ran out so fast that Sister Boniface didn't get a good look at her. Lindsey was on the floor laughing so hard that she didn't see the small nun until it was too late. For the rest of the school year she was forced to clean the faculty toilets and had secured a reputation as a foul-mouthed perpetrator of hooliganism. A real enemy of the Vatican.

Lindsey winced, recalling the incident. Thinking further, she supposed that everyone had thankfully forgotten about her eighth-grade antics, otherwise she probably wouldn't be standing here now with a job. She started to relax, and sipped weak coffee from a Styrofoam cup.

But she cowered when she saw the next teacher who arrived. It was Ms. Abilene, her seventh-grade nemesis. Shockingly, although fifteen years had passed, the woman looked not one day older than when Lindsey was a student. She wore the same flesh-colored hue of lipstick, and her hair was still styled in that Carol Brady flip that made it look as if a stiff baby octopus sat atop her head. Her inexplicably shiny complexion and fake-friendly smile were that of a wannabe-glamorous trailer-park mom, and her perpetual squint made the color of her eyes and pinpoints of her pupils indiscernible. She was no doubt the unholy lovechild of Renée Zellweger and Mr. Magoo.

Unnerved to see Ms. Abilene so untouched by the years, Lindsey was convinced that the seventh-grade dominatrix definitely had some Picture-of-Dorian-Gray thing going on. Want-

ing to disappear, Lindsey hid from Ms. Abilene by stepping behind a rotating rack of serial paperbacks, *Deeds of the Saints*.

After a moment, Sister Constance clapped her hands together and said, "Ladies, let us commence."

A few standard school announcements were made about the
stairwell lamps being out of service, end-of-year grades due,
and Boraxo to be used sparingly in the lavatories. Sister Constance caught Lindsey off guard when she announced, "And
I'd like to introduce our new office girl, an alum of St. Maude's
whom I am proud to welcome, Miss Lindsey Owyang."

One might have expected a few polite remarks, but no. Instead, Lindsey heard a few whispers, such as, "Cheeky, cheeky
girl," "Always acting the maggot, that one," and in a thick,
Gaelic accent floating from the back of the room, "She's no
better than a fishmonger's wife."

She bit her lip. Obviously, no one had forgotten about the
Pope shitting in the woods. These phrases uttered by the
teachers were the same ones used to describe Lindsey more
than once when she was a student. Although she hadn't
gleaned their meanings back then, today, if she had a copy of
501 Irish Verbs, she could look up their definitions:

Being Cheeky: acting in a manner worthy of being
slapped on either or both cheeks as many times as
deemed necessary by nuns of miniature stature.

Acting the Maggot: conducting oneself shamefully,
squirming about as does a maggot or other subhuman
larva.

Behaving No Better than a Fishmonger's Wife: sneaking around like a daft harlot, fool enough to be married to a "monger," whatever that was.

Despite the chilly welcome, Lindsey smiled and gave a little
wave. Sister Constance pulled her granny spectacles down with
her index finger to the tip of her broken-capillaried daschund
nose and tsk-tsked as she caught sight of Lindsey's pink nail
polish. Mrs. Mann clasped her hands together like a chipper
cruise director and in her clipped yet throaty voice reminiscent
of Miss Jane Hathaway on *The Beverly Hillbillies* said, "Miss
Owyang is at your disposal to perform any of your end-of-the-
year or summertime tasks. Just leave your instructions for her
on the office chalkboard. You needn't worry about her efficacy,
which is sure to be splendid because, as her student records
show, she routinely received First Honors and was Miss Perfect Attendance five years in a row!"

The small crowd disbanded and Lindsey looked to the pastry tray to see if any cookies were left. Blocking her view was a
mannequin-still Ms. Abilene, who suddenly turned to face
Lindsey, her false lashes quivering slightly like venus flytraps
coated in Maybelline mascara. Lindsey averted her gaze but
could feel Ms. Abilene's sand-speck pupils boring into her
head like weevils into a cotton ball.

Panicked, Lindsey decided to make a run for it. She bolted
for the door and made it safely to the hallway, which smelled
of rubbing alcohol and aerosol chalkboard cleaner. Terrified,
she scurried back to the foyer office to featherdust the portraits
of the archbishops.

Something Scuzzy This Way Comes

Lindsey always had vague aspirations of being an artist, but who had time to mope around all day in unsanitary, paint-splattered coveralls? Sure, she was creative, but her artistic inclinations hadn't yet propelled her to an MFA or a career as a graphic designer. Instead, she worked part-time as a museum gift-shop clerk.

When she first took the job, she thought the position might consist of expounding on color theory or debating the genius of the Fauves and Dadaists, but mostly she just spent her time convincing docents that their modernist jewelry looked "fabu." At the cash register she rang up an occasional copy of *Artweek*, but the store's assistant manager decided her real talents lay in massaging the egos of socialites and the Junior League set. As a result, she was oftentimes trapped in Zone Four, shilling miniature replicas of famous sculptures. Ladies who had just lunched would peruse the Calder- or Eames-inspired knickknacks and once in a while Lindsey would make a sale, perhaps a postcard of Picasso's *Les Desmoiselles d'Avignon* to one of the mademoiselles de filet mignon. Her commission was three cents per card.

Thursday afternoon, she left St. Maude's at four o'clock and took a short bus ride to the museum. Pushing through the heavy glass door of the gift shop, she walked past several matrons with glossy hair-helmets and gigantic Jackie O. glasses. In the back corner, she slipped behind an unobtrusive door that led to a warren of staff offices, and there she tied the required black apron over her clothes and adjusted her name tag. She consulted the schedule on a dry-erase board by the water cooler and found that tonight, yet again, she was assigned to Zone Four, the jewelry and tchotchke counter.

She emerged from the back office and greeted a few customers with her friendly yet reserved retail face. Working at a museum store required a demeanor somewhere between Gap giddy and Sotheby's solemn, and she remembered to walk with her hands folded behind her back like they had shown her in training.

Co-workers at *Vegan Warrior* magazine always bragged that practicing yoga made them stand taller, saying their whole body felt different. Well, Lindsey wasn't into yoga, but now that she worked retail she could honestly say that she held her body in a different way. Greeting customers in such a staid environment, she learned to trade her slouching for poise, and to look people in the eye instead of scanning the floor out of shyness and an overwhelming fascination for dustbunnies. When it came to conversing with strangers, she fought her casual dependence on "ums," "you knows," and the occasional swear word. And she trained herself, when directing people to exits and restrooms, never to point with a single finger, but to instead use a more polite, open-palmed gesture just like certain Disneyland employees and late-eighties Union Square mimes.

There was hardly anyone in the store, so she leaned against the counter and flipped through a Pottery Barn catalog that someone had left behind. One spread featured a dinette set, chandelier, and handwoven rug, but Lindsey paid little attention to the wares for sale, focusing instead on the prominently featured wall hanging of an old Chinese man wearing a mandarin robe, black boots with thick, white soles, and a hat with a horsehair plume.

"Oh, great," she thought. She imagined some designer thinking Chinese people added an exotic splash to any well-appointed home. She wondered what type of person displayed a portrait on their mantel of someone who wasn't even remotely related to them. As for her, she couldn't imagine hanging a gigantic picture of some random white lady in her apartment.

Actually, Lindsey knew exactly what type of person placed framed portraits of costumed mandarins in their house. Working at the museum put her in frequent contact with this exact type. In fact, she'd recently begun charting her sightings, and had hypothesized that the Bay Area was a teeming breeding ground and migratory destination for these particular lady-birds, distinguishable by the following markings: chunky jade or cinnabar jewelry, loose-fitting garments decorated with Asian motifs, a purse or contents thereof adorned with trinkets such as Buddha keychains, sandalwood prayer beads, ointment jars of Tiger Balm, or any other accessory that seemed to say, "I've purchased spiritual enlightenment for $7.95 plus tax."

Lindsey noticed these loyal fans of ethnic regalia fondling Asian pears at the farmer's market, ogling *blanc-de-chine* Quan Yins at antiques stores, and chowing down on seared scallops at the Slanted Door.

She called them the Hoarder Ladies. And yes, they were the female version of *Hoarders of All Things Asian*.

An addendum to her original theory:

While male *Hoarders of All Things Asian* focused mainly on the procurement of Asian love slaves, Hoarder Ladies seemed more concerned with the acquisition of fashion and home items, preferring to feather their nests with a healthy dose of oriental razzmatazz.

For quite some time she'd been noticing that the Bay Area's thirst for the Asian aesthetic in home décor was unquenchable. Even the museum gift shop had its own row of books that described how to arrange candles, statuary, incense, lacquered cabinets, and bamboo thingamajigs "*à la manière Chinoise*" to achieve the irresistible combination of sexiness and serenity. In one knick-knacky corner there was a small selection of slippers, purses, and blotting papers for shiny noses. Not to mention the best-selling item in Zone Four, which was a handbook of Taoist sayings that promised on its cover "to elevate shopping to a spiritual experience."

All these pseudo-Asian books and trinkets flew out of the store at an alarming rate. Lindsey could just imagine a Hoarder Lady telling her husband, "Honey, ancient Chinese geomancers say it's bad luck unless I buy all new furniture." To them, the translation of *feng shui* was "the more you buy, the more you save your soul."

Never mind what Buddha actually taught about renouncing material possessions. Who needed spirituality when one could just wear a yin-yang pendant and eat an eighteen-dollar salad grown at the Zen Center by people who may or may not have been thinking enlightening thoughts as they sprinkled charcoal-filtered water on the radicchio?

The Hoarder Lady phenomenon was even alive and well in Hollywood. Just the night before, Lindsey had been watching *Phat Cribs* on television and it had featured a top actress's "Asian Splendor Den," which was basically a hootchy-kootchy sex dungeon decorated like a Chinese restaurant but with better fabrics and crimson candles instead of fluorescent panel lights.

These women and their preferences for Asian decorations

were everywhere, and in the gift shop they bought up all the bracelets made of vintage mahjong tiles faster than Lindsey could restock them. Old Asian ladies certainly weren't buying them. Any old Chinese lady worth her salt would rather be playing mahjong and winning big bucks than *paying* big bucks to wear the tiles.

Which brought Lindsey to another matter. All this experience with older, upper-crust white ladies was doing nothing to help her understand one older Chinese lady in particular, namely, Yun Yun. An old white lady was a totally different kind of person from an old Chinese lady. One asked for ice cubes in her wine while the other never wanted ice in her drink, not even in water. Chinese ladies drank only hot, boiled water. Was it a habit left over from village days when everything needed to be sterilized? Or was it just to wash down greasy food?

For white ladies, grease was a night cream for removing makeup or erasing wrinkles. For Chinese ladies, grease was a main food group. For Lindsey, *Grease* was . . . a great movie.

At the museum, old white ladies took lemon and sugar in their tea and asked Lindsey to call taxicabs for them. In Chinatown, old Chinese ladies drank their *tcha* plain and took the bus. And Lindsey . . . well, she drank nonfat, decaf chai lattés and preferred to walk.

What did it all mean? Lindsey stood and wondered all these things as she cleaned the dead flies from the store's front window display. After "freshening up" the photography section, she replenished the artist monographs and hid from a couple of Hoarder Ladies. Maybe it was Lindsey's imagination, but it seemed she was a magnet for Hoarders, both male and female. Perhaps she sported psychic signage that advertised, "Everything You Ever Wanted to Know About Asians but Were Afraid to Ask—Free Consultation," or, "I Live a Fabulous Asian-American Life—Ask Me How!"

Hoarder Ladies in the store were always asking Lindsey questions, and not just, "Where's the powder room?" or "Do these earrings make me look jowly?" Instead, they approached Lindsey when she was rearranging the Jackson Pollock action figures or touting the age-defying effects of the museum's new *Forever in the Black* mascara, and they asked, "Could you please give me a brief summary on the last two thousand years of Chinese painting?" or "What was the purpose of the Cultural Revolution?"

As she emptied a dustpan into the trash, she kept her eye on a couple of Hoarder Ladies who were trying on the Andy Warhol limited edition wigs. She dreaded the possibility of one more person asking her about the uses of ginseng or the efficacy of acupuncture, so she positioned herself behind the jewelry cases and braced herself for the hours ahead.

Tonight she would be performing one of her most vital duties as a Gift Assistant. Prepping herself like a surgeon, she straightened her apron and slipped on the snug white gloves she was required to wear. She sanitized the glass countertop with streakless spray and wiped the area with a dust-free cloth.

It was her job to clean the fabric-covered, severed limbs of the gift shop's mannequins. The limbs may have appeared to be casually strewn throughout the store like prosthetics for sale in a doctor's office, but in reality, they had been strategically placed to optimally display high-priced necklaces, bracelets, and rings. To Lindsey's left, right, and above her head, bejeweled limbs hovered and waited to be stripped of their dust and dander. She knew the saleability of the precious jewelry depended on pristine presentation, so she had learned to groom the mannequin arms more meticulously than even her own body parts.

She got to work. Removing a chunky gold choker from a black velour bosom, she meticulously dragged a strip of

Scotch tape across the knap to eradicate any dandruff flakes or other unsightly particles. She repeated the action with a new piece of tape, symmetrically de-linting the faux décolletage until it was flawlessly devoid of specks. On her resumé she had boasted about her attention to detail, but she had no idea this would be her fate. She brushed the mannequin neck with one of those sticky rollers meant for pet-hair removal, lamenting the years she spent earning her college degrees in English and French Literature.

Moving on to the wrist and finger displays, she removed a few amber rings and gave the digits the Scotch tape treatment. A few minutes later, as she buffed the fake fingernails, her ears felt prickly and she sensed that someone was looking at her.

She looked up, and from a short distance she spied a set of eyes gazing at her from behind a book of nude photographs by David Salle. A giant ass was on the cover, and her admirer's eyes peeked over the top of the binding with arched eyebrows.

She watched the man inch incrementally closer until he abruptly dropped the ass-picture that was hiding his rosacea-blotched face. He thrust out his hand as if to shake, and said, "My name is Charles. I own a gallery in Big Sur and if you're an artist, I'd love to give you the opportunity to show me your stuff." At the word "stuff," his eyes looked down and lingered at her hoo-hahs.

She politely declined his offer and continued to de-lint a velvet arm with the pet-hair roller. But he was not deterred. Instead, he tried a new approach. Picking up a tube of lipstick from the nearby *maquillage* counter, he stroked the sides like it was a Vienna sausage-sized penis, and said,

"Is this what geishas wear?"

Lindsey ignored him.

He waved a hairy, Popeye-sized arm toward her and jerked his meaty hand in the air like he was catching a buzzing fly.

"Just look at you!" he said. "You'd be a good tea girl if you wanted to be!"

Lindsey opened a bottom cabinet and hauled out a box of extra mannequin limbs from behind the counter. Like an industrious beaver, she stacked a damlike barrier of miscellaneous body parts between her and the man.

He slid a business card beneath the thicket of velvet arms.

"Call me," he said, then made a puckering noise with his livery lips.

Lindsey felt dirty. Awash with cooties, she was unable to locate any Purell at the moment, so she sprayed herself with glass cleaner and patted her clothes and apron with her white gloves. Dismantling her makeshift dam, she knelt down to stow them back into their storage compartment under the jewelry case.

She heard a slightly Southern voice float down her way.

"Don't I know you from somewhere?"

She figured it was another randy retiree. Popping up from behind the counter, she stumbled back a few steps. As her arm flew back to catch her balance, her fingers got tangled in a display of chunky gold pendants suspended from leather cords.

"Oh," she yelped, then righted herself.

It wasn't an old guy. It was a young guy. Well, at least her age.

"Hi," he said. "We know each other, right?"

Lindsey looked at the smooth-faced, young Chinese man and was taken aback by his striking, "I play lacrosse" musculature and his remarkably hairless, smug beauty. Before she could say anything, someone bumped into him from behind and he turned his back to Lindsey, allowing her the brief opportunity to check him out quickly, yet thoroughly, without him seeing. She took in his sleek, healthy hair, suntanned neck, and fit body in profile. In mere seconds she speculated that he worked out at least three times a week, had expensive tastes in clothes, and had admirable personal grooming habits. He possessed a certain John-Lone-in-*Year-of-the-Dragon* coolness, but with his suede jacket and cowboy boots he also worked a Robert-Redford-as-Jeremiah-Johnson look. She found the overall effect to be sexy as hell, and was quietly alarmed.

"Uh, no. Um, I . . . I don't think so," she stammered, then turned and pretended to dust the computer keyboard. She kept her back to him and waited for him to walk away.

"Yeah, I'm sure I know you," he said, leaning his elbow on the counter and giving her a slow once-over.

"Um, no," she said, still avoiding eye contact. She tried to distract him by printing up a cash-register sales tape that made a lot of clicking noise. When he seemed undeterred, she left it turned on.

"Sorry, this register is closed," she said, then shimmied out from behind the counter and sprinted off. She pretended not to hear when he called out, "Hey, is your name Lindsey?"

On the way home from the museum, Lindsey stood on the bus and still felt shaky from her little encounter. That tall Chinese guy with the Diesel jeans, immaculately polished skin, and bare ring finger was not just any handsome stranger with bleached teeth and an adorable scar on his chin. She knew exactly who he was, and wanted no part of him.

Dustin Lee. For all of sixth grade she sat in the desk directly behind his. How could she *not* recognize him? She knew the back of his head like the back of her hand.

As a twelve-year-old newcomer to St. Maude's, Dustin had been noticeably different from the other Chinese boys in the class. For one thing, he had that funny way of talking. Not a Cantonese, fresh-off-the-boat accent, but a stretched-out way

of speaking, a way of taking time with his vowels and an innocent persuasiveness that charmed the teachers with its suggestion of lemonade, barbecues, and rodeos.

The beginning of that school year had come on the heels of
a particularly freezing and wet summer in San Francisco.
When the shivering and bored captives of St. Maude's first laid
eyes on their new classmate, he was wearing a Western-style
shirt with pearly snap buttons and stitched boots peeking from
beneath his flared Wranglers. He didn't have his uniform for
the first few days, and to Lindsey and the other kids, no one
seemed more fascinating than this boy who hailed from exotic
Houston.

Who knew they even *had* Chinese people in Texas? When
the kids all questioned him on the playground during that first
recess, Dustin insisted he wasn't Chinese at all, but a direct descendant of the great general, Robert E. Lee. No one was
quite sure what to make of the slender boy in his Tony Lamas,
but Lindsey took his delusional claim to be a sign that he, too,
was as ambivalent and confused as she was about being Chinese. With sixth-grade dreaminess, she fantasized that they
were kindred spirits, maybe even soul mates.

As the bus swayed, Lindsey recalled how Dustin quickly got
himself ostracized by the entire sixth-grade class. He was
freakishly obsessed with robots and the television show *Mork
and Mindy*, spending recess, lunch, and after school talking like
Mork or pretending he was one of the members of Kraftwerk
or Devo. He was downright bizarre from the get-go, and as a
newcomer who refused to conform, had set himself on a one-
way trajectory to getting pummeled.

Lindsey had overlooked Dustin Lee's eccentricities, secretly
hoping for a love connection. She suspected that he liked her,
too. Frequent swipings of her various vanilla-scented Hello
Kitty erasers were his main display of affection, and when he

returned them later in the day mutilated with his teeth marks, she was fairly certain that someday they would marry. On the playground she claimed to despise him, but she harbored secret affection for his Southern drawl and silly spurs.

And today, Dustin looked much the same, except with less baby fat on his handsome face, a more self-assured demeanor, and not a single trace of his spastic freakiness of yore. She had recognized him right away, especially when she spotted that crescent-shaped scar on his chin.

It was near the end of the sixth-grade school year, after eight long months of Dustin ruining upwards of ten of Lindsey's Hello Kitty erasers and breaking her Little Twin Stars pencil sharpener. Despite her secret affection for him, several times she asked that her desk be switched away from his. But her pleas went unheeded. Sister Constance liked him smack-dab in the center of the room, where she could see him, so Lindsey's only recourse was to stare for hours directly at the back of Dustin's head and wonder what it'd be like to touch his hair.

As it was, the class of pimply-faced pubescents was fraught with enough sexual tension. But to complicate matters, Lindsey wasn't the only person in the classroom to have a crush on Dustin Lee. While Lindsey's feelings were a secret, everyone knew for months about the other person's infatuation with the preteen Texan. Being subjected to the sight of daily public displays of affection toward Dustin made all the kids despise him even more.

It was Sister Constance who was deeply in love with him. On the first day of school, she took a fancy to the lad, and although his cowboy boots showed blatant disregard for uniform rules, she allowed the infraction, she said, as a special favor to the great Lone Star State. From that day on, every morning after recess, she sought out the opportunity to lavish particular attention on the boy. The students all eventually came to expect the commotions, and sometimes even looked forward to Sister Constance's bouts of inappropriate behavior as a break from the monotony of their schoolwork.

One day Dustin turned around and said to Lindsey, "It's a well-known fact that Chinese people eat rats. Do you eat rats?"

She tossed her eraser at his face and he yelled out with surprise when it bounced off his forehead.

Sister Constance immediately noticed the ruckus and stopped the math lesson. In her trilling singsong voice, like the haughty, deep-throated goose from *Charlotte's Web*, she said, "Bring that he-ere . . ." The whole class stopped what they were doing and breathlessly awaited what might happen next.

Lindsey stood up to bring the eraser to Sister Constance, but the nun waved her aside and said, "Not yoo-hoo. The boy. I want to see the bo-oy."

Even back then Sister Constance resembled a salt-and-pepper cartoon dachshund with a mustache and a habit. With her long snout and imperious demeanor, she looked exactly like the Doggie Diner logo. Her socks were frequently mismatched from either getting dressed in her dark convent hovel or tossing back a few too many Long Island iced teas in the faculty lounge. As Dustin listlessly trudged up the aisle like a death row inmate headed for the electric chair, Sister Constance dangled her black-stockinged foot out of her shoe with flirtatious abandon, savoring the approach of her beloved.

Everyone watched as Dustin made the familiar pilgrimage to her podium. When he reached the front of the classroom, he stood a few feet away from the nun.

"Come closer, Mr. Lee," Sister Constance said. She then proclaimed that his "enormous length" from her and his "flaccid posture" were a disgrace.

"Come forward and be erect, Mr. Lee," she commanded.

Once poor Dustin stepped within reach, Sister Constance grabbed him. She held his hands outstretched like he was J. C. on the cross, and silently devoured him with her bulging peepers as he stood helplessly and pleaded, "Sister, please."

Within seconds Sister Constance secured him in an amorous headlock, pressing his head into her woolen-cloaked bosom. While he attempted to hold his face to the side, Sister Constance stroked his hair, and like a purebred canine whose incestuous pedigree had warped its mind, she swayed back and forth and hummed Stevie Wonder's "My Cherie Amour." Cradled thusly, poor Dustin's head looked like a swollen, brown cabbage, as she stroked his neck and ears muttering, "Such a beautiful boy, such a shame to be so cheeky. Cheeky, cheeky boy. Such a shame to be acting the maggot."

Later that day out on the playground at lunchtime, Dustin resumed his teasing of Lindsey. He pointed at her robotically and said, "Chinese rat eater!"

When she didn't respond, Dustin went into a manic, Robin-Williams-as-Mork routine and started spastically flailing his arms and insisting that Chinese people ate rats for dinner every night.

Why was he calling her a Chinese rat eater, when he himself was Chinese? She wasn't able to decide which was more galling, his accusation or his voluntary affiliation with anything having to do with Robin Williams. Meanwhile, a circle of sixth and seventh graders formed around them.

The previous Sunday, Lindsey had seen *Whatever Happened to Baby Jane?* The image of the dead rat on the silver salver stuck in her consciousness. While kids began to congregate around them, she was mortified to think that anyone believed her family ate fricasseed rats instead of McDonald's Filet-O-Fish sandwiches which, at that time, happened to be all the rage amongst the St. Maude's preteen cognoscenti.

"Rodent eater!" Dustin said again, with Orkian detachment.

Standing there she thought of all the different kinds of rodents and how they might be prepared in Chinese cooking. She imagined marmots in black bean sauce, sweet 'n' sour gerbils, Peking squirrel with hoisin sauce, chipmunks cubed in a dry wok, and chinchilla chow fun.

She was not a rodent eater. Nor did she know any Chinese people who ate rats. As she considered what she might do next, it seemed, somehow, that the pride of her people was at stake.

The circle of kids closed in tighter around them.

Before her brain could talk her arm out of it, with dead calm, Lindsey picked up her *Dukes of Hazzard* lunchbox, wound back like she'd seen Atlee Hammaker do at Candlestick Park, and swung her weight forward, pivoting from the hip so her arm carried the full force of her body. She clocked Dustin square across the chin with her lunchbox. The sound of industrial-strength metal catching against his tooth enamel was quite unique.

"YEAH!" Cheers erupted from all around. Kids who hated Dustin slapped Lindsey on the back and offered her congratulatory remarks.

She noticed the bloody cut on her victim's chin and couldn't believe what she'd done. The kids began shoving Dustin and started chanting, "Rat Boy! Rat Boy!"

Stunned, Dustin still managed to affect his robot-voice and said, "I am not a rat. I am a homosapien."

Peals of laughter erupted. "He's a homo! He says he's a homo!"

"No! Not homo-*sexual*, homo-*sapien*. I am a homosapien like all of you . . ." He tried to explain the difference in meanings, but at the word "sexual" his audience howled even louder.

Like Mork from Ork at the end of each show, Dustin began tugging on his ears and exclaiming, "Na-nooh, na-nooh! Na-nooh, na-nooh!"

His defeat at the hands of a girl, his allusion to homosexuality, his Texan-ness, and his all-around dorkiness invisibly sparked what happened next. A mob of hormone-fueled preteens swept Lindsey aside, then proceeded to kick and pummel Dustin every which way they knew how. Girls yanked his hair, boys socked him in the face, and Franklin Ng performed an impressive, kung fu flying kick to the groin. Lindsey stood aside and watched the whole melée unfold like Shirley Jackson's *The Lottery*.

At 1:20 P.M., Dustin Lee lay in a crumpled heap. A few minutes later, Lindsey's class returned to their homeroom and Sister Constance noticed immediately that her beautiful boy was missing. Lindsey watched from the window as a few nuns hurried out from the convent to scrape him off the playground asphalt. When his silent whimpers turned to pained wails, Lindsey was relieved to know that she hadn't killed him.

That was the last day she saw Dustin Lee until today. Over the years she had, in fact, thought of him a couple of times, but mostly out of guilt. She'd wondered if the creepy romance that Sister Constance inflicted upon him had sent him off the deep end. She once speculated that he was dead, perhaps killed in a Texas tornado.

Well, now she knew. He was alive and well and living in San Francisco.

How She Learned to Stop Worrying and Love Broccoli Beef

Walking home from St. Maude's the next day, Lindsey peeled off a few layers of clothes as she sweltered in the afternoon sunlight. It had been damp and cold that morning, but now all the fog had burned off and retreated to the coastline, leaving just a few puffy clouds in the distance.

She was beginning to regret having told her dad she would spend the upcoming weekend helping clean Yeh Yeh and Yun Yun's house. In theory, she thought it was great that Chinese families were tightly knit and valued togetherness, but in reality she dreaded spending her Saturday unloading cases of Depends and Metamucil, having to make sure she kept a tight lid on her casual swearing for fear that Yun Yun might catch her uttering the f-word and administer a swift knuckle to her head.

As she crossed the Panhandle, Lindsey surveyed the street lined with Victorian houses. All the buildings looked as if they were painted in either 1875 or 1975, she couldn't decide which. One house was the curry-ochre of a Hari Krishna's dusted forehead, another the hue of a Willy Wonka peanut butter candy, and a few paces up ahead, a faded bungalow reminded her of a melted Creamsicle.

Crossing the street to avoid an oncoming hippie in a poncho, Lindsey made her way toward the intersection and passed a decrepit, pink mansion perched high on a cement foundation. She was admiring the impressive stone wall on the building's west side, when she had the sudden, eerie sensation of someone watching her.

Even without looking around, Lindsey had a hunch who it was. Over the last few weeks she had grown familiar with a certain pair of eyes that had been following her. Although overheated just minutes before, she now felt a chill around her neck.

The eyes belonged to an elderly Caucasian woman who lived somewhere in the neighborhood. Lindsey could see her now up ahead, her tiny, slippered feet visible just beyond a camellia bush. She seemed to be waiting, slowly biding her time—for what, Lindsey didn't know. She never said anything, but now that Lindsey spotted her, the snow-haired lady began to walk. Today she wore a lacy periwinkle shawl that rested on her sparrow shoulders, and the silky fringe of her wrap brushed the sidewalk, barely skimming the concrete.

Lindsey was fairly used to seeing the woman around, but each time she encountered the lady on the route to or from home she felt a skin-crawling twinge. The woman was like the garden statue of the prowling jaguar that Lindsey sometimes passed on Steiner Street. Both were gray specters that never touched her, but seemed to be watching her every move. Any time Lindsey passed either of them they bid a silent hello, one carved in still stone and the other, the human one, gazing through her with sparkling, amethyst eyes.

She didn't know the woman's name or where she lived, but Lindsey watched as she shuffled slowly in her low, silver shoes. When the woman turned and tilted her head a bit, Lindsey recrossed the street and disappeared behind a hollyhock to avoid being followed.

Many blocks later, Lindsey spotted the rounded turret of her apartment building. She ran up the steps and slipped the key into the lock of the brass faceplate. Once behind the leaded-glass panel of the front door, she finally felt safe.

Michael came home about an hour later and flopped down on the sofa, smelling of burnt plastic and fake butter.

He said, "One of the protein-starved interns forgot about her popcorn in the microwave and set off a trans-fat explosion in the office kitchen."

"Let me guess, she was smoking on the stairs while reading *Optimal Health*."

"Actually, someone told me they saw her in the bathroom trying to purge herself of some lime-flavored Pop Rocks because she realized they contained gelatin and hence, weren't vegan."

Lindsey smiled, almost missing the antics of her former workplace. She and Michael had met at *Vegan Warrior* magazine, where he was an editor and she had been the receptionist. She never really fit in with the group of militant vegetarians and could barely tolerate the mandatory "lifestyle sessions" on Friday afternoons, when they had to endure poetry slams and hackeysack tournaments. She couldn't understand how Michael could stand it, and she was actually kind of glad when she was ousted after being caught red-handed gnawing on a pork chop she had brought for lunch. Working at St. Maude's now, at least all she had to worry about was not eating meat on Fridays instead of hiding her carnivorous habits every day of the week.

Michael stretched out on the couch and patted the cushion beside him, signaling for her to come sit near him.

He rubbed his chin. "What else? The Druid wants me to use up all my rolled-over weeks of vacation time. Says it's a financial liability or something. Can you take time off? Maybe we could go to New Orleans and visit my parents."

Lindsey shook her head. "I'm too new at both my jobs. I haven't accrued any days off from either St. Maude's or the museum."

"Oh," Michael said. After a moment, he sprang off the couch. "I skipped lunch today. Are you up for an early dinner?"

"Sure," she said, and went to grab her jean jacket.

They walked hand in hand to their favorite Chinese restaurant. After sliding into a booth, they noticed an elderly Chinese lady at one of the front tables. Although she was sitting with her entire family—husband, children, and grandkids—the world seemed to melt away when she set her eyes on Michael. She stopped mid-chopstick and gaped at him.

A waiter came to their table and took their order, after which he collected their menus and shuffled away. The old woman from the front of the restaurant craned her neck for another eyeball-full of Michael, then put down a steaming beef bone and approached their table.

Walking fast, she stumbled to a halt, patted her hairdo, and beamed a partially toothless smile. She batted her sparse eyelashes and held her clasped hands beneath her chin. She pointed at Michael with starstruck awe and said, "You star in *Matrix* movie, eh?"

Lindsey stifled a laugh as she and Michael exchanged bemused glances. Gently, he replied, "Well, actually, no. I wasn't in that movie."

The woman was unswayed. "You can't fool me," she said. "Big secret, you probably on film location here, eh?" She winked at Michael as if she was keen to his little game. Looking him up and down, her gaze lingered from the top of his cowlick to the soles of his Stan Smiths. "Well, you look *velly niice*." She smoldered, looking like a Chinese Broom Hilda.

She turned on her orthopedic heels and did her best rendition of skipping away. Before sitting down with her family and her beef bone, she turned and gave a final little wave.

Michael good-naturedly waved back. While absentmindedly rearranging the condiments on the table, he said, "It's been a while since we've had real Chinese food."

Lindsey nodded in agreement. Just last week, Michael's sister had visited and they took her to a yuppified Chinese restaurant. The menus were in English with nary a typo, and they ordered touristy stuff—innocuous-sounding dishes like Orange Chicken and Imperial Rice. They ate sweet and fried things with goopy sauces. But it wasn't really Chinese food to Lindsey, or by now, to Michael either.

When they first started going out, Lindsey had to get over her anxieties about eating Chinese food around a non-family member, but over their two years together, Michael had learned to eat some hardcore stuff.

At banquets with Lindsey's family, he got used to eating things like pork guts in brown sauce and salted bottomfeeder in red oil. Her grandparents would order dishes in Chinese and when Lindsey asked what was coming, Yeh Yeh would explain, "duck with medicinal insect in soup," "third stomach of cow," "pig's trotters with pineapple and fungus," or sometimes, "mother-and-child-meet," meaning pigeon with pigeon-egg sauce. Literal English translation didn't always sound very appetizing.

But Michael had eaten it all, bless him. Even dishes that Lindsey wouldn't touch, like the seaweed that looked like hair, red bean dessert soup, and tripe. Michael had drunk the wine steeped with mice (for flavor, silly) and gnawed on the gnarliest of preserved fruit *mui*.

Lindsey's relatives loved to watch Michael mow down all

the Chinese delicacies. They listened with rapt attention when he described the pros and cons of baked *cha siu bows* versus steamed. He likened oxtail stew to Italian *osso buco* and compared Chinese beef tongue dishes to Mexican *lengua*. Lindsey would have loved Michael even if he was a fussy eater, but somehow their relationship was proof that the way to a man's heart was through sautéed cow stomach.

"Wow, that was fast," Lindsey said as their food arrived. She doused their potstickers with rice vinegar and chili paste, then stirred the *won ton mein* with *hom choi*, which was the house specialty.

Michael spooned some beef tendons and stewed turnips onto her plate, knowing it was her favorite. She responded by forking over some salt-baked tofu and a couple of pieces of almond-pressed duck.

While Michael ate with chopsticks, Lindsey used a fork because it was easier. They liked to take their time eating, but the food was so good they ended up stuffing themselves quickly. When they were done, they each washed down their meal with several cups of hot tea.

The waiter brought over orange slices and fortune cookies. As Michael paid the bill, he said, "Want to go for our walk?" She nodded, and they headed for the door.

There was about an hour of sun left before dusk, and they made their way toward Golden Gate Park. The windblown trees in the long, stretching shadows beckoned to them. Ducking below some overgrown foliage, they entered the cool green of a hidden path and held hands as they walked beneath a canopy of rustling leaves in dappled shade.

They strolled across bridges and through tunnels, behind bushes and around flowering, fragrant trees. As the air grew cooler, they stopped from time to time so Michael could rub warmth into her shoulders. Near the log cabin he let her trip him and they fell down on the grass to enjoy the weight of each other as they inhaled the scent of new-growth grass dotted with pipsqueak daisies.

Evenings like these, between five and eight, with their mixture of cool and warm air, kinetic energy, and laziness, were the bread and butter of their relationship. Their talks were sometimes serious or joking, and other times they didn't speak at all, just listened to the gentle, scooping slaps of their shoes.

She couldn't quite explain the feeling of Michael at her side, but she knew it was right. He never walked too far ahead or lagged behind, and they had a synchronicity while walking. When she reached out her hand, his was always there as if their fingertips had language without talking.

Lindsey held a handful of flat stones she had gathered along the paths. She carried them in case they ended up at Stow Lake, where Michael could skip them across water. Walking for a while, they instead ended up sitting on a bench, and she balanced the cool rocks on the inner part of Michael's forearm. His other hand in her hair, he whispered insipid nicknames in her ear that, if heard aloud, would undoubtedly gag the entire population of the city's hipper-than-thou pseudo-intellectuals. The sky was just getting dark now, and somewhere in the distance they heard the low, sonorous booms of detonating fireworks. Although they could see only a blank sky above them, it was exciting to know that somewhere not too far away, pyrotechnics were lighting up the evening with fizzy, exploding chrysanthemums.

Lindsey nestled her face into Michael's neck. After a moment he whispered in her ear, "Hey, did you hear the one about the Chinese newlyweds? On their honeymoon the husband says he wants to try sixty-nine and the wife says, 'What? You want broccoli with beef?'"

Lindsey smiled and swept the rocks off his arm with her hand, watching as they tumbled into the grass.

"Maybe we'll be newlyweds someday," he added.

Their eyes met for a second. Then she gave him a little shove and stood up, brushing herself off.

Back at home, Lindsey took a shower while Michael organized the recycling and dragged it down to the curb. After shutting off the water, she pulled open the curtain to discover that there wasn't a towel on the rack, so she stepped out into the hall and promptly screamed, startled to see Michael, who'd just thrown open the front door.

"Well, hi," he said, kicking off his shoes. Modestly trying to cover herself with her hands, she fumbled in the linen closet. Michael moved toward her and wrapped his arms around her from behind.

"Your clothes are getting all wet," she said, trying to wriggle free, but he held her tight.

"I don't care," he said, smooching her.

"Well, you should care," she said between kisses. "Dry cleaning is expensive, and . . ."

"Forget dry cleaning. In fact, I'm never washing my clothes again, and they're gonna get filthy and full of germs and I'm gonna hide all your Purell, and you're gonna love me anyway."

Lindsey turned around and undid several buttons of his shirt, unlatched his belt and pulled it through the loops of his pants.

She put her arms around his neck and he hoisted her up and carried her to the bedroom. Her wet skin was slippery, and as soon as they made it to the bed he clumsily dropped her on the mattress with a thud.

"Ow!"

He smiled, pulling his shirt over his head and falling on her. More kissing and fooling around eventually led to the hamster

dance. They laughed as several Hello Kitty plush toys catapulted off the bed and onto the floor. In time, the gravity of *la
petite mort* ceased all giggles. Moments later Michael rolled
over and they lay side by side for a minute or so, exhaling the
contented sighs of the recently nailed.

Propping himself on an elbow, Michael turned to face Lindsey and played with several tangled strands of her hair. He
gazed at her for a moment, then whispered, "I like how you
trimmed your bangs." He gently touched her forehead and
brushed a few wisps of hair to the side.

"Most guys wouldn't have even noticed."

He rolled over her and said, "I hope you like me more than
most guys."

She struggled as he playfully held her down. "I'd venture to
say I *very* like you."

Michael lay on his back and gazed at the ceiling. Staring into
space he said, "Remember when I rented *Fight Club*, and then
I thought it would be tough to get in that brawl with that giant
from Ireland's 32? That fucker knocked my lights out, but you
never said, 'I told ya so.' You just went and got an ice pack."

Lindsey turned to face him. "What made you think about
that?"

Michael was pensive and didn't answer right away. He continued on his own train of thought. He said, "Do you know
what I like about you?"

She looked at him quizzically.

He said, "When we get into arguments, even when you're
really pissed at me, you don't tear me to shreds like I know you
could. Even when you're hating me, you're loving me."

"Oh?"

"Yeah. I can see steam coming out of your little head and
you're simmering, but you never go for the jugular, and in the
way you look at me there's something, I don't know. It's like

you've already forgiven me. You're like a cat and I'm a mouse you've caught, and instead of sinking your teeth into me, you just let me go. I don't know what I'm trying to say."

"I know you're mine, so I let you live."

"Yeah."

Michael propped himself up on an elbow. "I'm glad you woke me up the other night when you had a bad dream. I need someone to make milkshakes for at two in the morning, and I want that person to always be you. I know you prefer it all smooth, but when I goof and leave the bananas too chunky you still say it's perfect and that makes me feel pretty perfect, too . . ."

He pushed up and rolled over her again, making sure not to squish her. He went on, "I hope that I make you feel as good, as happy and strong as you make me feel. In fact, I hope that you want to be with me for a really long time, as much as I, right now, very positively want to be with you. I guess what I'm trying to say is, well . . . let's get married. Will you . . . marry me?"

Lindsey couldn't quite believe what she'd heard. Did he just say . . . Yes. He said the word *marry*. This was not a joke with a punch line.

After all the marriage proposals she had watched in movies and on television she never once imagined how *the question* might be asked in real life, and more to the point, to *her* specifically.

Michael's words were still floating above her head as her mind sprinted off in several directions at once. She thought about when they first started going out. He always called when he said he would, not three hours later or even three days later, but exactly the time he said. In her dating universe before she met him, she had such low expectations that Michael's courtesy and common decency were a revelation. As their romance progressed, his everyday chivalry had quickly won her over.

She recalled how once he took her swimming along the American River, and he helped her climb down the steep embankment while simultaneously carrying towels, a cooler full of food, and a small tent so she would have shade to sit in. She carefully noted that he had quietly noticed her aversion to the sun and factored this detail into his preparations. The fact that he brought a tent had impressed her, and his tender attentiveness had melted her heart as well as her, um, panties.

Michael consistently considered her needs first. He always gave her the bigger piece of pie, the cake with more frosting, or the unburnt toast. He even claimed to like burnt toast so she wouldn't have to feel guilty. With these small gestures he taught her something she surprisingly had not quite believed at first, which was that she deserved kindness.

Theirs was not a romance of screaming tantrums followed by dramatic reconciliations, but she had come to realize that a clock-radio hurled at one's face at 2 A.M. did not equal passion. Pat Benatar was wrong. Love didn't have to be a battlefield.

She looked up at Michael.

"Tell you what," he said. "If you can wrestle me off you, you can say no. Otherwise, you have to say yes."

Lindsey grabbed him and pulled him down. "I don't need to fight you," she said. "Of course I'll marry you."

Po-Mo, Slo-Mo, Lacto-Ovo

Lindsey knew she was Asian because she was cutting meat with scissors.

She was preparing a special dinner to celebrate their engagement, and her menu reflected their particularly multicultural union. In addition to the sliced steak she was going to grill, she was planning on making lasagna, layering thin sheets of *wonton pei* instead of pasta between tomato sauce and Chinese mushrooms. Any moment now she was expecting Michael home from work, and for cocktails she was soaking freshly peeled lychees in vodka for "lychee-tinis."

"I'm home!" Michael yelled from the bottom of the stairs.

"Hi, Babycakes," he said, entering the kitchen and smooching her. "What's all this?"

"We're celebrating."

"Mmm," he said. "Looks . . . interesting."

He picked up an empty bottle of Chinese vinegar from the countertop.

"What's this for?"

"It was supposed to be for my special salad dressing."

"Do we need to go to the market?"

"Yeah," she said, "I ran out of fresh *wonton* skins, too." Washing her hands, she added, "The good thing about living in San Francisco is that even regular supermarkets sell all sorts of obscure Asian stuff."

Soon enough, they were in the car and on their way to Albertson's. As they made their way there, Michael informed Lindsey that he had some irritating news. He said, "Starting tomorrow, *Vegan Warrior* is sending me on a top-secret mission to the Psychic Food Ashram in Santa Barbara."

"What's that?" Lindsey asked.

"It's a ritzy getaway spot for aging hippies and New Age truth-seekers who trade cultlike devotion for tomato juice enemas and the opportunity to be ridiculed by a coterie of dieticians, yoga instructors, and self-proclaimed metaphysical healers. The ashram also supplies Southern California's restaurants with 'psychically clean' produce that—get this—is guaranteed 'free of bad vibes.' I'm going to investigate exactly what comprises bad vibes and how the ashram can prove such a claim."

Lindsey asked, "Isn't that a little short notice?"

Michael swung into the parking lot. "Yeah," he said. "The original reporter was taken off the case after nearly choking to death on a chicken bone hidden in the Tofurky hash. Behind the compound walls there've been allegations of late-night Krispy Kreme binges and genetically modified tomatoes that taste like bacon. Something's definitely amiss. Unfortunately, that means I'll be leaving first thing in the morning."

"How long will you be gone?"

"As long as it takes me to figure out if they yell at the vegetables to make them grow faster. Howard says that's against the laws of the Slow Food Movement. Also, that would definitely constitute bad vibes."

"Are you kidding?"

"Baby, I wish I was."

Just minutes after walking inside the store, Lindsey lost Michael. Standing in front of a row of pickles, she felt forlorn and confused. Every time they went to the supermarket they always lost each other within moments of getting there, and now she'd have to go looking for him. As she wandered past the rotisserie chickens, she ruminated on the strange inevitability of their separation. She was fairly certain she would find him on the arm of another female.

It was true that Michael Cartier had magic powers over women. Ladies of a certain age, that is. The Ethel Mermans, Carol Channings, and empress dowagers of the world adored him. It was as if he wore an invisible sign around his neck that read, NEXT HELPFUL YOUNG MAN, 52 MILES. When they saw him, elderly gals instinctively knew that he would be glad to help them reach a precariously perched can of herring in wine sauce, or fix the wobbly wheel of their shopping cart. He was the pied piper of the AARP, and Lindsey was forced to share him.

After gathering the items she needed for dinner, plus some extra-special treats for dessert, she went off to search for him in the "incontinents" section. But he wasn't there. After wandering all the aisles, she decided to pay for their groceries, and waited outside for him.

Standing in front of the store, she scanned the parking lot and spotted Michael's red Toyota. He was driving slowly in circles, and as he rounded one corner, Lindsey was perplexed to see someone sitting beside him. As she tried to make sense out of the strange scene, she noticed that the passenger was an old Asian lady, and she was leaning out the window and pointing. Lindsey watched as the car crawled though the lot and eventually stopped. She saw the old lady get out of the car, and

Michael helped her transfer her groceries into what was presumably her own car. Seeming to sense Lindsey's gaze, Michael looked up toward the front of the supermarket and spotted her. He waved, hopped back into his car, then whipped around to pick her up.

"What was that all about?" Lindsey said, hoisting her purchases onto the seat.

"You sprinted off down the ethnic foods aisle, and I realized I forgot my wallet so I came out to get it. The next thing I knew, this old lady gets in the passenger seat and orders me to drive around and look for her car. I couldn't say no."

Lindsey sat down and slammed the door. "That's how people get murdered, you know. She could've had a hatchet in her purse."

"I think I could've taken her," Michael said, pulling out of the lot. "Besides, if she were my grandmother, I'd want someone to help her." He smiled at Lindsey. "But don't worry. Now you're gonna be my old lady. I'll always carry your groceries, and won't help anyone else from now on if you don't want me to."

Lindsey gave him a sideways glance. Scooting closer to him, she ran her fingers through his hair. "No . . ." she said. "I wouldn't want to change that about you."

Michael drove slowly, making full stops at the stop signs and waiting for pedestrians as they made their way across the intersections. Lindsey said, "You know, you're not like any of the guys that girls in magazines complain about. You're not addicted to ESPN and porn, and don't have to win at Pictionary or Wiffle ball just to prove how great you are. I think because you were a busboy in college, you know what it's like to serve other people so when we go out you don't treat people like crap. I like that you give people the benefit of the doubt, and drive like a granny, and don't give slow drivers the finger. I used to think it was a show of weakness that you couldn't be bothered to get all pissed, but now I realize that, actually, it's strength."

She let go of Michael's head, and as she talked, she checked her own hair in the mirror on the passenger-side sun visor. She reached into her purse and proceeded to touch up her makeup.

Michael turned onto Steiner Street. He said, "When I first moved here, did I tell you I was on a Wiffle ball team? Incidentally, we did win."

"Yeah, I know, but that time when we were playing with those little kids in the park, it's not like you had to run them into the ground to prove you're a man. You let them win. And another thing, about moving here. A lot of people come to San Francisco and like it for a while, then leave or go back to wherever they came from. Other people, like you, once they get here they realize they can't possibly live anywhere else. I don't know what it is in a person that makes you become a San Franciscan, but even if the city has kicked your ass, or you've never been to the Mark Hopkins, Tadich Grill, or the Black and White Ball, you just feel it in your bones that you're home. I guess what I'm trying to say is that I like that you knew you belonged here even if you didn't . . . come looking to belong."

"But I was looking, I just didn't know it," Michael said, shooting her a smile. "When I first noticed you at *Vegan Warrior*, I liked that you never used to let people get away with their stupid shit. I remember when that editor, Lisa Dickler, insisted that everyone call her Topaz, you used to get on the intercom and say stuff like, 'package at the front desk for the Dickler.' And when that guy tried to play off that his name was pronounced 'Osshead,' you still called him Mr. Asshead, the way it was spelled. You were funny. And bold. I always knew you were smarter than so many people who worked above you, but you did all their dirty work without complaining. Actually, I kind of miss you at work. Now there's no one else to talk to."

"Oh, come on. You see me every day."

"Yeah, I know. But it's different. Did you know that when I used to hover over your desk, if I stood a little to the side, I could always see through that pinky-red blouse you wore? And I liked how, by the fax machine, you always unconsciously leaned in when I stood close to you. You always smelled faintly of citrus . . . and steak. Now I know it was your bergamot hair conditioner and Pau Pau's cooking, but back then, it was all so mysterious and sexy, in a domestic kind of way."

"Incidentally," he added, "I like to watch you put your lipstick on in the car when you think I'm not looking."

Lindsey blotted her lips on a tissue and replaced the cap on her tube of gloss. "Oh," she said. Still slightly shy of him, she looked away with a smile.

Arriving in front of their building, Michael parked the car and they unloaded the groceries. As they headed up their steps, he said, "Up until coming here, I moved around a lot, and the way you looked at me, and came to trust me, made me want a home. Made me think, for once, I could make a home with a girl who I wouldn't have to lie to just so I could get or do what I wanted."

"So are you saying that before you met me you were a liar?" She shot him a teasing look.

"Um, no." He smiled. "I'm just saying that you're the only girl I ever met where I wanted to be honest in everything. See, like you have this lipstick smudge right . . . here." He reached over and rubbed a tiny spot near her mouth, then leaned over and kissed it quickly.

She noticed an old lady across the street watching them, and aware that they were being stared at, she said, "hey," and nudged him away.

"Nope," Michael said, playfully pulling her toward him. "You have to do what I say now. You're my wife."

"Not yet!" she yelped in protest as he pushed her through the door and shut it behind them. Gently pushing her down on the inside stairs, he let the groceries fall willy nilly to the side. She said, "You're squishing my cupcakes!"

"That's the whole idea," he replied, continuing to bump his cucumber against her fruit basket. His mouth traveled down her neck and to her belly button where he deftly unfastened her miniskirt. They decided they couldn't wait until after dinner, so there in the dim stairwell, he devoured her cherry pie.

Digging Up Dirt

The next morning, Lindsey watched Michael from the window as he ran down the steps to the car and threw his luggage into the backseat. He started the engine and waved one last time, and as he zoomed off she already missed him.

When she arrived at St. Maude's, the doors were locked. She'd forgotten that the school was closed for Ascension Day. Turning around and heading back home, she was sorry that she got dressed and rushed all the way to work.

As she walked, cars sped by on Oak Street. She noticed how strange it was that there were no other pedestrians. She passed overgrown gardens spilling through cast-iron fences and rows of cracked, marble stairs. Soon enough, she had that familiar feeling of being watched. Near the corner of Fulton and Laguna, she spotted the old lady with her white witch's pompadour and velvet shawl. The woman tread softly and silently in the distance. Lindsey detoured down to McAllister Street, and for the rest of the way home wondered how Michael would survive more than three days without eating a hamburger.

As she walked up the steps to their apartment she unconsciously said a couple of Hail Marys. Once in the kitchen, she put down her purse and picked up the phone. She dialed her parents' house.

"Hey, Dad."

"Oh, hi. What are you doing calling? Are you at work?"

She explained that Michael had gone to Santa Barbara and that she had the day off.

"Oh," he said, "since you've got nothing to do, why don't you get a head start cleaning Yeh Yeh and Yun Yun's house today?"

She reluctantly agreed, hung up the phone and went to the bedroom to change her clothes.

Out on Thirty-Eighth Avenue, Lindsey approached the yellow stucco house. The exterior was covered in exhaust particles from the nearby traffic on Geary Boulevard, and large sections of peeling paint in the open-air stairwell barely clung to the walls, as if the soot were the only thing keeping the paint stuck to the building.

As she walked through the gate and up the stairs, she wondered what the place might look like inside. She hadn't been here since she was a kid, and didn't remember anything. By the look of the weeds and dead grass out front, it appeared that her grandparents had really let things go.

Her dad had given her the key the night of Yun Yun's party, and she turned it in the lock and entered. The place was completely dark, except for a bright, coin-sized spot of sunlight that shone through a hole in the heavy curtains.

"Hello?" she said, knowing that Yeh Yeh was most likely in Chinatown minding his grocery store but unsure if her grandmother was home. Waving her hand to clear the air, she immediately began to sputter and cough, choking on decades-old dust that mushroomed up from the hall carpet as she felt her way along the walls looking for a light switch.

Across the dark hall, a bedroom door was half-shut but she could hear a television. She figured Yun Yun was probably in there. Approaching, she knocked softly.

"*Wa?*"

Lindsey slowly pushed open the door and saw her grandmother sitting in the bedside chair, fully clothed with her size-four stockinged feet resting on a plastic-sheathed ottoman. The rest of the room consisted of a bed with a floral bedspread tucked neatly around the mattress, and a vanity with a can of hairspray and a bottle of Jean Naté after-bath splash. A pair of miniature pink slippers sat by the bed.

"Hi, Yun Yun."

"Mm," her grandmother replied, half-hiccupping, half-grunting. She didn't ask Lindsey why she was there, and didn't seem to care anyway.

"Am I interrupting something?" Lindsey asked, and received an annoyed glance.

After a moment, Lindsey apparently hadn't observed the obvious and Yun Yun answered with a single word, "*Matlock.*"

She saw Andy Griffith on the television and nodded. "Well, I'll get out of your way. I'm just going to clean up a little." As she turned to leave, her grandmother asked, "You gain more weight?"

Lindsey backed out of the room and shut the door behind her. Every time she talked to Yun Yun she felt like Charlie Brown trying to kick a football. Her grandmother was Lucy Van Pelt, inevitably snatching the ball away at the last second, and Lindsey always seemed to fall flat on her back. Every time she was duped by Yun Yun's initial niceties, she knew she should have known better. Yun Yun would begin conversations with deceptively kind remarks like "Colorful sweater," or "Nice shoe," only to add a moment later, "look like Bozo clown," or "hunchback toe fall off yet?"

Feelings of insecurity were inevitable around Yun Yun. As Lindsey shuffled toward the front of the house, she wondered if she had, in fact, gained a few pounds.

Contrary to popular belief, not every Chinese grandmother was wise or kind. Some were downright ornery and didn't want you around. They didn't give you candy or say you were smart or that they loved you. Yun Yun was just this type.

A force of nature in the Owyang family, she was a gnarled and prickly thing, like an old rosebush growing out of a pile of rocks with branches entwined around a chain-link fence, having produced nary a blossom over the last thirty years. Yun Yun could prove her thorns were sharp, and often did, with caustic comments that stung worse than any pricked finger.

Lindsey feared her grandmother but was at the same time curious about the origins of her surliness. Somewhere in the soil beneath Yun Yun's rocky terrain, below that dry and tough exterior, was a tightly wrapped root ball. Lindsey wondered about that root ball. Down in the dirt, something had to keep it pulsing and alive. Lindsey wondered what Yun Yun's story was. She had read that trees required careful pruning to thrive, but how could she get close enough to cut a sprig and see what might develop? Most likely she'd be punctured by the sharpest of thorns.

Lindsey had also read that indoor plants used their leaves to purify the air, turning carbon dioxide into oxygen. Yun Yun, who often sat as still as a houseplant, transformed things as well, but in the opposite way. She actually sucked air *out* of the room. She could take happy feelings and holiday good cheer and with one scowl or cutting look, fill a room with dread.

And Lindsey wasn't the only one who felt this way. Her brother, Kevin, had often complained that their grandmother despised him. Just as Yun Yun had often told Lindsey that listening to music was a waste of time, she also had scolded

Kevin, saying that playing basketball would cause an early on-set of osteoporosis and "too thin blood." To drive her point home, she always ended with the comment, "And you, already so short. No longer growing. Short man for life."

Lindsey walked to the window in the living room and parted the thick wool curtains with her hands, setting off an avalanche of powdery dust that rained all over her arms, shoulders, and head. Covered in gray dustbunnies, she looked like she was wearing a shag carpet. *Jeez*, she thought, *it's like Mount Saint Helen erupted in here*.

From the looks of things, neither Auntie Geraldine or Uncle Elmore had been coming around to clean the place like they were supposed to. Lindsey went into the kitchen to find a wet rag, but was so overcome by the mess that she forgot what she was looking for. Every square inch of linoleum and tile was splattered with multiple layers of every kind of food and beverage imaginable, as if a hundred cans of soup, spaghetti sauce, and various condiments had exploded in 1998 and been left to dry. It looked like Chef Boyardee had broken into the place and tagged the walls and floor with Franco-American graffiti.

Violent splashes of spilled coffee accented the floor and drips of brownish gravy made stripes on the lower cupboards, ending in dried blotches and pools that were then smeared with footprints. She wondered how two old people could make such a mess.

She stumbled around looking for cleaning supplies, puffs of dust following her like she was Pigpen from the Peanuts gang. In the broom closet she found unopened rolls of gift wrap from the fifties, boxes of swirly patterned Dixie cups, and unused packages of luncheon napkins in chartreuse, avocado, and other vintage colors unseen since 1969. She could just imagine Yun Yun reasoning, "Still good! No need throw out."

Under the sink she found some ancient sponges. They were bundled in their original packaging with the price tag still stamped on the cellophane. Fifteen cents for five sponges. When had they bought these, during the Cold War? She stacked the dirty dishes and let them soak in the sink while she investigated the rest of the house.

The dining room was entirely dedicated to trash. She found grocery bags filled with various items: scraps of miscellaneous string, sugar packets from restaurants, and saved twisty ties from a thousand loaves of bread. She found sacks filled with crumpled paper bags in various sizes, and within one of those bags, inexplicably, a single plastic cup. Or a sock. She sifted through boxes of dirty rubber bands and piles of expired newspaper coupons so old they had turned yellow. Walking through a maze of stacked magazines and expired telephone books, she headed toward the mantel, where she saw a statue of Buddha resembling Baboo the Genie wearing balloony, CP Shades culottes. Dusting off his rotund belly, she then made her way down the hall to the other bedroom.

From what Lindsey could see, Yun Yun was Felix Unger to Yeh Yeh's Oscar Madison. Her room had been neat as a pin, but Yeh Yeh's room was another story. Lindsey opened the Levolor blinds and looked around. She saw a sad, twin-sized cot in the corner and a scuffed-up dresser. After noting these two pieces of furniture, there was nothing left to do but stand back and stare at the staggering mountain of junk that took up half the room.

She had often wondered what type of person bought all the novelties at checkout counters and gadgets advertised on late-night television. Now she knew. Yeh Yeh apparently bought them all. Stacked from the ceiling to the floor she saw ten-piece baking sets, flame-resistant oven mitts, lights that turned on at the clap of a hand, leather-repair kits, and the Whispertron 2000 for eavesdropping on conversations up to fifteen feet away. As she gazed at the tower of boxes, it occurred to her how dangerous it might be if Yeh Yeh's teetering tower of bargain merchandise ever toppled onto his bed at night. She could just imagine the headline: CHINESE MAN FLATTENED IN BIZARRE CHIA PET ACCIDENT.

She took a moment to play with the novelties that required human interaction. Dropping a coin into his desktop toilet-shaped bank, she listened as it made an authentic flushing noise. She pushed a button to make the Big Mouth Billy Bass sing "Don't Worry, Be Happy." After pressing the paws of several kung fu gerbils that began to twirl their tiny nunchuks, she triggered the motion sensor on a plastic Frankenstein head that played a rendition of "Who Can It Be Now?" by Men at Work.

On the floor by the window were various piles of junk mail. Sifting through some envelopes, she noticed that some were postmarked as far back as the seventies and eighties. Kneeling down, she picked up a stack and found little reminders scrawled here and there. Written in dull, soft pencil were notes such as, "milk and toilet paper," or "Tuesday senior special at Chick-n-Coop."

It was then that she noticed the yellow Post-it notes stuck all around the room—on the doorknobs, the metal cot legs, and on the windowsill. One read, "hide in ditch," another, "drop and roll," and by the closet, "duck and cover." Each upper-right corner was marked with a corresponding disaster—"tornado," "earthquake," or "stray bomb." Yeh Yeh was obviously prepared for any worst-case scenario. Lindsey was somewhat comforted to know that her grandpa would be ready should a rogue cyclone ever tear through Chinatown.

Back in the kitchen she threw out trash and wiped down the countertops. Here and there she found more Post-its that Yeh

Yeh had stashed. Cleaning the toaster, she found directions on how to escape during a flash flood. Inside an unwashed coffee mug in the cupboard, she discovered how to cure a snakebite.

She flicked on a lamp in the living room and took a closer look around. The space was divided into a tidy section and a sloppy one. There may as well have been a line painted down the room to delineate the "his" and "hers" sections. By the fireplace was a single, orange-upholstered chair and a tiny area rug. That must have been where Yun Yun sat and picked her teeth. Five feet from the chair was a smallish television set with a bouquet of plastic violets sitting on top. That was all.

The other half of the room was much like Yeh Yeh's bedroom. She stared at the hill of trash and yet another tower of stacked boxes against the wall. She found unopened miniature screwdriver kits, teeny wrenches, and itsy-bitsy fondue forks that read, SOUVENIR OF NIAGARA FALLS. Since everything was still perfectly encased in the original packaging, she deduced that neither Yun Yun nor Yeh Yeh actually used any of these things, but were well prepared for a fabulous party that they'd probably never give.

After making a bologna sandwich and a cup of hot tea for Yun Yun, Lindsey swept, mopped, and scoured. As she worked, she became more and more curious about her grandparents. Their house was generic and spoke of a very boring life. She wondered about their marriage and, lightheaded from the Tilex and Comet fumes, started to think that hidden somewhere in the place must be a clue to some sick and twisted secret life they had, either together or individually. Lindsey had always had an overactive imagination, and now that she was hungry, tired, and high from Windex, a really bizarre idea popped into her head.

Porn. It was disturbing to think of parents watching dirty movies, but to go a step further and to think of grandparents getting smutty was downright sick. Nonetheless, once the possibility, albeit far-fetched, popped into her brain, she couldn't stop thinking about it. The idea of Yun Yun or Yeh Yeh having a secret stash of nudie mags was so disgusting that her mind had to go there. Half-jokingly, with each closet and drawer she organized, she searched for a cache of whack material hidden amongst the domestic rubble. They simply *had* to have more of a life than Publishers Clearinghouse sweepstakes forms and U.S. commemorative coins. As Lindsey cleaned, she secretly looked for *Penthouse* or *Juggs* magazines but found only periodicals titled *Caring for Houseplants*, *Pet Canaries*, and *Terrier Fancy*. In the bathroom, what she thought might be a couple of dildos turned out to be underwater flashlights.

Several hours later, organizing the last of the bathroom drawers, in a box full of electric razors and unopened shaving cream canisters, she found a black, rectangular box. It was buried deep underneath some vintage Gillette replacement blades and samples of talcum powder, and she almost missed it. It was a videotape in an unmarked sleeve.

She read the typed label:

"You've taken your first step to fulfilling your needs. You may be embarrassed, but we guarantee you will be completely satisfied after you watch . . ."

Aha! This was it! She'd found something nasty in her grandparents' house! She ran to the living room and popped the tape into the decrepit VCR. Its innards sluggish, the machine hissed and whined. Turning on the television, after some static, Lindsey watched as words appeared onscreen:

"Don't be ashamed . . ."

She braced herself for bondaged nurses or Playmates fornicating with sheepdogs. What she saw was far worse:

"You know you want it . . . your deepest desire come true . . . A CURE FOR TOENAIL FUNGUS."

It was a video infomercial about a condition that infected the feet of one in nine Americans. As numerous examples of yellow, mangled toenails flashed onscreen, Lindsey covered her face with her hands. Repulsed, she turned off the VCR.

During a final pass with a broom, Lindsey's curiosity turned more serious. She realized she didn't know Yun Yun and Yeh Yeh at all. She knew they had lived in Locke, near Sacramento, but where had they each been born, how did they meet, and why did they get married? Did they love each other?

By late afternoon, she was closing the blinds in her grandfather's bedroom, and she spied something under the twin cot. She fished it out from against the wall, and found that it was a dusty photo album. Flipping through the sticky pages, she checked that it actually contained pictures, then she calmly slid it into a paper bag.

Poking her head into Yun Yun's room, she was relieved to find that her grandmother was taking a nap, eliminating the need for any potentially acerbic conversation. She tucked the album under her arm and headed out the door.

Back at home, Lindsey sat at the kitchen table and carefully slipped the photo album from the paper sack. She dusted it off and took a breath before opening the cover.

Flipping through the pages, she came to a few fuzzy snapshots of her dad as a teenager with backdrops revealing crates of fruit that looked like peaches and pears. In other photos, Yeh Yeh or Yun Yun sat unsmilingly in the foreground holding an already chubby Auntie Geraldine and baby Elmore. She didn't recognize any of the snapshots as being from their San Francisco house. She figured all these pictures had been taken in Locke. Thinking for another moment, she could have sworn Yeh Yeh had once mentioned growing up in the city. When had they moved?

Lindsey thought more about how little she knew of Yeh Yeh and Yun Yun. She had never given much thought to them as people in any context other than being her grandparents. For that matter, she hardly thought of her parents as regular people either. Other than the day-to-day interaction of family life, she never discussed with any of them their personal aspirations, political views, or how they felt about art, recycling, begonias, or anything.

Reflecting now, it seemed ridiculous that she knew so little about their hopes, desires, childhood dreams or disappointments. When she was a kid, her nuclear household had been like a small factory in which conversation was designated by and limited to one's role in the family. Any tangential conversation irrelevant to the smooth operation of cooking, shopping, cleaning, or getting to and from school or other sanctioned activities was considered superfluous and barely tolerable.

Enough toilet paper in the closet? Homework and dishes done? Car, fence, or broken zipper need fixing? These topics were all acceptable. Lindsey, Kevin, and their parents filled every evening with matter-of-fact conversation about pick-up and drop-off schedules, piano practices, SATs and hair appointments. The guys talked about sports and occasionally Lindsey and her mom talked about jewelry or the latest plot of *Murder, She Wrote*.

Never a peep was uttered about depression, existential angst, or subverting any dominant paradigm. Her mom and dad would freak out if they knew her liberal high-school and college curricula were teaching her that the American Dream was fraught with ennui, alienation, and personal malaise.

As Lindsey scanned through the photos she thought of the many Chinese immigrant families in which children as well as adults worked from sunrise to sundown, barely making ends meet. After all their toil, presumably there wasn't left-over time or patience for complaining or chitchatting about vague, personal dissatisfaction. Even though Lindsey's parents were prosperous enough to have leisure time, still, a Chinese way about things—a cultural despondence—gripped them and pervaded their lives, each so separate beneath one roof. Like most Chinese families, they never talked about feelings. It was as if they were scared of the brutally honest things they might say if they ever got started. Or, perhaps, like everybody else in the rest of the country, they were just bored with each other and were more interested in watching *American Idol*.

Instinctively, each member of the Owyang family kept to themselves. Perhaps as children Lindsey and Kevin had absorbed through osmosis an invisible Chinese rule about not overstepping one's boundaries. Their parents never cursed or spoke out against injustice—in the world, workplace, or anywhere—and personal feelings of any kind were hardly expressed. Each Owyang unit was individually shrink-wrapped and bound in an airless sheath.

It was into this environment of unspoken thoughts that Lindsey had sometimes uttered a simple question and was met with either feigned deafness, confounded silence, or a dismissive, noncommittal response such as "not sure," or "some other time."

Over the last couple of years, she had asked a lot of questions and only received the vaguest answers.

"Where did you grow up?" she might have asked.

"Oh . . . in the valley."

She was left to wonder which—the San Fernando Valley, or near Sacramento, or in some random "valley" in China?

She had occasionally asked how Yeh Yeh and Yun Yun met, or where they grew up, and her parents provided no suitable answers. As unlikely as it seemed, it crossed Lindsey's mind that perhaps her father didn't even really know. Seeing as how she knew so little about her dad, it wasn't that outrageous to think that he, in turn, might also be uninformed about his own parents. Maybe he never asked and they never offered any clues. A generation closer to the old Chinese way of thinking, her dad had been steeped longer in the traditions of minding one's own business, not rocking the boat, and biding one's time. Maybe he didn't care to know, or else his curiosity had eroded like silt on a riverbank. Why dredge up mud when the water was clear now?

But to Lindsey the water was still murky. For a couple of years now she had been trying to gather bits of family information. She was like an early Californian panning for gold, believing in her right to discover buried secrets. However, the strong current of verbal reticence that invisibly gripped the nearly dried-up Owyang riverbed hardly ever yielded a shiny pebble of insight. She was exasperated that her quest for answers had turned up mostly sand and hardly any nuggets of truth. Everyone else acted like there was no value in what she was so diligently searching for, and they discouraged her folly by throwing her off their scent with incomprehensible mumblings. Her elders routinely stonewalled her by turning up the volume on the radio or TV, and only occasionally flitted a morsel of information her way before fleeing to another room, stopping up their mouths with another chopstick-full of *jai,* or jabbing the words back between their teeth with another toothpick.

Whenever her tenacity appeared to have slackened, they seemed relieved. But Lindsey secretly took notes in her head, filing away all the bits and pieces of information she gathered over the years while listening to whispered conversations when no one thought she was paying attention. She had to piece snippets together and figure out in her own head what was real about the past. Details were like old pennies she saw in the street and could have left in the gutter, but she always decided to pick them up, quietly slipping them inside a mental pocket. Here is what she had sifted and sewn together thus far:

She knew that Locke had been a bustling, all-Chinese town once upon a time, and that her grandparents worked in the asparagus and pear fields. As a boy, her dad helped them fold cardboard boxes, then picked fruit with them as he grew older. Each adult had made a dollar a day back then, and Yun Yun sometimes augmented the family income with small sewing jobs for one of the white ladies who lived on the River Road. Lindsey once overheard her grandmother talking in Chinese about a woman's measurements, conducting her conversation in Zhongshan dialect, her guttural sounds interrupted by phrases such as "huge bazooms."

Lindsey had heard vague rumors that Yun Yun was from a broken home, and that she and Yeh Yeh had met in San Francisco before they moved to Locke, but she was unsure. Yeh Yeh sometimes referenced selling vegetables on the street long before he ever had his grocery store, and he once mentioned knowing Yun Yun as a young girl. But Lindsey could have been wrong. She had compiled a Frankenstein creature of stitched-together stories and hearsay, and some details were mismatched. But it was the best she could do, so far. Anyone who could possibly know anything acted like they were in the Witness Protection Program, as if the corroboration of information was so dangerous that the knowledge of it could still get themselves, their offspring, or future generations whacked, deported, or barred from American success should any hundred-year-old indiscretion be revealed.

Needless to say, Lindsey didn't understand why everything was so hush-hush. She was raised during the Oprah-Geraldo-Jerry-Springer era, when people routinely parlayed careers out of gabbing convivially about White House lap dances with underaged metrosexuals. She was used to E! Channel confessions and didn't get why anyone would want to keep secrets in this day and age when divulging your bullshit made you rich and a hero for at least fifteen minutes. Unlike old-school Chinese folks, Lindsey would hardly consider one person's disgrace a mark against Chinese people as a whole.

Sighing, she closed the album. She felt a little guilty for swiping it, but vowed to replace it when she returned to her grandparents' house for another round of cleaning. She was scheming about how to further excavate details of her grandparents' earlier days when the phone rang and interrupted her train of thought.

It was Michael. He told her the vegan *owsla** had confiscated his phone and he was calling from a booth in the hallway of his ashram cellblock. He said that he convinced them he was an

---

*This was the Psychic Food Ashram's term for their "peace officers" who roamed the dormitory halls in search of contraband items such as outside food that tasted too good. The enforcers took their name from a hierarchical group of rabbits in *Watership Down* because they thought themselves peaceful, vegetarian animals. Although one of the ashram's tenets was that eating meat created aggressive behavior, Michael said he found the *owsla* more intimidating than any carnivore he had ever met, especially when they searched his suitcase and ruthlessly confiscated a peanut butter sandwich that Lindsey had packed for him. They said commercial peanut butter possibly contained pork hormones and claimed they would throw it away, but Michael suspected they just ate it when no one was looking.

acolyte seeking spiritual guidance and was dedicated to ingesting only raw legumes and fruits that were free of bad vibes. No one trusted him yet, and in fact, he thought the phones were tapped because he kept hearing clicking noises. Or perhaps that was just his TMJ, which acted up when he didn't eat enough protein.

The ashram had recommended he begin his stay with a three-day fast. He said, "If I don't call you within two days just drive down here with a rib eye in a bag and throw it over the fence."

"You'll be fine," she said.

Jook Singin' in the Rain

"My tour bus is about to leave, but real quick, could you just explain the history of Chinese painting?"

That's what a Hoarder Lady said to Lindsey just as she was about to take her fifteen-minute break.

"No hablo inglés," Lindsey said, then walked away.

She left the gift shop and took the elevator up to the third-floor gallery. Strolling around for a while, she eventually settled on a bench to study a Chagall painting. She stared at the watery blues and a floating bride, and as she sat there a little longer, tapping her feet on the floor, she suddenly felt hot cigar-breath wafting from behind her head.

She had hoped that today she would be left alone, but she was wrong. Hearing a familiar hissing noise, she anticipated the question she heard every time she tried to wander through the museum like a normal person.

Since the first day she started working in the gift shop she had been harassed by the security guards, all older Filipino men. It seemed they couldn't wait to set her up on dates with their nephews or themselves, and every week they approached her and wiggled their long eyebrows and chewed their bottom lips as they studied her. Today was no different. As she sat and waited, the uniformed man eventually asked the inevitable question:

"Are you married?"

She kept her eyes on the painting and sighed, ignoring him in hopes he would saunter away. Instead, he walked in a circle around her and waited for her reply.

The security guards seemed to have a running bet over her exact ethnicity. Last week as she studied an Yves Tanguy surrealist painting, a guard popped into her field of vision. "Filipina?" he inquired with a tinge of hope in his voice. A minute later, over by the ladies' room another blue-uniformed gent sauntered by and ventured, "Korean?" Then, by Rauschenberg's *Erased DeKooning*, "Thailand girl?"

Lindsey felt a sense of déjà vu as she glanced now at a different but equally persistent guard.

"Married?" he said again, stepping closer. Annoyed, she stood up and walked away. She contemplated alerting security to the routine harassment she'd been enduring, but she supposed that would have been futile.

Her fifteen minutes were up, so in a huff she got into the elevator to head back down to the lobby. As the doors shut, she found herself squished behind a group of rowdy twentysomethings. They jostled and shoved one another, paying no mind to the few passengers who were not part of their herd.

Someone said, "Hey, press 'two,' wouldja?"

Another guy responded, "What do I look like, a freakin' *Chinaman*?"

Smashed against the elevator's back wall, Lindsey was taken aback by what she heard. She fumed and wanted to say, "Let me up front, I'm Chinese! I can push the button!" Instead, she stayed quiet and silently hated them all.

Back in the gift shop, she slipped her apron and white gloves back on. After de-dandruffing a Warhol wig, she blew out the bangs with a can of compressed air and used a pick to tease the synthetic strands to rat-nest perfection worthy of the pop icon. Placing the wig back on a Styrofoam head, she saw someone approaching in her peripheral vision. He came forward and was zapped by a crackle of static electricity as he touched the counter. With a spastic motion, he jumped back.

"Ow!" he said. Then added, "Yang!"

She jerked her head up.

Yang was right. Her hippie aunt, Shirley, referred to sexy guys as "yummy and *yang*," as opposed to "*yin*," which meant feminine. Dustin Lee struck Lindsey at this moment as a good blend of both—handsome and muscular with masculine *yang* but also graceful and well-groomed with perfect skin and feminine *yin*. Either way, there was no denying this time that he was the hottest Chinese guy she had ever laid eyes on, and tonight he was a welcome sight.

"Hey, Miss. I'd like to complain that your carpet just gave me a terrible shock," he said.

"Well, you shouldn't shuffle your feet, then go around touching things. Didn't you learn anything in science class?"

He smiled. "I don't know if you remember, but I was here before."

"Yeah, I know."

"So, do you have any idea who I am?"

"Let's see," she said. "Your name is Dustin Lee, and you may or may not be a direct descendant of the great general, Robert E. Lee. When you were twelve you were uprooted from Texas and went to St. Maude's Elementary School, where you accused other Chinese kids of being rat-eaters and in your spare time worked on your Devo impersonations. Am I right?"

He smiled and leaned in close. "You're fantastic, you know that?"

She allowed a small smile to show, but with trepidation.

"I was so happy when I bumped into you last week," he said. "You turned out really, um, all-right-looking."

Lindsey blushed. Not only had Dustin turned out to be not bad-looking himself, but as they chatted, she noted a certain charisma that made other patrons in the store turn around and notice him. He carried himself like a celebrity, and said, "How's it goin'?" to complete strangers who nodded and smiled, seeming to feel immediately better about themselves because someone far more beautiful than they had just acknowledged their existence.

Dustin leaned over the glass counter and said, "You really do look great." Then he made a fake-sad face and gave her a puppy-dog look. "But you don't seem all that happy to see me."

His flirtation was boosting her ego but she decided to play it cool. She said, "Let's just say I'm glad you're not dead."

"Well, at least that's a start."

He reached across the counter to touch her hand, and when she hesitantly lifted it away from his, he grabbed and squeezed it, pressing a small, rectangular thing into her palm. He kissed the back of her hand, and said "I'll be in the bar across the street. Come see me when you get off." Then he abruptly turned and walked away.

Dazed by his sudden appearance and quick departure, Lindsey watched him stride out the door. Uncurling her clenched fingers, she found a peace offering, a Hello Kitty eraser. She brought the small, pastel square under her nose and inhaled its pleasing vanilla scent.

Alas, Hello Kitty was like kryptonite. Who knew that pink, plastic crap could be so intoxicating? But, oh, it sure was. For an Asian girl, and presumably others, there was something about that new, plastic smell that consistently delighted. Maybe it was the nostalgia of childhood revisited, the promise of a perfect world where all the pencils were sharp and colors were bright like candy. In the Sanrio world, everyone was a chum, with silly clothes and perky bows. Faces were innocent, wide-eyed, and friendly with no mouths to utter ugly words or get you in trouble with French kissing or fellatio.

The rest of her shift flew by, and by nine, she was counting out her register and replenishing Zone Four with supplies. She freshened up her appearance with the hair-and-makeup kit she kept in her staff locker for nights when she and Michael planned late dinners out. With Michael in Santa Barbara, she rationalized that there was no reason to return so soon to their dark, empty apartment. She headed across the street to where Dustin awaited her.

It was drizzling outside and Lindsey didn't have an umbrella, so she held the edge of her coat over her head. As she stepped off the curb on a green light, she was nearly plowed over by a brown Trans-Am with a flaming, gold eagle painted on the hood. She jumped back, terrified.

Under the streetlight in the well-lit intersection, she could see that the driver was a middle-aged man, an *Asian* man, and as he slowed his car he simultaneously revved the engine. Leaning out the window, he eyeballed her from head to toe, then sneered.

"Look where you're going, you dumb bitch."

Lindsey stood paralyzed as she watched the driver peel across the lanes, burning rubber. Still standing dumbly in the crosswalk like Rainman, she eventually regained her senses, ran to the bus shelter at the curb, then spontaneously burst into tears.

It was raining now, and as she sat there and waited for the patter to lessen, she felt like she had just been assaulted. She

took a few deep breaths and considered what had just tran-
spired with the Trans-Am driver. A sudden tide of frustration,
resentment, and confusion swelled in her heart, and in her
mind she launched into an unspoken tirade against a phenomenon that had troubled her all her post-pubescent life:

The Angry Asian Man. She encountered him every so often,
and he could take many forms: a young guy, an old guy, businessman, skateboarder, store clerk, restaurant worker, pedes-
trian, or like tonight, a guy in a car. An Angry Asian Man was
always a stranger, but someone whom, with a single look, a
curt word, or with silent body language communicated something to her that struck the core of her being.

The Angry Asian Man inexplicably hated her. When she encountered him she was always caught unaware, perhaps walking innocently when a stream of saliva would land mere inches
from her shoes. She would look up to see someone whose
physical features made it appear that he could possibly be her
relative, but whose unblinking glare and sneering look of disgust let her know in no uncertain terms that he found her—her
appearance, her presence, her *being*—deserving of nothing but
derision.

An Angry Asian Man never looked or spoke to her with any
semblance of civility, but in the second or two that he made
himself known to her, a sexual tension dominated the exchange.
Young or old, immigrant or not, whether he blew smoke at her,
made a small noise, or silently glared, one particular gesture was
consistent. Every encounter with an Angry Asian Man had involved a split-second moment when he drank her in with his
eyes. Without fail, his gaze traveled up and down her body in a
quick once-over, and this appraisal of her physique always struck
her as a crucial and humiliating focal point of each incident.

In her experience, being a slightly built Asian-American
woman with a California accent and primarily pink wardrobe

was its own ticking time bomb. When an Angry Asian Man looked at her, she knew his reaction to her had everything to do with the battle of the sexes. It had to do with the tension specifically between Asian men and Asian women, and also between Asian men and non-Asian women, and to say that such a thing was not a sore spot would be a lie.

Lindsey knew of the struggles of Asian men and the history of bachelor societies in the early days of immigration. She knew of the hardships of fathers and grandfathers who were beaten down—sometimes literally—in mining camps and on railroad crews. She knew Chinese men took jobs as cooks, houseservants and laundrymen, swallowing their pride to do "women's work" lest their families starve. She admired that ingenuity, loyalty, and humility for the sake of survival, but somehow, to an Angry Asian Man, she did not deserve the right to offer sympathy. And he certainly did not want her pity.

She didn't expect an instant lovefest every time she met an Asian man on the street, but it really troubled and shocked her that the Angry Asian Man never even gave her a chance. He immediately shut her out, but also seemed to resent her for not knocking at his door, for not falling down at his nonexistent welcome mat and beating her breast while wailing to be let in. Was she supposed to hold herself to an invisible sense of racial honor and stand in the corner like a wallflower until an Angry Asian Man flicked his cigarette her way or deigned to find her attractive?

Screw that noise.

Lindsey sat at the bus stop and dried her tears. She pulled out a tube of lipstick and with three quick smudges put her game face back on. Standing up, she headed toward the bar.

Dustin was sitting at a table right near the door so she spotted him immediately. He hugged her and said, "So, what's up with you these days?"

She tossed her bag down and slid into the seat next to him.

"Asian guys hate me."

He laughed, then briefly turned away to order their drinks from the bartender.

"That's not true. I'm Asian and I don't hate you."

"Well . . ." she hesitated.

"C'mon, tell me your problems," Dustin said, setting a drink in front of her and sitting down.

Without engaging in the usual small talk or polite niceties, Lindsey launched into a description of the Angry Asian Man phenomenon. She explained, "Maybe it only happens twice a year, or maybe once every couple of years, but these guys do exist. I've never mentioned it to anyone, and actually feel kind of silly talking about it now."

Perhaps it was the combination of Dustin being sort of a stranger, but also somewhat familiar that made Lindsey feel comfortable enough to spill her guts at this moment. Maybe it was just the intent way he was staring at her. For whatever reason, she continued,

"I don't know. Angry Asian Men resent me for reasons I'll probably never know. Summing me up by my clothes, or whatever, their disapproving stares are so intense they both scare me and piss me off. Are they prejudiced against me because they think I was born with advantages, or do they disapprove of choices they think I've made? They act like they already know all about me. I don't know why my appearance inspires such vitriol, but I feel like a bull's-eye in a mysterious, hostile game of target practice within my own ethnic group."

A moment before, Dustin had signaled to the bartender to keep the drinks coming. As another round arrived, Dustin considered her words carefully, and nodded. He said, "If it's any consolation, Asian girls hate me, too."

Lindsey's interest was piqued. "Really?"

"Yeah. You and I have a lot in common." He picked up his glass and held it up to the light. "See, if you were a beverage, I bet you would be a peppy soda pop rather than a heavy, murky tea. As I recall, when you're not belting me with a lunchbox, that's your personality for the most part. When white people see you and realize you wear the same kind of clothes as they do and you don't speak with an accent, they probably welcome your hint of Chinese flavor, assuming you're filled with empty calories but are nonetheless . . . refreshing. They like that you're different enough to be entertaining, but not strong enough to upset their stomachs. On the other hand, some Chinese people, Angry Asian Men included, take one look at your packaging and immediately judge you. They assume you're too bubbly, or have some kind of gimmick. They might think you're too sweet to be any good, or think you've designed yourself to cater to Western palates. In all of two seconds of seeing you, they take it upon themselves to proclaim that your character consists of inferior ingredients devoid of any authentic Chinese flavor."

Lindsey looked Dustin in the eye, fairly impressed. She'd never heard anyone explain her predicament so succinctly. He obviously knew where she was coming from. Wherever he'd been and whatever he'd done since the sixth grade, he certainly had shared some of her sticky experiences. Trusting him, she said, "I know this city has exponentially more white guy /Asian girl couples than the other way around. If Angry Asian Men view this type of mixed couple as an unfavorable phenomenon, there isn't anything I can do about it. I don't feel responsible for any relationship other than my own.

"Likewise, if Angry Asian Men want to date blondes, I

don't care. If blondes don't want to date them back, that equation has nothing to do with me. I do feel, however, that somehow Angry Asian Men blame me for these . . . social discrepancies, or whatever. They seem to regard me as an enemy who contributes to a greater whole of racial inequalities, never empathizing even for a moment or perhaps considering that I, too, have to deal with people's misconceptions."

Dustin looked up from his drink and grinned. "So," he said, "I take it you date white guys."

She nodded sheepishly.

"Yeah. I date white girls."

There was a pause, then they both burst into laughter. Dustin ordered more drinks, and after a moment, he said, "So, you're really burning a path to the top, what, working retail?" He rattled the ice cubes in his glass and took a gulp of whiskey.

Her legs had gone slack against the banquette panel, and she noticed now that Dustin was eyeballing her thighs. She nonchalantly pulled her skirt down and closed her legs.

"Don't do that," he said, winking at her.

Embarrassed, she tried to think of something to say. "So, what happened to you? Where did you go after sixth grade?"

"I went to boarding school. Military. Texas. Pure hell. I was the only Chinese kid and got my ass kicked, like, every day."

Dustin scanned the semi-crowded bar, and his eyes lingered at some grungy girls in tank tops who were making cow eyes at him. It was hard for Lindsey to believe that a guy who turned out so handsome was ever a runt that people picked on. He turned his attention back to her.

"Actually, it's not exactly true that Asian girls hate me. I just hardly ever meet any. However, the ones I do see don't seem to want to have anything to do with me. I don't have a big, fat CLK Mercedes, or look like a doctor, or anyone with money or a future, or anything."

"Not all Asian girls are looking for guys with money," Lindsey said.

Dustin shot her a look.

Lindsey thought about the Chinese Math Vortex. Her cousin Sharon. The invention of the abacus.

"Um, what do you do, anyway?" she asked.

He looked straight at her. "My family owns the Golden Phoenix chain of Chinese restaurants. Second biggest in North America. I don't work. I'm a mooch." Changing the subject, he asked, "So how come you don't date Asian guys?"

She had promised Michael she'd keep their engagement a secret for a month or so, until he found her the perfect ring, he said. So instead of telling Dustin she was off the market, she just replied, "What am I supposed to say? After my whole life of not hanging out with other Chinese people at school or at work, am I supposed to walk up to someone and say, 'I'm ready to embrace my Asianness now. Will you be my friend?'"

Dustin nodded and stared into his empty glass. He said, "Believe me, I know what you mean."

And Penguins Is Practically Chickens

People with tiny heads cannot be trusted. That's what Lindsey reminded herself as she used a toothbrush and a cup of diluted bleach to clean between Jesus's toes on the hallway crucifix. Today, the tiny head in question belonged to Sister Boniface. Lindsey could see her now, bawling out a little Chinese girl down by the third grade classroom. As Lindsey continued her Son of God mani-pedi she watched Boniface's beet-red face and quivering puff of orange frizz like a pom-pom of pubic hair poking out of the top of her wimple. She was gesticulating with her tiny fists, hard and mauve like new potatoes, and she boxed the air like a mechanical, menacing garden gnome. The little girl bowed her head in contrition, and Lindsey suddenly imagined herself standing there in those Mary Janes, feeling the pain of the past, reliving the terror she herself felt when she was a St. Maude's student.

To think of Sister Boniface, Lindsey inevitably had to remember the Era of Lost Chinese Children. Under the diminutive nun's tutelage, Chinese children had a particular way of going bye-bye, and Lindsey had always feared she would be dropped down a trap door to a fiery, dungeon furnace.

The first kid to go had been Beethoven Sing. Beethoven was a sullen and grumpy kid from the first day of kindergarten. He hardly ever talked or moved, which was usually considered good behavior by Sister Boniface, and he just sat and stared into space no matter what the other kids were doing. Lindsey and the other children drew maps of the world, learned the names of the planets, and nodded their heads as their militant leader performed scientific experiments too advanced for their age group. The tiny nun showed them how to make explosive devices from everyday items such as baking soda and vinegar. She wired up her contraptions with mangled coat hangers, and presto! Just because they couldn't read yet was no excuse not to engage in a cottage-industry of do-it-yourself domestic bombs for household use. All the kindergartners cheered when Boniface exploded a papier-mâché piñata, but Beethoven just sat there with a tight frown, his greasy bangs twittering in the breeze from the open window.

Sometimes Lindsey tried to talk to him. When one of the parents made cupcakes to celebrate Annunciation Day, Lindsey asked, "Beethoven, do you want vanilla or chocolate?" He sat stock-still like a P.O.W. who refused to utter a sound under questioning. Sister Boniface interjected, "He doesn't get a thing. His mother says he's allergic to chocolate, milk products, yeast, dust, and fun." His left eyelid twitched and several kids took it as a sign that they could eat his cupcake for him.

As the months unfolded, the kindergartners made nifty napkin rings out of pipe cleaners and learned the alphabet. They sang "Waltzing Matilda" and "My Bonny Lies Over the Ocean." For two whole months Beethoven sat motionless in his plastic chair. Sometimes the rest of the class forgot he was even there at the back of the room.

That is, until the day the kindergarten classroom received a new record player.

In addition to being an enthusiastic proponent of noontime calisthenics, Sister Boniface fancied herself a music aficionado. She called the newfangled device a phonograph and played religious records for the children. Near Christmastime, Lindsey and the other kids learned "Hark, the Herald Angels Sing," "Away in a Manger," and "Joy to the World." The old LPs were made of colored vinyl, and one day Sister Boniface removed a turquoise disc from its sleeve and placed it on the turntable. After a few crackles of the needle, two or three notes played through the speaker and Beethoven suddenly sat bolt upright. It was as if all the past months he was a deactivated toy and this music instantly unlocked a secret code in the corroded microchip of his brain.

The song was "O, Little Town of Bethlehem," and as the other kids sang with lazy, slack tongues, each of them couldn't help but notice the effect this particular tune had on the little, spiky-haired curmudgeon. Beethoven sat on his hands and began to rock. He started out slowly, taking in the soothing, lulling lyrics. His shoulders then unlocked and propelled his neck back and forth. By the second stanza he was pitching his head forward as if knocking against an imaginary wall, and his chin banged against his chest. At the third verse, he really put his lower back into it. He rocked harder and harder, like a heavy-metal headbanger. All he needed to complete his performance was to bust out in an air-guitar solo.

"And in the dark street shineth . . ." the children sang hesitantly, worried about their little classmate. Sister Boniface tried to alleviate their concerns.

"It's okay, children," she said. "I'm going to box his ears!" With the deliberate, slow-motion steps of a trained assassin, she quietly snuck up behind Beethoven, whose bangs, by this time, were flying wildly out of control. The legs of his chair wobbled from the force of his weight. Sister Boniface spread her fists wide and was about to administer two crushing cauliflower ears on the poor fellow, when suddenly the song ended and Beethoven's flailing torso also came to an abrupt halt.

He immediately returned to his previous catatonic state and once again stared straight ahead without moving a muscle. Sister Boniface stood behind him, her arms still outstretched. She looked disappointed that her opportunity to smash the boy's head like another papier-mâché piñata had now so cruelly been torn from her grasp.

They all stared at Beethoven as "We Three Kings" began to play. Through two choruses they eyeballed him, none of them singing, just watching expectantly. He was exactly like that singing frog in the cartoons, sitting now like a lump after a rousing performance. They stared at Beethoven until the end of another song. He remained completely still as if nothing had happened. They all began to suspect that they had collectively imagined his rhythmic flailing.

Sister Boniface tiptoed to the turntable and returned the needle to the beginning of the turquoise disc. As the notes of "O, Little Town of Bethlehem" began again, sure enough, the little froggie came back to life, throwing his body back and forth like a daredevil riding a roller coaster. The other kids were all just spectators watching sheepishly from the sidelines.

The recess bell rang and the students ran from the classroom, all except Beethoven, who was still hooked on a feeling. Thirty minutes later, when they returned from the schoolyard, Beethoven had disappeared. No one ever saw that grumpy little boy again, and it crossed Lindsey's mind that perhaps the nuns had simply killed him.

Two weeks later, the kindergartners were invited to the first-grade classroom to visit the older kids' newly acquired pet guinea pig. Suddenly, it all made sense. Lindsey knew exactly what had happened to Beethoven. The docile rodent's fur was the same jet-black color as Beethoven's short-nap hair, and he twitched just the same way. She was convinced the boy had been transformed into the little animal. Every kid knew that nuns had magical powers. This spell they had cast on Beethoven was just the sort of thing Lindsey suspected was their forté.

The first graders described how the guinea pig liked to eat apples and lettuce. A couple of Lindsey's classmates who also suspected sorcery piped up, "He's allergic to chocolate. Don't feed it to him!"

"That's right. Chocolate is bad for animals," Sister Colleen affirmed. "Any other comments?"

"And no milk!" another girl advised.

"Keep his cage clean. He hates dust!" Lindsey interjected.

They all filed past the cage and took turns petting the creature's soft fur. When it came Lindsey's turn, she scratched Beethoven's neck and vowed that next year, when this would be her classroom, she would stay after school every day and sing "O, Little Town of Bethlehem" to him. She imagined a gaze of gentle gratitude in Beethoven's eyes, and it was then, at the tender age of five, that Lindsey wondered if Beethoven's being Chinese had anything to do with his sealed fate.

For the next few weeks, when she wasn't working in her religion notebook and coloring in Jesus's muttonchops just so, Lindsey studied the other Chinese kids in her class:

Dorcas Foo was thick-faced with wiry hair. Nelson Fong had sad eyes and buck teeth. Jefferson Lee was a silent genius. And Ima Ho was skinnier than a piece of Scotch tape. During class it was difficult for Lindsey to scrutinize her Chinese brethren for lurking evil, so eventually she decided to perform her anthropological study on the playground. Over the course of several months, here is what she discovered:

The St. Maude's playground appeared to be a childhood wonderland with its crisply outlined hopscotch squares, tetherball courts, and drinking fountain of gleaming white porcelain and multiple stainless-steel spigots. One day, as Jefferson Lee innocently hydrated himself at the trough, someone pushed him and he cracked his skull wide open, his melon spurting like a giant pomegranate. He was rushed to a nearby hospital, never to be seen again.

The hopscotch corner was where slow runners such as Gina Fang were pummeled with Nutter Butters during tournaments of freeze tag and four square. The various tetherball poles made excellent locations for immigrant-girl Dorcas Foo to be tied to the stake like Joan of Arc until she confessed a crush on Scott Baio. Lindsey suspected that poor Dorcas didn't even know who Scott Baio was, but that somehow made extracting her confession all the more tantalizing to the brats who tormented her.

Lindsey had, in fact, joined in on the torture of her classmate. It was fun to reenact the Salem witch trials and pretend to burn her at the stake. At least it wasn't Lindsey who was being picked on, and she wanted to keep it that way. Even at five years old, she knew she didn't want to be a helpless Chinese victim lashed with Red Vines.

Neither Ima nor Dorcas returned the following school year. It gave Lindsey pause for thought.

By the second grade, Lindsey was the only Chinese girl in class and Nelson Fong was designated as her "boyfriend" by the rest of the class for the sole reason that they were both Chinese. She hated being asked, "When you marry Nelson Fong, will you live in Hong Kong and play Ping Pong with King Kong?" She heard that at least five times a day.

By the fourth grade, two new boys arrived, Franklin Ng and John Goon, but by midyear, young Mr. Goon also vanished. He was sick one recess and cut a path through the handball courts with a series of projectile barf grenades. The schoolyard erupted in mayhem as all the kids ran the gauntlet of spent pasta-shell casings and half-digested cherry Pop-Tarts that lay like splattered, exploded land mines on the battlefield that was the St. Maude's schoolyard. Some speculated that he had the plague, but Lindsey didn't ask any questions. When he didn't return for science class, she just figured that he met the fate of the other Chinese children at St. Maude's. He had either been killed outright or transformed into a furry animal.

After what happened to Dustin Lee at the end of sixth, she became completely convinced that associating with Chinese students slated for certain termination would most definitely worsen her prospects in the afterlife. If she socialized with the unsaved on earth, there would be little chance St. Peter would pluck her from the slush pile of purgatory, especially since all those more deserving, innocent pagan babies were down there wrecking the curve for everyone else.

As the years proceeded, in addition to her mounting concerns over her potentially Satanic destiny, she began to wonder what benefits there were to being Chinese, if any. As far as St. Maude's was concerned, none.

An inventory:

Total students at St. Maude's: 240.
Number of Chinese students: 26.
Number of Chinese boys, school-wide, ever chosen to
    play Joseph in the Christmas pageant: Zero.
Number of Chinese girls ever chosen to play Mary: Zero.
Number of Chinese altar boys: Zero.
Number of Chinese children forced to sit in the back pew
    of the church during Friday-morning mass: 26.

Twenty-six. That was every single Chinese kid in the school. Since St. Maude's charged non-Catholics a steeper tuition, weren't those Chinese dollars worth sitting a couple of pews closer to the action, especially when there were sixteen empty pews between them and the rest of their classmates? Didn't their fees earn them a Chinese Mary in a holiday skit every once in a while? Lindsey would have settled for being the innkeeper or even one of the barnyard animals, but she was always crammed anonymously into the chorus, where she resented missing her chance to bleat piously. If the three wise men were supposedly from the "Orient," why couldn't Franklin, Nelson, or another Chinese boy ever be chosen to play one of the "Orientals"? Year after year, Chinese robes and feathered turbans were donned by freckle-faced Irish kids with painted-on pointy eyebrows and slanty eyeliner.

Still cleaning the crucifix, Lindsey dabbed a Q-tip on the Lord's nether regions and was shaken from her daydreaming by Sister Boniface screaming at the little Chinese girl at the end of the hall. The nun's bellowing echoed through the corridor: "If you do it one more time . . . this . . . means . . . WAR!" She thrust her arms into the air and outstretched her hands, wiggling her wee fingers like a squirrel on its hind legs begging for food. Lindsey could practically see the steam shooting out of Sister Boniface's ears as she watched the little Chinese girl nod obediently, looking contrite for whatever transgression she had committed.

As she watched the Chinese girl walk back to her classroom in the wake of Sister Boniface's fury, Lindsey took a moment to wonder what school life was like for the little moppet. Was she as frightened as Lindsey had been? Maybe if Lindsey befriended the girl she could help her feel less alone. She vowed to keep an eye on her from now on.

Even Asian Girls Get the Blues

"Hello?" Lindsey said sleepily. It was two in the morning.

Michael's voice was low and soothing. "Hi, Cutie Pie. It's me. Sorry to call so late, but the Owsla are asleep so it's the only time I could get a chance to call you."

"How's it going?" she asked, awake now.

"Okay, I guess. The food's crap. How are you?"

"I don't know," she said vaguely.

In all honesty, she hadn't been doing so great. She'd been restless and lonely, and since her encounter with the Angry Asian Man and her talk with Dustin, she'd been reflecting on her dearth of Asian friends. Furthermore, despite the fact that she was positively in love with Michael, she'd been thinking about the finality of marriage. For a single gal, the dating world was a smorgasbord, at least in theory. The idea that she'd never spin the lazy susan again just made her a little nervous. Would she really be happy forever without ever tasting again from the banquet of hotties she imagined were out there somewhere?

Michael interrupted her thoughts. He said, "What's on your mind, Babykins? Just because I'm down here in this wasteland of good vibes doesn't mean we can't talk. Just pretend I'm in bed right next to you, talking like we always do before we go to sleep."

"Have you ever noticed," she said, "that we don't hang out with many other Asian people?"

"We hang out with your family all the time."

"They're relatives. They don't count."

"Oh?"

"I think I'm having an Asian identity crisis."

At two in the morning on a Tuesday night?"

"I know it sounds kind of ridiculous."

"No it doesn't. Tell me."

Lindsey collected her thoughts as she readjusted a pillow under her neck in the dark. "Well," she began, "to be my age, Chinese-American, and raised in San Francisco is practically synonymous with going to Lowell High School, listening to Kool & the Gang, and experimenting with permanent-wave hairdos. I've never drag raced a souped-up Honda down Nineteenth Avenue, gone out for midnight snacks at Golden Dragon, or stood in the freezing cold tinkering all night with a midget-sized pocket bike. And Asian guys who do that sort of stuff would never look twice at me."

"That's good for me," Michael interjected. "But go on."

In the sleepy darkness, Lindsey's thoughts turned wistful. "Maybe from my experiences at St. Maude's, I give off a vibe that tells Chinese guys that even talking to me would render them jinxed or zapped into a guinea pig. It probably doesn't endear me to them that I went to a private high school where I subscribed to a kind of teen conformity that had me wearing safety pins in my ears and Doc Marten boots while pogo-ing to ska music, instead of sporting hair scrunchies and L.A. Gear cross-trainers while slow dancing like a metronome to the latest by El DeBarge."

"Yeah?" Michael said patiently.

Lindsey continued, "Lowell had a huge Asian contingent, but at my school I was one of a total of five Asians. Instead of banding together in solidarity, we all stayed away from one another. We never acknowledged our Asianness to one another. I've been thinking about it and have come to the conclusion that we each had our hands full trying to fit in and dared not risk doing anything that would further exclude us from the J. Crew world.

"There were two of us girls, me and a girl named Leslie. We shared several classes and the teachers always mixed up our names, which sucked. Of the boys, there was one exchange student from Beijing, and the school counselor tried to play matchmaker with us, even though we hated each other. When no one else was around, he called me names in Chinese, one of which was *jook sing*. I went home and asked my mom what that meant, and she told me it meant 'hollow bamboo,' like I was an empty shell of a Chinese person. She goes, 'Who called you that? Some fresh-off-the-boat *fob* with "little emperor" syndrome?'"

"What about the other Chinese guys?"

"The other Chinese boys paid no attention to me whatsoever. One was pounded every day after school on his way to working in his family's restaurant. Of course, carrying a violin didn't help his coolness quotient. The other boy had actually reached the upper echelons of the Super Clique, so far out of my social league that it would have been laughable for me to even attempt touching the purposely frayed hem of his designer clothes. By the way, thanks for listening to me. You're being really patient."

"I want to know," Michael said. "You've never told me any of this before."

He was right. Lindsey didn't know why it was all pouring out now. Maybe she wanted to make sure she told him all about herself before they got married, as if there was stuff he hadn't figured out in their two years of living together. Maybe she wanted to let him know what he was getting into, that he was marrying a "hollow bamboo." Perhaps she wanted him to judge for himself if that was a good or a bad thing. Maybe if he assured her that he accepted her the way she was, she could stop doubting her self-worth.

She said, "In college I didn't make any Asian friends either. Can you imagine that? At Berkeley, where everyone is Asian. During lunch I sometimes found myself in a deluge of O-Chem students just released from their lab, but the geniuses were too busy thinking about molecular structures and cures for cancer to notice me. And I dismissed them all as nerds because they weren't in Art History. When I tried to befriend the few Asians who were in my English classes, my attempts left me feeling like the troll I was. Like the time I approached this haughty Korean girl who wore lacy Jessica McClintock frocks, cameo pins, and white gloves every Tuesday to Shakespeare. I asked how her midterm paper was coming along, and she said, 'Why are you even talking to me? You're not in Honors.'"

Michael interjected, "Didn't you tell me you read *China Boy* in a Multicultural Literature class?"

"Yeah, when I handed in my first assignment early, the T.A. said, 'I hope you don't expect preferential treatment just because we're both Chinese.' When I asked what he meant, he replied, 'Oh, I think you already know.' I always remembered the way he refused to make eye contact and fluttered his eyelids like a malfunctioning slot machine. Whatever."

She knew that Michael hadn't called to listen to her ramble, so she stopped talking. "Forget it," she said.

"Cheer up, Baby. We can talk more when I get home."

"Okay. I love you, Mister."

"I love you, too. Now get some sleep."

Fellowship of the Ming

The next day at St. Maude's, Lindsey checked the office chalkboard to see which tasks Sister Constance had assigned her for the day. In perfect nun cursive it read,

Pick up sheet music and missals from Mrs. Yee's home.
Store in basement for archives.

A mild jolt of panic reverberated through Lindsey's bones like a note through a tuning fork. She looked at the address on the chalkboard and recognized it immediately as the location of her childhood piano lessons. She would have to go *there*? *Today*?

Lindsey knew the route well. As she trudged to Mrs. Yee's place, she felt like she was back in fifth grade on the way to her lesson. She walked slowly, stalling because she wasn't quite ready to face her childhood memories of Mrs. Yee's dark, airless abode. Nonetheless, she headed toward the border of Chinatown, and made her way to the red door across the street from the 76 station that used to have the numbers in Chinese on its giant, fiberglass orange ball.

She approached the iron gate with the double happiness geometric design, and rang the bell. Standing there, she waited in the sunlight and tried to make eye contact with the gas-station attendant across the street so there might be a witness just in case she disappeared behind the red door, never to be seen again.

After a minute, the door opened, and there stood Mrs. Yee, just like all those times before.

"Hello," Lindsey said, trying not to stare at the droopy wiglet that sat atop Mrs. Yee's head like a small animal. Look-ing into the woman's black-outlined cat eyes, she noticed her false eyelashes were lopsided and coming unglued.

In an affected, childlike falsetto, the piano teacher said, "I've been expecting you."

Lindsey stepped inside the narrow doorway. She stood against the gold wallpaper in the foyer and waited as Mrs. Yee retrieved the hymnals for her to take back to school. Lindsey stood in the quiet darkness, and after a few moments Mrs. Yee called down to her from the hallway, "Could you come back here and help me, please?" She sounded as frail and demented as Michael Jackson.

Lindsey headed down the cramped hall toward the room where her childhood piano lessons had taken place. She rec-ognized the Esther Hunt prints of Chinese children, the bamboo-style picture frames with black ink lithographs, and the japanned cabinet which she had always imagined was a repository for shrunken human heads. She stopped and stood against the black shelves overstuffed with books about séances, past lives, Atlantis, and the mummies of ancient Egypt. The musty room radiated a kind of moist heat, like the kind of damp warmth rising from a worm-rich compost heap, or, she imagined, the air inside a sealed mausoleum.

"I'll just take the hymnals and get going," Lindsey said, hoping to beat it out of there.

Mrs. Yee adjusted her rattan bracelets. "Won't you stay? I'll just play one song, for old times' sake . . ."

Before Lindsey could protest, the woman sat down and began to shake out her wrists as she had always done before playing. She patted the piano bench, signaling for Lindsey to sit down.

So frightening with their perfect red lacquer, Mrs. Yee's fingernails were mesmerizing. Overgrown, they curved slightly inward. Lindsey sat perfectly still as Mrs. Yee twirled her wrists hypnotically and clicked her nails together like Mr. Burns from *The Simpsons* contemplating an evil deed. Resting her fingers against the keys, she eventually began to play. She launched into a song Lindsey knew well. The click-clacking of her talons on the ivories conjured the chilling sound of a skeleton dance.

Lindsey recalled how Mrs. Yee used to place her cold, veiny hands atop hers to manipulate her fingers. Mrs. Yee's tapered digits felt shriveled and boneless, like waterlogged segments of baby corn. Pulling her hands away, Lindsey would watch Mrs. Yee's wrists and fingers prance along the keys like a marionette's. When Mrs. Yee invited her to follow her moving hands, touching the plastic-feeling nails reminded Lindsey of the time she once poked the dead, glass eye of the taxidermied antelope at the natural history museum.

As Lindsey sat now and prayed for the song to be over, she glanced out of the corner of her eye at Mrs. Yee and cowered slightly at the sight of the woman's sagging cheeks. Her skin was bluish-white and seemed bloodless beneath smears of rouge that reminded Lindsey of the overapplied handiwork she had seen on corpses at funeral parlors. Starting to get really creeped out, Lindsey suddenly stood up.

"I have to go!" she said, scooting out from the piano bench. She grabbed the stack of hymnals and sprinted down the hallway.

Mrs. Yee stopped playing and swiveled her neck slowly as she watched Lindsey bolt for the door. In an eerie, monotonous singsong just like the voice of the dead-bride hologram at the end of Disneyland's haunted mansion ride, she said, "Hope you'll return . . ."

When Lindsey emerged into the late morning sunlight, she felt like a mole that could barely see. Had her soul been sucked from her body during *Fur Elise*? She patted her chest and knocked herself on the head to make sure she hadn't been rendered a zombie in those ten minutes of darkness. She hurriedly walked down Stockton Street until she was safely away, far enough so Mrs. Yee couldn't see her with those Cleopatra eyes. In her fright and paranoia Lindsey speculated that perhaps Mrs. Yee always wore that wiglet to hide another set of peepers in the back of her head. Maybe she could pop one of those eyes out and hold it in her palm to look around corners.

Glad to be several blocks away now, Lindsey was so near to Chinatown she figured she would pick up some lunch before heading back to work. Turning down Washington Street, she was comforted to see the curly edges of the pagoda rooftops in the near distance. Her mood lightened as she approached the bright turquoise lampposts with their red and gold dragons reaching toward the blue sky.

She was reminded of Arnold Genthe, a German photographer whose pictures of Chinatown in the late nineteenth century remained the oldest existing record of any American neighborhood. Lindsey owned a book of his pictures, and even though she knew some critics thought his work perpetuated stereotypes of Chinese people, she was grateful he had taken the time to record the old scenes. He even had the foresight to store his glass negatives in another part of the city so they were spared destruction in the 1906 earthquake and fire. She didn't mind too much that he was a white person who filtered Chinatown through his own lens, perhaps having added artistic details to heighten the exoticism. She figured that without him there would have been no pictures at all.

Staring at the ornate balconies of the second-story temples, Lindsey thought of another person from the past, Look Tin Eli. After the earthquake had destroyed the original Chinatown, politicians in San Francisco wanted to move all the Chinese people to the outskirts of the city, but Look Tin Eli, a Chinese-American, convinced the city elders to keep the original site. He promoted the idea of Chinatown as a tourist attraction reconstructed with Chinese architectural flourishes. Partnering with white builders, he helped resurrect the neighborhood as a picturesque Asian wonderland that played to the public's fantasies of the East more than it represented any specific place in China. As Lindsey looked above and enjoyed the sight of the tiled rooftops, she wondered, if Look Tin Eli were alive today, would he be lauded as an innovative businessman or criticized as a sellout? Personally, she couldn't imagine Chinatown without its bright colors and unique, sinocized buildings.

On Grant Avenue she passed a plaque that marked the spot where the first rickety tent had been erected in the old city, then called Yerba Buena. Ducking into a storefront that sold dim sum to go, she grabbed some snacks, then zigzagged through a couple of alleys, stopping to munch on a piping-hot *ha gow* shrimp dumpling. Looking up, she spotted a familiar sign.

Her dad had once mentioned that Yeh Yeh spent every Tuesday at the Family Association visiting his cronies and playing cards. Lindsey wondered if her grandpa was there now. Still standing in the alley, she scarfed down a couple of *siu mai*. Then, on a whim, she decided to peek inside the brick building.

She walked up the stairway, her shoes hitting the aluminum floorstrips and making a flat, clapping sound. When she reached the top, she navigated a complex hallway with sharp turns, dips, and inclines that suggested that the layout of the building had been reconfigured many times. Eventually the maze opened onto a large room sparsely populated with a few gray-haired men. One was hunched in the corner, a trio sipped tea, and another read a Chinese-language newspaper, flipping it from back to front, which, she remembered, was the way Chinese books opened.

Lindsey noticed that all the men were wearing suits—dark gray—with white shirts. A couple even had fedoras by their sides. They all looked vaguely the same, like in pictures of men from a bygone era when everyone wore a suit and hat, no matter how rich or poor (or Chinese). From the odor of cigars she knew she was in a men's club, and the white walls, fluorescent lights, and minimalist decor gave the place the aura of a waiting room in heaven.

A man approached.

"What you lookee for?" he said. "Lookee nice shoppee?"

How bizarre. It wasn't like Lindsey was a constable coming to shake down a money-laundering dry cleaner. Why was this old Chinese man putting on his ching-chongy "I'm talking to whitey" voice?

She stood for a moment without saying anything. The man seemed to be in his late seventies, with slicked-down hair and smiling eyes. As he nodded and bowed, Lindsey felt uneasy.

"Um, I'm looking for . . . Yeh Yeh," she said.

"Yessee?" the man waited for her to say more, still nodding in the meantime.

"My grandfather," she said, "Yeh Yeh."

The man smiled patiently. "Yessee, many Yeh Yeh here." He stood there as if he could smile all day long.

Uh-oh. Trying to think of her grandfather's name, her mind drew a blank. Thinking she was being clever, she told the man, "I'm here to see Mr. Owyang."

He looked at her for a moment, then erupted in a high wheezing laugh. "You funny, Missee! All Mr. Owyang here!" He pointed to the black letters on the frosted glass door, which read OWYANG FAMILY ASSOCIATION.

Stymied, Lindsey then figured she'd describe Yeh Yeh, but what was she gonna say—he's Chinese, with gray hair, hella long earlobes, and a coupla moles sprouting hair? That described every old guy in the place.

Just then, another man shuffled over.

"Hey, I know your face," he said. "Long time ago you hang out in Jackson Street grocery store."

Lindsey was puzzled for a moment, then said, "Yes! That's Yeh Yeh's store."

As she stood expectantly, the two Chinese men conversed in Cantonese. From their intonations and gestures, she could tell that the second man was explaining to the first that he recognized her, and she strained to hear any names, especially American ones, being mentioned. They went back and forth with questions and explanations, after a while seeming to forget she was even there. Shifting her weight from foot to foot, she concentrated on trying to remember Yeh Yeh's name.

Feeling like an idiot for not knowing it, she picked her brain but couldn't come up with anything.

This is ridiculous, she scolded herself. Then she thought, *Wait a minute. I have to know this. Think! Start at the beginning.*

She figured that her grandfather had been given a Chinese name at birth, but like all Chinese babies, he was probably just called "Bi Bi" for a while. Some Chinese received a different name when they became adults, and another when they got married. Not that those names would have stuck either. Relatives probably just called him things like "Uncle's brother," or "second son," or whatever. In Chinese, the individual didn't matter as much as the family as a whole. Who you were in relation to everyone else was what defined you and determined how others addressed you.

In addition to the numerous monikers a single Chinese person like Yeh Yeh could have, he probably had an American name too. Lindsey didn't know whether the phenomenon was specific to San Francisco or not, but Chinese who were not given English names at birth often adopted American names, like George or Jenny. She understood why that was useful if your Chinese name was unpronounceable for Westerners, but why was it necessary if your name was Ming? And then there could also be American names heaped upon already-American names. For instance, her dad's name was Earl, but some people called him Bill. When she once asked him why, he just shrugged and said, "same thing," as if neither mattered much anyway.

To confuse things further, there were also nicknames. After having a myriad of Chinese baby names, adult names, familial titles, and then an American name like Maisy or Tom, then, for unknown reasons, on the streets of Chinatown, some people just came to be known as Shorty, Limpy, or some other term of endearment. Lindsey's dad had friends named Chubby Chin, and Dutch Dang. One guy with a thick Toisanese accent used to call the house and simply refer to himself as Uncle Zippy.

Maybe there were lots of old guys shuffling through Chinatown with names like Chuckles Chan and Jingles Jang. It was like the Old West, and everyone seemed to be guarding their true identity to avoid deportation even though their family had already been here for a hundred and twenty years. Old names were forgotten, but no one seemed to object. Maybe it was just easier to forget the past and concentrate on the here and now when you're suddenly just called "Smiley" instead of Serene Mountain of Jade Amongst the Swirling Heavens.

Lindsey thought it was all unnecessarily complex. Her whole life, she'd only thought of herself as an individual, not as someone whose every action could potentially disgrace every Owyang from here to Dailang, China. But then again, maybe the constant reminder of who someone was in relation to you made you think before doing something stupid. Something stupid like asking questions that might be better left alone.

Finally, one of the men seemed to remember that Lindsey was standing there and turned her way. He nodded and exclaimed, "Ah! You lookee Mistah Owyang."

Well, I could have told you that! she wanted to scream. Instead, she just followed the man down a hallway to another large room at the back of the building. She looked around and saw men playing cards and mahjong while others watched television. She spotted her grandfather by a long table, cutting a huge portion of apple pie with a plastic knife.

"Yeh Yeh?" she said, approaching.

The elderly man sat down at one of the folding tables and proceeded to eat his pie. He didn't seem surprised to see Lindsey, but didn't acknowledge her presence either. After a moment, Lindsey took the seat next to him.

"I was in the area and thought I'd visit you," she said.

Yeh Yeh nodded and continued to chew. Beneath his dandruff-sprinkled overcoat he wore a gray sweater vest, a clip-on tie, and gray pants. His horn-rimmed glasses and mild demeanor gave him the appearance of a weary FBI agent on a coffee break.

"I have extra rain jacket if you need," he said.

Lindsey looked across the window to the bright, sunny sky. "Oh, no thanks," she replied. Screwing up her courage, she added, "I wanted to ask where you grew up."

Yeh Yeh's eyes darted back and forth, and Lindsey wondered if he was mulling over an escape plan in case of a flash flood. He sucked pie through his teeth.

"I grew up right here," he replied. After a moment of quiet, Lindsey heard what sounded like low singing, but the idea of her mild-mannered grandpa breaking into song seemed fairly preposterous.

But she heard right. Yeh Yeh was softly singing the lyrics to "San Francisco."

She looked at him with a puzzled expression until he finally said, "I learned that when I used to empty spittoons in a real, old Frisco brothel!"

Lindsey had never heard her grandpa say something so wacky. She was curious, but unsure how to proceed. It suddenly occurred to her that a man dressed for blizzard conditions on a hot, sunny day might have other Walter Mittyesque delusions.

Nearby, two ancient Chinese men who had been arguing in Chinese switched to perfect English. Lindsey eavesdropped as they discussed the dissent among members of the Chinese Six Companies, debating what to do about the rift between their group's Sun Yat Sen loyalists and others who favored Communist ideas. As their conversation grew louder, Yeh Yeh retreated further into his own world.

"What was your father like?" Lindsey asked.

He stabbed at a few pie crumbs. "Chinese labor build all of California. You know that wall that hold up Mark Hopkins Hotel? My grandpa helped build it by hand. No tools, nothing."

"Really?"

"Sure, sure. Chinese do all work in this city no one else want to do. Dig ditch . . . There's even tunnel right by Golden Gate Bridge, dug by all Chinese hands. Dynamite blow your finger off!"

He coughed, then pulled his coat tighter around himself. Tapping his fingers on the table, he said, "Bridge game start at twelve noon."

Lindsey looked at the clock on the wall, and realized that Yeh Yeh was politely waiting for her to leave.

"Can I come see you again?" she asked.

Her grandfather pulled his woolen cap down past his ears. He replied, "I work in grocery store on Wednesday through Saturday, sometimes different schedule if Elmore is busy. But you can see me there."

Lindsey nodded, then leaned over to give her grandfather a hug. He did not return her embrace or acknowledge in any way that another human being was touching him. He seemed uncomfortable, but managed to say "Okey-dokey," before nudging away from her. Lindsey patted his shoulder, then gathered her things and left.

Permanent Records

Sitting on the bus on her way back to St. Maude's, Lindsey listened to The Violent Femmes on her discman and thought about the Permanent Record.

For her entire school career at St. Maude's, Lindsey had lived in fear of the Permanent Record. It was the threat that all teachers had dangled over students' heads since the beginning of time. Caught chewing gum in the hallway? On your Permanent Record. Ate meat on Good Friday? Jotted down for all eternity. God saw everything and nuns remembered everything. Lindsey wondered if there was a giant, fluffy cloud in the sky upon which a massive card catalog floated, the lesser saints periodically updating a venial sin here or there in red pencil. In her imagination, heaven was too dignified to go digital.

She entered the building and returned to her desk to find a note from Sister Constance requesting that she clean the taxidermied baby alligator that resided in the seventh-grade homeroom. After checking her voice mail to see if Michael had called, she went to the closet to find some latex gloves, then proceeded to the classroom. She was jittery as she made her way along the squeaky floors and up to the third floor. However, upon arriving at the door to the seventh-grade room, she was relieved to find a posted card which pronounced that Ms. Abilene had gone to lunch.

Turning the brass key, she quickly stepped inside. She made sure not to slam the door because the heavy glass windows had a tendency to rattle. She stood by the chalkboard and surveyed the rows of desks, the shelves of encyclopedia volumes, the coat rack, and the student-made mobiles that floated overhead. The room seemed smaller than she remembered, but the smell was the same: anxiety, deceit, sexual confusion. And what did that smell like? Vaguely: acne astringent, Mop & Glo, preteen sweat, and Gee Your Hair Smells Terrific shampoo.

Ah, the seventh-grade classroom. The scene of many crimes.

Atop a shoulder-high bookshelf, the taxidermied alligator squatted with jaws agape and eyelids peeled back. The creature's head was thrown back and its tail whipped up to the side, coiled in a permanent attack position as if it might lunge forward at any second, despite having been stuffed for at least twenty years. Lindsey took a deep breath and spritzed the animal with a can of compressed air. She hopped back as clumps of dust blasted from between the reptile's sharp teeth and wafted down to the floor.

As Lindsey continued to clean the baby alligator, she glanced around nervously. Being inside the seventh-grade room, she couldn't help but remember another St. Maude's incident that had resulted in the demise of a Chinese boy. It was a bizarre story that involved conspiracy, strappy sandals, and poo-poo.

While the Mork Incident at the end of sixth grade had presumably sent Dustin Lee back to the land of rodeos and chain-saw massacres, Texan charm had revisited the St. Maude's population in the shapely form of Ms. Kathleen Abilene, the new seventh-grade teacher. As Lindsey and the other students sat through her introductory speech, they watched skeptically as she spelled her name on the chalkboard and explained that, coincidentally, she had also been born and raised in a town called Abilene, located in glorious central Texas. The kids immediately were suspicious of her, not only because she was the first non-nun teacher they ever had, but she also had a strangeness about her, a kind of Terminator-cyborg quality, like she was actually a mechanized robot underneath a skin of living tissue. In addition, the details of her life were too perfect to be true. Her name was Abilene and she was *from* Abilene? *Come on*. The kids weren't dopes. Ms. Abilene's story was the kind of fiction created by former criminals and actresses with questionable pasts. Although Ms. Abilene managed to act somewhat normal, the savvy seventh graders were convinced she must have been a showgirl in her sordid dust-bowl past.

The leggy, titian-haired cyborg's appearance contributed much to the kids' imaginations of her. They were used to seeing plain black smocks and nary a stray hair revealed from the nuns' headbands. In contrast, Ms. Abilene's fiery, harlot hair tumbled against her jewel-toned dresses in such a way that they knew a vixen lay beneath those polyester ruffles. Also, there was a fallen-flower quality about her that the students were too young to fully understand, yet they knew that something wasn't right. Oftentimes she didn't sing the hymns in church and didn't seem to know the standard prayers by heart. This led Lindsey to suspect that Ms. Abilene was like Faye Dunaway in *Little Big Man*, the wife of a preacher who was just pretending to fall for the Jesus crap while spending her off-hours sponge-bathing the succulent contours of Dustin Hoffman's naked booty. Additionally, Ms. Abilene's face was always shiny, inspiring further speculation about potentially sweaty nights engaged in un-Christlike activities. She oozed a kind of Christian-swinger vibe which convinced the kids that their seventh-grade teacher liked piña coladas and getting caught in the rain.

Early in her seventh-grade year, Lindsey had noticed that Ms. Abilene wore a jade ring. The fact that Ms. Abilene favored the gemstone of Lindsey's people was very distressing. Ms. Abilene also liked to wear embroidered kung fu slippers with her stirrup pants, and instead of Sanka, she sipped oolong tea from a cup with longevity symbols.

One afternoon Ms. Abilene stopped to ask Lindsey if she liked her jade ring and slippers. Lindsey didn't say anything, but just shrugged. When she failed to respond favorably to her teacher's choice of body adornments, Ms. Abilene shot her a cold look and Lindsey knew she just made an enemy for life. She watched as Ms. Abilene walked to her desk and unlocked a drawer. The woman calmly scribbled a few words on an index card, then promptly locked it away.

Ms. Abilene's right-side drawer was the safekeeping place for an enamel box decorated with cherry pies and innocuous red letters in Betty Crocker-style writing that spelled RECIPES. The old-fashioned script suggested the box contained down-home, step-by-step directions for baking only the most dee-licious TexMex comfort foods. But Lindsey and the other kids suspected otherwise.

Sure enough, it was Ms. Abilene's treasure box of smack-talk.

Every time she moved more than five feet from her desk, Ms. Abilene always made a spectacle of locking the drawer that contained the enamel box. Naturally, childlike curiosity being what it was, it was only a matter of time before the kids' devious little minds started to plan the drawer's unhinging. The moment finally came one afternoon after Ms. Abilene left the classroom to take a phone call (no doubt to confirm a tryst with the part-time basketball coach for banana daquiris at happy hour).

Nelson Fong picked the lock. In seconds he had the enamel box out in the open and they all gathered around the desk to watch him lift the lid as if it was the Ark of the Covenant. Just like a regular recipe box, the tin was filled with index cards. But instead of ingredients, these cards recorded the kinds of things any grown person should've known better than to commit to writing. For instance, under "miscellany" they discovered that their third-grade teacher, Sister Ada, had not actually retired and gone back to Ireland, but instead had been a compulsive eater of laundry detergent and inadvertently poisoned herself with a midnight snack of Calgon and a Downy chaser. In her spidery handwriting, Ms. Abilene had written that Sister Ada "was no angel." This opinion was followed by a detailed transcript of how she and the nun had had a quarrel in the teachers' lounge regarding a bottle of Bushmills stashed in the hollow underside of the fiberglass Christmas nativity manger.

The recipe box revealed other school trivia as well. By perusing the cards, the kids also learned that Mother Frances had a pacemaker, and Mr. Prospect, the eighth-grade science teacher, had asked Ms. Abilene out for Harvey Wallbangers.

When they flipped through the alphabetized section, things got really juicy. On the top of each line was a child's name and a list of qualities that had nothing to do with academics. Each of the students took turns looking up his or her name and discovered Ms. Abilene's secret thoughts about them.

One kid's card read, "Stringy hair. Cliquish and degradingly flirtatious re: boys."

Another's read, "Just plain stupid. Unteachable with annoying Hispanic accent."

Before they all scrambled back to their seats, Lindsey shuffled through the cards until she found her name. At first she
noticed just a big, blank space and she breathed a sigh of relief.
But then, as she lifted the card completely out of the box she
spotted three little words along the bottom line: "Arrogant
Little Twit."

Lindsey looked around at the faces of her classmates, who
all snuck peeks at their cards. The group sat and felt the collective heaviness of their crumbled little hearts. Allowing themselves to be stricken for just one moment, they quickly
reminded themselves that they were no longer babies. They
were seventh graders.

Cue the music. It was time for Ms. Abilene to die.

They had posted a lookout at the classroom door, and after
a few minutes, he whispered, "Here she comes!" They all slid
back into their places as the doorknob turned and their teacher,
clad in fake Halston, entered the room. She strode directly
over to her desk, turned her key in the drawer, and made sure
her recipe box was safely inside. The kids had replaced it exactly as it had been. Silently they glanced at one another and
quietly schemed how they might exact their retribution.

The following day was the kickoff for many strange classroom happenings. All chalk was suddenly "misplaced." Text-
books disappeared and whole lesson plans needed to be
reworked because the teacher handbooks were all of a sudden
missing random pages. The manual pencil sharpener was
booby-trapped and broke apart, raining dusty shavings down
onto Ms. Abilene's Easy Spirit pumps. On Wednesday, Ter-
ence the turtle was set free, and on Thursday Ms. Abilene's favorite African violet plant, with the dainty blossoms of which
she was so proud, mysteriously shriveled to paper wisps, poisoned it seemed, by an overdose of strawberry Yogloo.

On Friday the most horrifying thing of all happened. Dur-

ing recess someone snuck back into the classroom and took a
shit on the floor behind Ms. Abilene's desk. Its brownish mass
could best be described as fetidly defiant.

Ms. Abilene forced them all to kneel on the linoleum floor
with their hands on their heads until the defecator revealed
himself. (Face it. It had to have been a guy.) As they kneeled in
silence, Ms. Abilene paced the aisles like a death-row prison
guard and swatted thighs with a yardstick anytime anyone sat
back on their heels or tried to lower their akimbo elbows. They
stayed that way for one hour and twenty-two minutes.

Ms. Abilene tapped her cloven hoof on the floor and threatened, "We have all day. Even after school." The minutes ticked
by. Lindsey's kneecaps ached, but it was worth it to see Ms.
Abilene so pissed. Her eyes sweeping from kid to kid, Ms. Abilene resembled a komodo dragon slithering through the aisles
in search of her prey.

Finally, an arm was raised. Muscle-free like an uncooked
strip of bacon, it quavered in the air and immediately grabbed
the attention of the entire room. The arm belonged to Nelson
Fong. With abject fear, he opened his mouth and managed to
let out a peep of a noise. Then he cleared his throat and said, "I
did it."

Ms. Abilene hadn't given anyone permission to move, but
all the kids—all except Nelson—dropped their arms and began
to straighten their legs. When the bell rang, all the kids ran out
of the room, leaving the two adversaries alone—one kneeling
with his grimy hands clasped over his head in contrition, and
the other in strappy seventies heels, rubbing her chin as if unable to decide which excruciating punishment in her extensive
repertoire she might exact on the fellow. Lindsey turned back
for one last look, and stretched across Ms. Abilene's beige-
glossed mouth was a vengeful smile, the grimace of a Southern, trailer-raised she-devil who knew whuppings more exotic

than the likes anyone had ever seen west of the Rio Grande.

Even now, so many years later, Lindsey didn't like to think of whatever must have happened to poor Nelson Fong that afternoon. All she knew was that the following Monday the shit was gone, and the following year they all advanced to eighth grade, minus one Chinese boy.

Still meticulously detailing the preserved reptile, Lindsey wondered if Ms. Abilene still kept a tidy box of trash talk in her desk. She was suddenly desperate to know. Hmm . . . it occurred to her that she did have in her current possession a giant steel ring full of the school's master keys. Reaching into her pocket, she grasped the jangled mass of metal.

It was the eighth key that tripped the lock on the desk. With an easy click, she had the drawer open. A few Erasermate pens, rubber stamps, thumbtacks, a confiscated beeper, two broken staplers, and . . . well, now. There it was. A box. Not the same box, but a blue, cloisonné one with pink peonies. She quickly stopped and listened for footsteps. Hearing none, she made a mental note that the door was securely locked. Convinced that she was safe, she opened the box.

She didn't recognize the names of Ms. Abilene's current students, but the same wispy writing detailed their offenses. She read a few:

Anna: Gaining weight. Will be fat by eighth grade.
Taylor: Spoiled brat, but cute father.
Kristen: Eats boogers. Needs Ritalin.

Lindsey felt triumphant in her devious discovery, but then a mild worry struck her. "What am I doing?" she asked herself. Realizing she had better get out of there, she crammed the index cards back inside the box. Having trouble shutting the lid, she rearranged a few cards and saw one with an asterisk and a notation:

See Permanent Record, Basement Room 6.

Aha!

So, the Permanent Record was a real, physical thing. Maybe it was a massive, corroded filing cabinet locked away in a top-secret chamber. Naturally, she would have to investigate, and there was no time like the present. Who knew what she might find in the dank depths of the St. Maude's basement? She gave the alligator a final spritz, left the seventh-grade homeroom, and flew down the stairs.

"Leaving for the day?" asked Mrs. Grupico. She was wearing one of her typical outfits, red polyester pants and a black blouse with huge white polka dots. With her bloated neck, she looked like a gigantic chicken with a thyroid problem.

"Yes. See you tomorrow," Lindsey replied, retrieving her things from the cloakroom. She waited until Mrs. Grupico left, then pocketed a flashlight from the utility closet.

Instead of heading out the front door, she detoured across a short hallway to a narrow staircase where she'd seen many a nun appear and disappear. As she descended the dark stairwell she began to detect a mildew smell, the same odor that permeated the Pirates of the Caribbean ride at Disneyland. But this was no amusement park. This was her old grammar school, and she was headed into unchartered territory equipped only with a pink sweater, a flashlight powered by the weakest of batteries, and lip gloss. She was determined to find the Permanent Record, but what would happen if she was discovered? If any emergency arose, she would have to think fast. If worse came to worst, the only weapon she had against certain doom was . . . charm.

She tiptoed down the snaking stairwell. Her path was illuminated only by her dim flashlight and the small, stained glass windows that shone amber and ruby light on each landing, every fourteen steps or so. At long last she came to a hallway that was so quiet it seemed a vacuum for all sound, including her own breathing.

She clutched the keys so tightly that her fingers began to cramp. As noiselessly as she could, she tried a few keys in the brass lock of a heavy wooden door with iron fittings. None of the regular Schlage or Medeco keys worked, so she inserted one of the spooky old skeleton keys at the end of the ring. It fit perfectly.

Opening the door a crack, she reached one skinny arm into the black space and felt around the ice cold wall for the light switch. She found a thin chain. She pulled it.

A high lightbulb *plinked* on and illuminated the room. Broken church pews. Stands for sheet music. An old upright piano. She didn't see any file cabinets, so she turned to leave. Just as she was about to turn off the light, she noticed some dusty picture frames stacked against the wall in the far corner. Stuffing the keys into her coat pocket, she walked across the room for a closer look. Kneeling down, she dusted off a pane of glass with the palm of her hand.

She secretly hoped she might find some old class photos of her and Dustin, but what she discovered was far more intriguing. Along the bottom of the photo was a caption, "St. Maude's Rescue Mission, 1907." Lindsey saw three withered nuns standing behind about twenty girls. Twenty *Chinese* girls.

Flipping through the other frames, she discovered similar posed photos, except with different girls and different years up through the 1940s. The girls' ages ranged from about four to fifteen, and in that particular Chinese way, no one was smiling.

Lindsey had read about rescue missions for Chinese girls. In the late 1800s, women like Donaldina Cameron had helped girls escape poverty and prostitution. Some girls were given away by their own families, or kidnapped from China and sent to San Francisco on boats. Others had been promised prosperous lives only to be sold on arrival as slaves. Lindsey didn't know that St. Maude's had been a place of refuge. Who were all these Chinese girls anyway, and what had happened to them?

She sat on the floor cross-legged and took a moment to study the photos. In 1908, the girls had short pageboys or hair pulled back in buns with a few Chinese hair ornaments like satin headbands. In 1918, the girls wore matching white smocks and plain skirts. A 1934 photo showed bland facial expressions and one girl with finger curls. The nuns all looked the same from year to year, wearing nurselike uniforms and black veils covering their hair. Except for crucifixes around their necks, they resembled the fuddy-duddy matrons who worked at See's Candies.

Lindsey scooted across the cold floor to a different row of frames. "Oh, here are the twenties," she thought to herself. She flipped through, looking to see if any of the girls had Josephine Baker hairdos. She scanned 1924 and then moved on to 1925, and then 1926.

The photos transported her to a different time, same place. In some pictures she recognized the stained-glass window of St. George slaying the dragon from the landing on the northeast stairwell. She looked at the next frame, and as she scanned the faces of the 1928 girls, a creepy, twilight-zone chill slowly traveled from the top of her head down to the small of her back like an invisible finger tracing the curve of her spine.

Her eyes fell upon one girl's face in particular. Time slowed down for a moment as she studied the girl in the third row, second from the left. Her eyes were transfixed by the image. It was a girl who looked not just a little, but exactly, uncannily, precisely, unmistakably like Lindsey.

She knew her own face. She knew that rabbit-in-the-headlights expression she sometimes got when she was tired. The girl in the photo had wide-set eyes and particularly sparse eyebrows, just like Lindsey's—well, exactly like Lindsey's—each morning before she gave them the MAC eyeliner treatment.

And what of those narrow shoulders, and that particular way of slouching? This specter had even appropriated Lindsey's bad posture. Did they even *have* bad posture in 1928?

Lindsey was spooked. Something was very, very wrong. All she could think about was the end of *The Shining*, when the camera panned across the old party photos from the haunted hotel, then focused on the image of a young Jack Nicholson. Had he lived before, or was he a ghost?

She wasn't sure what to think, but before she could ponder what to do next, she heard a noise by the door.

"Well, hello there."

Lindsey practically jumped out of her skin. She spun around on the floor and looked up to see a figure, motionless as a wax museum mannequin, calmly leaning against the doorjamb. It was Ms. Abilene. Slowly, the woman brought her hand to her face, wiped the corners of her mouth, and smiled menacingly.

Panicked, Lindsey wondered what Ms. Abilene was doing down here. Lunch? Maybe she just returned from one of the cellar dungeons, having just devoured a unicorn to keep herself alive.

Lindsey stood up and brushed herself off. Having read many a fairy tale, she should have known that basements and attics were almost always guarded by hideous beasts. *Think fast*, she told herself.

"I . . . I was just wondering where Sister Constance wanted me to put those hymn books." Straightening her posture in an attempt to exude confidence, she added, "In fact . . . I was looking for someone . . . I'm glad I found you."

Ms. Abilene tapped her fingernails against the wall. She leaned forward and said, "I'm glad . . . I found you . . . too."

Lindsey and her former seventh-grade teacher stared at each other for a long moment. Lindsey suddenly remembered why she herself was down here in the first place—to search for the Permanent Record. She speculated that perhaps it was down the next flight of stairs, along with skeletons shackled in rooms littered with the tattered remains of snack-tacular children.

One thing was for sure, she wasn't going to get down there now, not with Ms. Abilene here. She figured her best bet would be to get out of there as quickly as possible.

She said, "Well, I've got to go!" and dodged past Ms. Abilene. She peeled up the stairs, careening around the turns.

"Wait . . ." Ms. Abilene said softly, but Lindsey was already gone.

Keeping Up With the Ahchucks

Not far from the Owyangs' home, near the Moraga Street Hill overlooking the Sunset District, was a beautiful, courtyard-style Chinese house that belonged to the Ahchucks. Months ago they had sent out glossy, red invitations with gold lettering and scented return-envelopes for a thirty-fifth wedding an-niversary party that was to take place this evening.

The Owyangs had known the Ahchucks since "the old days," but Lindsey wasn't sure how long that was exactly. No one ever said. "The old days" could have meant anything—since her dad was in college, or maybe back when Yeh Yeh first opened his grocery store. Maybe it meant back when the fam-ily lived in Locke, or maybe it went back another generation, back to the village days, back to Zhongsan or some other part of southeastern China.

One thing was for sure, the Ahchucks had been in Califor-nia long enough to get rich. With better views and twice the lot-space as the Owyangs', their home was decorated with a rock garden in front and well-trimmed bonsai within a hard-wood fence with geometric detailing. Surrounding their prop-erty was a cinder-block wall in a key-fret design, and the roof was topped with gleaming, ceramic tiles and mythical animal figures on the upturned corners to protect the property from evil spirits. The place was painted a serene moss color, and the interior was filled with blue and white porcelain and rosewood furniture.

When Lindsey was young she hated the Ahchucks' house. She loathed visiting them, and was embarrassed by how Chinese their home was. She felt that the Ahchucks were purposely calling attention to their otherness, and was uncomfortable in the midst of all the Asian motifs.

She remembered one time when the Ahchucks had invited her family over for dessert and tea. She and Kevin, nine and eleven respectively, rolled their eyes as their parents marveled at the traditional landscape paintings and green jardinières in the foyer. Everything screamed of ancient China, and even the patio panels were decorated with carved Chinese lettering. Lindsey and Kevin were asked to take their shoes off and were supplied with embroidered slippers, a custom that struck them as foreign and weird because they were used to flapping around everywhere in flip-flops and checkerboard Vans. They stared at the Ahchucks' daughter, Janice, who was Lindsey's age and wore one of those Mandarin tops that looked like pajamas. Lindsey was so embarrassed for her. She herself was wearing a yellow T-shirt with an iron-on decal of the *Welcome Back, Kotter* cast, and when Janice pointed to John Travolta and asked who he was, Lindsey was dumbstruck that the girl had never heard the name Vinnie Barbarino.

The Owyangs and the Ahchucks shared jasmine tea and polite conversation around a low table while Lindsey quietly shuddered, noticing additional Asian details. On the Ahchucks' deck were tall, grassy bamboo trees planted in pots decorated with dragons, and a miniature wooden bridge overlooked a koi pond. Lindsey felt stifled. Sitting there, she was relieved to know that at least her own home looked more like the interiors on old television shows like *Family Affair* and *The Courtship of Eddie's Father*.

She wanted to leave and rudely kept asking, "Can we go now?"

Her parents shushed her and complimented the Ahchucks on their beautiful grand piano, which, unfortunately, triggered a command performance by Janice. The girl got up and played a classical masterpiece to perfection as Lindsey and Kevin squirmed, bored to tears. After Janice finished and the Owyangs politely clapped, Mr. Ahchuck asked if Lindsey knew how to play, and her mother answered, "of course," as if it was widely accepted that all Chinese girls were natural piano geniuses. When Mrs. Ahchuck suggested Lindsey play something, her dad must have seen the abject fear on her face and maybe he intuitively knew that she could only play "Chopsticks," despite twice-weekly lessons with Mrs. Yee. The adults proceeded to faux-bicker until the Ahchucks inferred that the Owyangs were humbly refusing to show off Lindsey's prowess lest she put Janice to shame. *Oh*, they seemed to realize. *Lindsey is obviously a virtuoso. The Owyangs are ever so gracious not to point out our daughter's inferiority.*

At the end of the visit, the Ahchucks bowed and nodded their heads like the Chinese servants in movies. Lindsey disdained their subservient style. Thank God her own parents shook hands like normal people. Kevin hid his impatience a tad better than Lindsey, but both could barely wait to get out of there as the adults lingered in the hallway and heaped compliments on one another.

Not long after they had visited the Ahchucks, Lindsey became self-conscious about the small nameplate on the front of their own house that spelled THE OWYANGS. She had always been somewhat uncomfortable with such a pronouncement of their Chinese presence, and she worried if the small sign had something to do with their welcome mat being pelted with rotten fruit in recent weeks. At first she thought some raccoons had knocked over the trash can on a garbage-collecting night, but that explanation didn't account for the outside wall also being splattered with debris. She had an inkling that something was wrong, but hadn't mentioned it to her parents. In the mornings, however, she noticed her dad sometimes scraping the front door and hosing down the driveway before leaving for work.

One Saturday she awoke early, and as she watched cartoons and worked on her third bowl of Sugar Pops, she detected a rustling sound near the kitchen window. She heard laughing, and then some splooshing noises against the window pane, like heavy rain. In her nightgown she shuffled to the side of the window and through the glass, she saw two neighbor boys, Greg James and Steven Kilroy, throwing stuff at the house. When they exhausted their supply of mushy berries and bologna sandwich crusts, one said to the other, "Stupid chinks." Then they left.

Lindsey stood there as her milk moustache dried on her upper lip, and then she calmly returned to eating her cereal. She wasn't quite sure what to do or how to feel. About a half hour later when her mother came into the kitchen to turn on the Mr. Coffee, Lindsey didn't mention what she had seen.

"You're up early," her mom said, and Lindsey only replied, "Uh-huh." She knew that sooner or later her mother would open the front door to retrieve the newspaper, but didn't known how to warn her about what she would find.

Lindsey was fully engaged in watching *The Superfriends* when she heard her mother go to the door, and from outside Lindsey heard her groan, "Oh, no." Her mother came back in and woke Lindsey's dad. When they both emerged from the bedroom they were quiet. Once again, her dad went out and cleaned up the mess, and pretty soon it was a normal Saturday morning with her mom sipping coffee and her dad mixing the Bisquick. The only thing anyone asked her that morning was, "How do you want your waffle, Linds? Crispy?"

Kevin woke up later and after their parents were out of sight Lindsey told him about the neighborhood kids throwing stuff at their house and calling them stupid chinks. The weirdest thing was that just last year Kevin used to play with Greg. The boy used to beg Kevin to get bottle rockets and smoke bombs for him in Chinatown, and he had even been inside their house and eaten marmalade sandwiches on Wonder bread that their mom had made for him. Now he was throwing stuff at their windows.

"We have to do something," Kevin said.

"Yeah, I know," she agreed.

"Dad always says not to cause trouble in our own neighborhood," Kevin said. He explained how, a few months ago, when Steven stole and wrecked his jacket, Dad forbade him to retaliate. He refused to allow Kevin to let the air out of the boy's bike tires, doorbell ditch his parents, or throw anything at his house. Lindsey agreed with her brother that they would only get in trouble if they did any of those things now.

The siblings decided to do the only thing they could. She didn't remember how they agreed, but they had. They planned to do something really terrible.

There was a neighbor across the street who always let his German shepherd take a huge crap in front of the Owyangs' house. He never cleaned it up. The turds would pile up and eventually Mr. Owyang would knock them into the bushes with a shovel, but every day there was more shit, and they all knew it was the same guy and his same damn dog. Once again, her dad never talked about it, but everyone in the family knew it happened.

So that afternoon, Kevin and Lindsey got a large plastic bag and went outside. As expected, they found a pile of steamy poop on the sidewalk and used a garden trowel to pitch it into the bag. That step accomplished, they went back into their house and retrieved a carton of milk, and poured it into the bag with the smelly turds. Kevin twisted the bag shut and shook up the nauseating concoction.

Then they went for a walk. They hiked up ten blocks, ducking behind trees along the way. They peered around to make sure the coast was clear, and tiptoed up the landscaped walkway. As Lindsey stood by, Kevin wound up his arm like a discus thrower and catapulted the bag of milky shit onto their target. The slimy, splattering noise was both disgusting and satisfying at the same time. They felt vindicated and laughed as they ran away. The Ahchucks front door was left dripping and smeared with shit.

She and her brother never talked about what they did. Lindsey herself hadn't thought about it for a long time. The Ahchucks probably never knew it was they who had vandalized their home, and perhaps Mr. Ahchuck, like Mr. Owyang, had calmly cleaned it up without blaming anyone.

The Ahchucks, so kind and gracious, had been an easy target. Lindsey was only nine and didn't understand her emotions or the reason behind why she did what she did. But feeling conflicted about being Chinese and retaliating against other Chinese people was a lot easier than blaming her tormentors. As illogical as it seemed, even after the neighborhood boys had vandalized her house, in the weeks that followed, she still wanted them to like her family and perhaps come over for sandwiches as if nothing had ever happened.

That was the thing about fitting in. Being a kid and wanting desperately to be liked, she didn't focus on other people's motivations or prejudices. It was just easier to doubt herself.

Looking back now, she realized she was more willing to accept the possibility of her own family being deserving of derision than the idea that any white person was actually wrong. Had years of watching *The Brady Bunch* warped her brain that much? Even though she had never informed anyone, including the neighbor boys, of what she and her brother had done to the Ahchucks' house, at the time she thought that having thrown the shit proved she could be prejudiced against Chinese people better than anyone, and didn't that mean white people could trust her better now?

Suddenly Lindsey was jarred out of her reverie by a wave of guilt. She'd always known the Ahchucks hadn't done anything to deserve what she and Kevin had done, and now that she reflected on the incident, she was full of regret.

She felt thoroughly rotten. This evening her whole family would be going to the Ahchucks home, and how could she look anybody in the eye knowing what she had done? As she showered and dressed, she wondered if she should apologize to someone tonight, or even mention it at all.

Just then, the telephone rang.

"Hello?" she answered.

"Hey, Cutie. It's me."

She dropped her voice to a whisper and said, "Do you need me to FedEx you some SlimJims?"

"No." Michael sighed. "I'd probably never see them, anyway. They'd be confiscated. It's like a gulag with Pilates here."

"When can you come home?" she said.

Michael lowered his voice so she could barely hear him. "I'm still digging up dirt for the exposé. Not only do they heat their supposedly raw food higher than a hundred and eighteen degrees, but their mesclun mix includes shoots from carnivorous plants."

"So?"

"Well if you don't eat meat, but you're eating plants that ate meat, by association, you ain't no vegetarian. The good news is that it's a huge story. The bad news is I'm going to be here at least another two weeks."

Lindsey was crestfallen. "That long?"

Just then, her Call Waiting beeped. "Hold on a second," she said to Michael, then clicked over. It was her brother. He snapped, "Where the hell are you? We're all waiting at the Ahchucks. People have already started eating."

"Okay, I'm coming," she said to Kevin, then clicked back over to Michael.

"Are you sure you can't sneak out of there any earlier?" she asked.

"I'll try. But don't think I'm having any fun down here. It's all quinoa and compost tea. Oh, damn, here they come. Gotta go. Love you, Baby."

She hung up the phone and finished getting dressed.

Arriving at the Ahchucks, she approached the house with its elegant, tiled roof and immaculately landscaped garden. She admired the leafy trees that lined the walkway and the branches of the Japanese maple that formed a canopy over the deck. Paper lanterns illuminated the perimeter of the house as well as the elegant red umbrellas that decorated the spacious courtyard. She walked up the slate pathway and passed a trickling waterfall with a Buddha statue. At the end of the winding path bordered with lavender and rosemary, Lindsey cringed as she passed through the front door she had once splattered with milk and dog feces.

Once inside, she was impressed by the beautiful antiques and simple yet luxe decor she had once thought embarrassing. As party guests mingled in the main house and some others gathered in the garden, Lindsey looked for her family and found them outside at one of the round tables decorated with fresh crimson peonies and lucky bamboo stalks.

She said hello to everybody and sat down. Yun Yun was sitting primly in one of the folding chairs slipcovered in red cotton, looking fairly innocent. As Lindsey removed her coat and pulled a chair out, she caught sight of her grandmother knocking her knuckle against the side of Yeh Yeh's head. She scowled, "Why you wear same old overcoat here? Embarrass me!"

"Big party. Twenty tables," her mom said.

"Shall we?" Kevin got up and headed for the buffet.

"I'll get plates for you two," Lindsey's dad said to Yun Yun and Yeh Yeh. He and Lindsey's mom got up and joined the line.

Lindsey sprang from the table and sidled up to her brother.

"Kevin," she whispered. "Do you remember what we did?"

"What?" he said, and Lindsey reminded him of their terrible deed.

"Don't talk about that *here*," he admonished her.

"Do you think we should apologize to someone?"

"Are you crazy? Just forget about it. It's best to pretend it didn't happen."

They reached the front of the line and servers began piling fried chicken wings, roasted pork, and a smattering of seafood items on their plates.

"But it *did* happen," she said, jogging to keep up with her brother. She stumbled a little as her heel caught in a divet on the lawn.

Kevin shushed her, and as they returned to their table Lindsey didn't have a chance to bring it up again. Mr. and Mrs. Ahchuck, Janice, her husband, and the rest of their entourage arrived to thank them for coming and to offer a champagne toast.

"*Ai-ya!* Thirty-five years! Congratulations!"

"Happy anniversary!"

Everyone yelled in celebration, except for Yun Yun, who stuck her index fingers in her ears as Yeh Yeh just sat very still and nodded. "Congratulation," he mumbled, but no one was paying attention to him.

Removing her fingers from her ears, Yun Yun said, "Where's Mabel Ahchuck? She's the only reason I came here. Where is she?"

Looking around, Lindsey's dad said, "I don't see her."

Everyone went back to eating and drinking, while Yun Yun reached over and yanked the sleeve of the host's tuxedo. "What's wrong with you? Don't bother to go pick up your mother? You lock Mabel in closet? What a terrible son!"

Mr. Ahchuck looked around, unsure of what to do. He laughed nervously, but before he could say anything, someone at the next table grabbed him and pulled him into the toasting crowd.

Lindsey's family settled down, while in the distance Lindsey spotted Uncle Elmore and Auntie Geraldine arriving through the front door.

Shortly thereafter, a commotion inside the house signaled the arrival of another guest, a particularly loud and obnoxious woman whose squeal was heard well into the garden. "Hel-lo, where are all the men?"

Lindsey turned and recognized Uncle Elmore's ex-wife, Dee.

"This ought to be good," Kevin cracked.

Auntie Dee was an extreme narcissist. If she suspected a man found her pretty she would unbutton the top button of her blouse and lean forward as she talked to him. If she felt at any time during their conversation that his eyes had strayed from her effulgence, she would scan the crowd for another specimen of manhood to pounce on. She was convinced that every man she saw wanted to sleep with her. It didn't matter who he was—her neighbor's son, the mailman, or an old guy driving by.

Her marriage to Uncle Elmore had been an exercise in cosmic retribution, seeing as how they were exactly the same. They both suffered from the same adult-onset illness, which Lindsey referred to as Electric Slide Disease. It flared up in the presence of any member of the opposite sex, hindering both Elmore and Dee with uncontrollable shakes and wandering eyes. After their wedding, they were both still on the make and ready to trip the lights fantastic at the drop of a satin hat. Too many disco songs over the years had thumped through their gray matter while under the influence of multiple tequila sunrises, and now they both had the "push, push in the bush" mentality 24/7.

According to Lindsey's mom, in the 1970s Auntie Dee had all the guys in Henry Africa's and Lord Jim's at her beck and call. She acted bored when they cruised her in her UFO jeans and her cowl-neck sweaters, but preened when they called her "foxy little mama." In high demand, she had guys chasing her down the street in their AMC Pacers while she zipped around in her Ford Mustang just like the one Farrah Fawcett drove on *Charlie's Angels*.

Uncle Elmore had fallen hard for Dee. He had been watching her in the local fern bars for several months, when they happened to meet at a costume party happy hour at El Torito one fateful Halloween. Elmore was dressed as Ponch from *CHiPS*. He flashed her his badge and she flashed him her crotch. The rest was history.

They had a huge wedding reception with a Chinese lion dance, and for a while enjoyed being married. But eventually their lives took on the tragic ennui of a Billy Joel ballad. Their simultaneous restlessness began to show at family events. At parties Auntie Dee danced with every man who wasn't her husband, and once advised Lindsey, "Sleep around while you still can." Uncle Elmore sidled up to Kevin at holiday dinners and offered words of wisdom such as "Condoms are for chumps."

At Chinese banquets they began to air more and more of their dirty laundry while everyone else was left to stare at one another uncomfortably. Once when Lindsey spun the food on the lazy susan toward her uncle, Auntie Dee reached out and stopped her, chiming loudly, "Elmore can't eat spareribs. He's impotent." Later, when the rock cod was being served, Uncle Elmore commented, "None for me. I sleep with a cold, dead fish every night."

Now Kevin and Lindsey watched as Uncle Elmore and Auntie Dee eventually spotted each other and headed in opposite directions.

"How sad," Lindsey said to her brother, "They spent their youth doing the bump. Now they can't even stand to bump into each other."

Kevin nodded, then took off in search of hard liquor. Her parents got up to mingle with various people and Lindsey was soon left sitting alone with her grandparents. After a minute, Yun Yun began to cough, so Lindsey offered to get some water.

Near the buffet table she sidled up to her dad. Fueled by two glasses of champagne she felt loose enough to ask her dad something she might not have, had she been sober.

"Dad," she said, "How did Yun Yun and Yeh Yeh meet?"

Her dad shot her a surprised look. "How am I supposed to know?"

"Well, you are their son. Haven't you ever asked?"

Her dad stared into his paper plate. He studied his piece of cake, then said, "Oh, yeah?" His response made no sense. Another second passed and he said, "Want chocolate with raspberry or lemon with buttercream?"

After he sauntered off, Lindsey considered quizzing either

Uncle Elmore or Auntie Geraldine who, after all, were also Yeh Yeh and Yun Yun's children. However, when she spied Uncle Elmore drunkenly pissing against a cedar and Auntie Geraldine behind a jade plant scraping individual portions of cake one by one into a shopping bag, she changed her mind.

Leaving the courtyard, Lindsey wandered into the house and caught up with her mother near the bathroom. Inside, she sat on the toilet lid as her mom combed out her perm with an afro pick from her purse.

"Hey, Mom," she said, "do you know anything about Yeh Yeh and Yun Yun before Dad was born?"

"Not much. They've always been so quiet about things." Her mother paused to dab concealer below her eyes and went on, "Been driving me crazy ever since we first got married. No one wants to talk about anything, so I stopped asking. Why do you want to know?"

Lindsey looked at the floor despondently. "I dunno," she said softly. "I just think it's important to know our family history."

"Well, good luck." Despite her words, her mom wasn't the least bit encouraging. She drew a burgundy outline around her lips, shut her compact, then added, "Better leave it alone. Do you want people knowing about all the bad or embarrassing things you did?"

Her mom's words prompted her to think again about the dog-shit incident. Lindsey was certain her mom would be horrified if she knew, and she herself was too mortified to even think about it much longer. Maybe her brother was right. Maybe her mom was right. Maybe things should be left alone and not talked about. She understood that remembering could be embarrassing, even painful. But what if she couldn't forget?

Oh hell, she'd forgotten all about Yun Yun's water. Lindsey ran back to her family's table with a cup for her grandmother. As she held it out for Yun Yun to take, Yun Yun's face turned into a sneer and Lindsey realized she was holding out the cup with only one hand, instead of the Chinese way with two hands to show her grandmother proper respect. Yun Yun reached out with a slightly shaky hand to take the water and then sipped from the edge of the cup.

"*Ai-ya!*" she said, tossing the cup down onto the table in disgust. "Why you bring me cold water? You want me freeze to death?"

Lindsey fumbled for the cup. She had forgotten the old Chinese lady preference for hot water.

"Sorry!" she yelped, then turned to flag down one of the caterers.

"Oh, forget it!" Yun Yun moaned. "Go ahead and just forget me."

Lindsey walked back to the buffet table with its silver samovars. She retrieved a cup of hot water, but when she returned to the table Yun Yun refused to drink it.

She got up and looked for either of her parents or her brother, but didn't see them anywhere. She found Uncle Elmore and said, "Could you please tell everybody I'm leaving?"

"So soon? They're about to start the dancing," he hollered after her. "You're gonna miss the Electric Slide!"

Lion Dance With a Stranger

On Thursday nights the museum was open late, and after her shift at the gift shop Lindsey went to the adjoining café to meet Dustin. He had called her at work and since she didn't have anything to do anyway, she agreed to meet him. As she entered the eatery, she scanned the tables filled with evening museum-goers, but didn't see him. After ordering a latté, she made her way across the crowd to an empty spot by the window so she could people-watch as she waited. Looking out at the purple, almost-summer sky, she watched for her old school chum with nervous excitement.

She heard a voice. "Is this seat taken?"

He was about eighty, wearing an old-man windbreaker, and had mostly white hair with a sand-colored swath swooped over from one side, held down by the miracle of Dippity-do and a single, amber-colored bobby pin. And he was holding a catalog from the Asian Art Museum. *Ah so.* He was a *Hoarder of All Things Asian*.

Looking around, Lindsey noticed other café patrons sitting at more spacious tables—a black man with a laptop, an older woman emptying a packet of Sweet 'n' Low into her coffee, a white guy with dreadlocks who'd finished eating and was now just sitting there. It bugged her that this senior Hoarder wanted to share her tiny, twelve-inch-diameter table while other singletons occupied spaces three times bigger. In the unspoken, random hierarchy of public seating, it seemed that everyone assumed that Asian girls would be most accommodating. People never seemed to fear that a 120-pound Chinese gal clutching Hamtaro Ham Ham stationery was going to say no, pound their face into the dirt, or pull out a .45 and blow 'em away.

"I don't bite," the old man said. "See, dentures!" He stuck his finger into the side of his mouth and wiggled his entire top row of teeth at her as though they were a delightful finger puppet. Before she could explain that she was waiting for someone, he pulled out a chair and sat down. With pen and paper strewn about the table, it seemed fairly obvious that she was in the middle of writing a letter, but he proceeded to gab away like they were old friends. He began, "When I was in the war . . ."

This first sentence was a clear indication that the conversation would not be short. Lindsey was certain he was going to talk forever. She was plotting her escape when she heard him say, "and I had me a girlfriend in Hong Kong that looked just like you." He reached over and poked her in the chest, trying to play off that he didn't just basically touch her boob. He rested his gnarled hand with white knuckle-fur an inch from hers on the table.

Lindsey spotted an empty two-top across the room and started to pack up her bag, stowing her unfinished letter to her friend Mimi in a side compartment.

"You can have this table," she said, standing to leave.

"Don't go! I bet you can't guess my name."

"No thanks." She turned away, but was slow in escaping because a big group at the next table had also just stood to leave.

As she waited for them to collect their coats and get out of her way, the old guy said, "Wait! Have you ever seen a glass eye? I got a whole collection at home in my candy jar. If you guess how many I have, I'll give you a Kennedy half dollar!"

This last comment struck her as particularly *Silence of the Lambs*, so she hopped between a couple of empty chairs and bolted. She dodged past some artsy guys with goatees doctoring their mochas, and discreetly raced an old lady for the last window seat. Throwing down her backpack to stake her claim, she sat down and realized she'd forgotten her latté.

Just then she heard a roar outside that rattled the café's plate-glass windows. It was a black, vintage Norton motorcycle that had zoomed up onto the sidewalk just outside the café. Propping the beautiful machine on its kickstand at a rakish angle, the driver pulled off his helmet and Lindsey saw that it was Dustin. As he sauntered inside, people turned and looked at him. Lindsey noticed other girls and several guys sliding their eyes his way, and she thought to herself, "Okay, it's not just me. He's gorgeous."

He walked up to Lindsey with a smile.

"That was quite an entrance," she said.

"Nothing less would do," he said, taking off his leather jacket. "I'm trying to get in your pants, y'know."

No, she didn't know.

"Want me to get you something?" he said.

"Latté?"

He nodded and walked off, and she couldn't help but enjoy the back view of him.

When he returned, Lindsey thanked him and said, "Something you said the other night . . . What, exactly, do you mean when you say you only date white girls?"

Dustin took a sip of his coffee. "Well, it's not really on purpose. It just turned out that way. I guess no Asian girl has ever liked me back. Maybe I never wear the right kind of jacket, like other Chinese guys. I've never had a Derby, a Sir Jacques, or a Members Only, which I suppose all the natty Asian dudes were sporting back in school."

Lindsey stirred sugar into her coffee and considered what Dustin was saying as he continued, "In high school, the kind of music you listen to is everything, right? There were zero Chinese girls in Texas who were into New Wave." He chuckled a little. "I was so superior to everybody and everything back then. I think I actually had a T-shirt that said, 'Death to Poseurs.'"

Lindsey nearly jumped out of her seat. "So did I!" she blurted in amazement.

As Dustin continued to talk about high school and college, Lindsey felt as though he was describing her own experiences. It was evident that they had both had a hard time making Asian friends.

"Anyway, I guess part of the reason I moved back here is because I just broke up with my girlfriend in Austin. Incidentally, she was a blonde. Miss Abilene."

Lindsey nearly spit out her drink. "WHAT?"

Dustin was surprised by her response. "Hey, take it easy. I said she was Miss Abilene, but it was, like, three years ago, and just one regional competition. She never went on to any of the big beauty pageants."

Lindsey breathed a sigh of relief. For a split-second her mind had conjured the disturbing image of Dustin fornicating with her seventh-grade nemesis.

She tried to explain, "I thought you said *Ms.* Abilene. You know, from school. Oh, wait. I forgot. You left in the sixth grade, so you don't even know who I'm talking about. Forget it."

They talked some more and exchanged similar stories about how neither of them had ever managed to find their niche in an Asian peer group. As Dustin talked about his vacations in Europe, Lindsey looked into his handsome face and let her imagination wander. She began to think that had he not been pummeled out of her life in sixth grade, they might have really gotten along. If their first romance had been with each other, their path to same-ethnicity dating could have been launched on a whole different trajectory. As it was, neither of them had ever hooked up with another Chinese person, and frankly, staring at his full lips and smooth skin, she was beginning to wonder what he would be like in bed.

Guiltily, she erased that scenario and thought instead about Michael. Growing up, he had always "passed" for white. And although it wasn't his fault that he hadn't attracted harassment, he never experienced the ambivalence, subtle cruelties, or outright hostility that she had. She sometimes doubted if Michael could really ever understand.

But Dustin could. Over the next hour, they got to know each other even better. They each related similar tales of hating their names, insisting on eating only American foods in front of classmates, hating piano lessons, and cutting Chinese school.

Dustin said, "Once in my college dorm I detected the unmistakable odor of *hom hyreur* wafting down the hall from some Chinese guy's microwave. Some white girl walked by and was like, 'Eew, what's that smell?' and I said, 'I don't know,' as if I hadn't eaten stinky, salted fish my whole frickin' life."

He finished his coffee and added, "All that stuff you described about not fitting in with other Asian girls with their spiral perms and their AP Calculus classes—that was the same way I felt around Asian guys. I never felt smart enough around them and they just thought I was an asshole. Do you think Chinese guys are all predestined to become doctors, engineers and CPAs?"

"I dunno. Are you?"

"What, can't you tell by my snazzy clothes and expensive motorcycle? I'm a *flaneur*, a gadfly, a man-about-town." He paused, then added, "Unemployed. A leech on society. Like I told you before, I live off my family. But get this. Now my dad says if I want to get my inheritance, I have to marry a Chinese girl. Doesn't that sound straight out of a movie?"

Lindsey nodded.

"Unfortunately, it's my life. My dad is on some kick about preserving our heritage. Well, he should have thought about that before he moved us to the middle of nowhere, where people think Chinese food is 'crab rangoon' with cream cheese."

"Actually," Lindsey said slowly, ". . . *I'm* getting married."

She had promised Michael she wouldn't tell anyone until he got the ring, and she hadn't even told her family yet, but she couldn't hold it in any longer.

"Really?" Dustin said.

"Yeah!"

She suddenly felt really excited, and made a mental note to pick up some bridal magazines on the way home. She beamed, "Isn't it great?"

Lindsey had assumed Dustin would be mega-ecstatic for her, like any girl would be. But instead of jumping for joy and acting giddy, he just looked perplexed.

He shifted his weight in the chair and with his head cocked back, said, "This boyfriend of yours, what kind of things is he into?"

She replied, "We walk in the park, watch movies—"

"Oh, I see. He's boring."

Lindsey was annoyed to be interrupted, and on top of that was further irritated by his comment. "He is not. We're in love—"

"Snore! Where's he now, anyway?"

"He's on a trip for work. I really miss him."

"Oh, I bet he's so *nice*. Mr. Nice White Boring Guy. When he's here I'm sure he makes you lunch for the next day and it's waiting for you on the kitchen counter in the morning."

"He's not really white. I mean he is, but not really. Anyway, what's wrong with nice? And for your information, he does make me lunch, and it's sweet." She was in such a hurry to defend Michael's considerate nature that she fumbled the explanation that he was a quarter Chinese. Before she could elaborate, Dustin took another jab at her.

"That's so bourgeois. All you Asian girls end up wanting the same thing— suburban security. Minivans. I thought you were going to be different, but nope. It's nothing but minivans for your future."

Lindsey felt her cheeks burn. It was as if Dustin instinctively knew that the word "minivan" really riled her up. She hated minivans!

She didn't like that he made a sweeping generalization about Asian girls, and plus, it wasn't even accurate. Furthermore, while she was Asian and was also a girl, she certainly did not appreciate being lumped in with nameless, faceless others.

She sulked for a moment, trying to think of a witty comeback. Only an ascerbic rebuttal would do in this situation. But she wasn't fast enough and soon the chance passed. She needed to distract herself from the fact that she was failing at snappy reparteé, so she just finished her latté, which had gotten cold.

She wasn't sure why she felt such pressure to be clever around Dustin. Maybe it was a psychological remnant from their combative sixth-grade relationship. Although they had just talked about so many similar experiences and found things in common, she now found that they'd suddenly regressed and

resumed their roles as preteens who could rely only on taunting to ease the sexual tension.

She was wondering what Michael was doing at this very
moment when Dustin said, "Hey, want to go for a ride on my
motorcycle? If you come with me, you'll be the first Asian girl
on my Norton. I've had a lot of different motorcycles and a lot
of girls who rode with me, but no Asian ones. See, you're all
snug in your minivans. You Asian girls never say yes to a ride,
especially if it means you have to spread your legs." He shot
her a lascivious grin.

She scoffed, unable to decide if he was being a jerk. Keeping
her wits, she said, "Maybe we just don't want to ride anything
with *you*."

Dustin ignored her scolding. He looked around the room as
the crowd emptied out, then turned to her and said,

"Well, do you want a ride or not?"

She felt the need to disprove his impression that Asian girls
were no fun. In spite of herself, she wanted to distinguish herself from the imaginary crowd.

"If I go, it's just a ride home, okay?" She freshened up her
lipstick.

Dustin grabbed his jacket and stood to leave. "I know, I
know. You love your boyfriend, blah, blah, blah. C'mon."

They walked to his motorcycle and she put on his spare helmet and threw her leg over. He revved the engine, and before
zooming into traffic he turned around and said over his shoulder, "Try not to cream your panties!"

She felt awkward having her arms around a guy who
wasn't Michael. She tried not to embrace Dustin too closely,
but his erratic driving, especially with the sharp turns, made a
firm grip necessary. As he careened through traffic and she
held on for dear life, she was aware that she was squeezing

him. She was not at all comfortable with the way the motorcycle engine vibrated through the leather seat against her crotch and thighs. Dead kittens. She told herself to think about dead kittens.

Once they arrived at her house, he took off his helmet and waited for her to get off. For half the ride she had been planning what she would say at the moment of dismount, so it confused her momentarily when he, not she, uttered the exact words she was thinking.

He said, "Look, I really hope you don't expect me to kiss you good night. You know, I'm with someone."

She actually felt a strand of jealousy until she realized he was making fun of her.

"Oh, buzz off," was all she could think to say.

He got off his motorcycle and propped it on its stand. Following her to her door, he said, "I love you, Lindsey," mocking her in a singsong voice as she ascended the stairs. "Maybe we'll get married and I'll buy you a *minivan* . . ."

She was fairly annoyed and was planning on shutting the door in his face when Dustin suddenly called out, "Wait!"

He caught up with her, grabbing her hand.

"Hold on a second," he said. "I'm just joking. Don't be mad."

She turned around and looked at him.

"Look," he said. "I'm really sorry about being a jerk to you in sixth grade. I only acted that way because I had a big crush on you."

"Really?" she said, her voice creaky.

He said, "I'm sorry we didn't get to know each other . . . before. Maybe if we'd been in high school or college together, neither of us would have felt like such freaks."

As they stood in the cold stairwell, Lindsey looked at Dustin and suddenly felt a tenderness toward him. The side of him that was a swaggering jerk temporarily melted away, and she saw something of herself in him—a little bit of a misfit, but doing what he could to figure things out.

After a moment he said, "After all we've shared, how about a kiss good night?"

She shook her head and said, "I don't think so."

He took a step closer to her. "Oh, c'mon. You're not married *yet*. In fact, there's still time to . . . marry *me* instead."

She knew he was just teasing her, but nonetheless, she was flattered and embarrassed by his suggestion.

"I don't even know you," she said, swatting at his jacket.

"I could 'know' you right now. Upstairs."

Lindsey crossed her arms. Since it was chilly, and he was kind of getting to her, she didn't want him to see her raisinettes peeping from her thin, cotton sweater.

He changed tactics. With puppy-dog eyes, he said, "I got beat up for you."

"Mork, you brought that on yourself."

He laughed. "C'mon!" he said playfully. "Have you ever kissed a Chinese guy? Are you saying you're gonna get married and live your whole life without kissing a Chinese guy?"

"That's not going to work, either."

"Hey, you're racist! Just one kiss. Or maybe you're afraid you'll like it too much."

"Bye, Dustin."

She closed the door behind her, and bounded up the interior stairs. Mmm. She was definitely afraid she'd like it too much.

Jacked up on caffeine and giddy with flirtation, Lindsey put on an apron and decided to clean the whole apartment. She swept and mopped the floors, scrubbed the kitchen and bathroom sinks and the bathtub, and even sprayed that foam stuff in the oven and wiped it down. When she finally exhausted herself, she took a shower and flopped onto bed.

An hour later she was still awake. She still wasn't used to being in bed without Michael, and besides, something about that sixth-grade boy who was now a well-muscled braggart with amazing cheekbones had gotten under her skin. After another hour of lying awake she felt like the punch line in that joke about the agnostic, dyslexic insomniac—but instead of lying awake and wondering if there really was a dog, she lay there and wondered what it would be like to kiss Dustin just once. She couldn't stop thinking about him. Tossing and turning, she finally gave in to temptation and touched her Monchhichi.

Helllooo Kitty.

Mulan Rouge

Mid-May was turning out to be downright hot in San Francisco. As Lindsey walked to work at eight it was already seventy-five degrees and the temperature was steadily rising. A pleasant wind rustled through the bottlebrush trees across the street, and overhead, acacia pollen, like bright yellow, powdered sugar, wafted down onto her head.

Pinching her nose to avoid a sneezing fit, Lindsey spotted her stalker in the intersection. The old, white woman was chasing a silken shawl that had gone airborne in a sudden gust of wind. With her hair blown loose and her blue-veined hands thrust skyward in pursuit of her scarf, the withered lady looked like the wicked witch of the Western Addition conjuring a tornado. Before the creepy granny could spot her, Lindsey detoured down Baker Street.

Arriving at St. Maude's, she gave a little nod to Mary in the foyer before heading to the office. On her desk she found a stack of papers and a note from Sister Constance that read,

Confirm faculty expense reports. Give to registrar when complete.

She slumped in her chair and frowned. It had never occurred to her that holy people like nuns and priests shopped till they dropped or were even responsible for buying their own clothes or necessities. She really wasn't looking forward to approaching her superiors face-to-face to ask things like, "Sister Boniface, did you really need these tummy-trimming support hose for a sleek silhouette, or are you really using them to make a bomb?"

She looked at the multiple lists with attached receipts and saw that Sister Constance had already made V-shaped checks next to obviously fine purchases such as five nightlights in the shape of Jesus's head for $7.89 and thirty plastic figurines of saints for $23.89 at the religious supplies bookstore. Other items were marked with red question marks, such as the gym teacher's *butt floss, black* for $18.99 at Thongs 'R' Us and Sister Hubert's *mustache wax, chestnut brown* for $14.67 at Hair Hut, A Place for the Distinguished Man.

Picking up the phone, Lindsey dialed the interoffice extension number for Mrs. Grupico, the registrar. Mrs. Grupico was not the type of person who had time for idle chatter so she bluntly asked Lindsey what she wanted. Lindsey said, "Sister Constance left the expense reports on my desk. Are you sure I'm the right person to confirm these?"

She heard Mrs. Grupico take a long drag off a cigarillo. In her hoarse, smoker's voice the woman replied, "Listen, hon. I typed your job description myself. This task falls under 'duties as needed.' Good luck, kid." And with a cackle, she hung up.

Lindsey sighed and replaced the phone receiver. Flipping through a few pages, she found the following:

Father Hanson had purchased Odor-Eaters, bunion cream, and an Odwalla Mango Tango smoothie at Walgreens. Lindsey made a blue checkmark next to the amount of $ 22.75 and flipped to the next page.

Miss Mullen, the second-grade teacher, had submitted a receipt for crayons, construction paper, and Dixon Ticonderoga pencils from Rite Aid. Printed on the next line was a four-ounce tube of K-Y jelly, but Miss Mullen had had the good sense to cross it out. Lindsey made checkmarks next to the school supplies and moved on.

Sister Rita had bought thirty-six cans of chicken and liver senior cat food at PETCO. Lindsey wondered if nuns were even allowed to have pets. It crossed her mind that maybe Sister Rita was stowing the cans beneath her mattress for late-night snacks. She drew a question mark in the margin and flipped ahead.

The last submission was Monsignor Rathburn's. Lindsey scanned the items, which, among other things, included a pair of shoes for $320 at Bruno Magli, and a receipt for *Special Ordr. Case Whisk, Sing. Malt* at Plenty O'Jugs that set St. Maude's back $420.

Compared to the others' modest expenditures, Monsignor Rathburn's receipts suggested that this most humble servant of the Lord spent his evenings partying like it was 1999. Lindsey knew it was not her place to judge, but it *was* her job to confirm the validity of his items' necessity. She was suddenly outraged by the audacity of the man's luxurious shopping spree. Determined to ferret out injustice, she pulled up her socks and, like a foolhardy Eliot Ness, sprang up and headed straight for the lion's den.

The easiest way to the rectory was across the schoolyard and down a short alleyway near the church. As she made her way down the mezzanine-level steps she wondered about the other passageway that led to the rectory, the one that was connected to the convent by the small chapel. The only reason Lindsey knew about it was because her class had gone there in the eighth grade.

One afternoon Sister Constance had announced that the

soon-to-be-graduating class was to be rewarded with a special treat. As all the kids excitedly anticipated cupcakes or an excursion to Great America, the nun built up the surprise by saying, "You've all been extra good, so I think you deserve it."

They all gleefully lined up outside the classroom as instructed. Were they taking a bus to the movies? They excitedly whispered about where they might be headed. Sister Constance said, "I know you are aroused, children! Patience, and you will be rewarded!

They snaked out to the schoolyard and lined up against the stucco wall of the convent. Quieting down, they waited for Sister Constance to speak.

The nun smiled proudly and as she took a deep breath, the swelling air in her lungs made the crucifix on her chest heave up and down.

The kids all beamed with excitement, and some even clapped. What would their surprise be?

"And now, finally," Sister Constance said. "You have all been such grand children that today you are going to a very sacred place. We are all going inside the convent. Yes, you have been so good that today you will be allowed to spend recess praying in our private chapel."

They were all paralyzed into stunned silence. *They would be going where? Into the belly of the beast?*

Sister Constance turned her key in the lock and swung open the door with its heavy, grid-lined safety glass. They entered a dark hallway and passed high-ceilinged rooms filled with mysterious storage boxes. The air smelled stale. As they hugged the walls and each other, the kids' knees knocked as they walked by an expansive kitchen filled with antiquated appliances, most noticeable of which were the industrial-sized electric mixers. It seemed unlikely that the nuns spent weekends baking like Keebler elves, so the students were only able to assume that the confectionery equipment was used to cook naughty children into delectable meat pies.

Lindsey had been disturbed to think that somewhere nearby was where the nuns slept. She wondered if they wore their habits to bed. As she and her classmates descended three steep stairwells to the convent basement, some kids were so spooked Lindsey thought they might pee their pants. No one asked where the bathroom was because they were fairly certain that convents had no toilets since nuns didn't pee.

When they finally reached the chapel, they entered a cramped, low-ceilinged space with slender wooden pews and flesh-colored walls. They filed in and knelt down. The room's feng shui was such that all they could do was stare up and affix their gaze on the most enormous crucifix they had ever seen.

As if they weren't all trembling enough, even the biggest and bravest kids were near whimpering when they caught sight of the bloodiest, nakedest Jesus of all time. Streams of red, oozing plasma trickled down to His barely concealed privates. A teensy loincloth the size of a beverage napkin outlined every embarrassing detail of the Lord's weinerdog. Lindsey wondered how the groovy lad with the swarthy muttonchops had sunk so far.

Passing the convent now on her way to the rectory, she realized that the eighth-grade visit had probably been a last-ditch effort on the part of the school to impress upon the graduates the ultimate suffering of Jesus in order to instill long-lasting guilt and fear of pubic hair. Perhaps it was St. Maude's way of saying, "Be good! As you go off to high school and encounter the temptations of wine coolers and tingling genitals, remember the Messiah's bloody crotch!" The Lord never even Did It, and look what happened to Him.

Lindsey shuddered at the remembrance of her class's visit to the chapel. As she walked across the scorching hot asphalt of the empty schoolyard, she could see the rectory up ahead. Shading her eyes with her hand, she remembered how she and the other kids always speculated about what went on behind the walls of the priests' quarters.

Through the screen door they sometimes saw Monsignor Rathburn kicking back on his recliner enjoying a cocktail while watching *Family Feud*. A housemaid used to bring him snacks and fluffed a ruffled pillow beneath his black nylon socks. From the yard the students were able to see curtains decorated with rickrack, plush sofas, and a sparkly set of highball glasses resting on an endtable.

Monsignor Rathburn's life seemed pretty cushy and he acted nice enough to the kids in front of the nuns, but all the students knew in their hearts that he was an agent of evil. If his face was painted red and horns affixed to his head, he would have been the spitting image of Satan with his pointy eyebrows, piercing eyes, and demonic grin. Everyone had heard the parish rumors about him amassing a personal fortune by bilking elderly ladies out of cash they had stashed beneath their mattresses for safekeeping. Supposedly, Monsignor Rathburn guaranteed generous ladies half-court seats in heaven if they would sign checks over to the church in his name. No one had any proof of these accusations, but every Friday after mass, the kids all snickered at the women who responded favorably to Monsignor's handsy squeezes. Lindsey noticed the other ladies as well, the ones who clutched their handbags more firmly in his presence as if they, too, suspected he was not an instrument of peace, but a common purse snatcher hiding behind his starched collar.

As Lindsey made her way across the yard, a loud bell suddenly rang and kids immediately spilled out from the multiple school exits. Instantly the quiet, concrete expanse turned into a riotous swarm of running children. They laughed and yelled, and Lindsey quickly found herself dodging basketballs, jump ropes, hopscotch games, and clusters of scheming girls huddled in circles. As she cut a path toward the rectory she noticed that the hearselike black Cadillac that was always ominously parked out front was missing. She slowed as she neared the bungalow, not quite sure how she would address the monsignor about his affinity for pricey whiskey.

In the alley that separated the rectory from the church, Lindsey did a double-take as she spotted the little Chinese girl, the one who was recently yelled at by Sister Boniface. She was standing against a brick wall doing nothing, so Lindsey approached her.

"Hi," Lindsey said. "What are you doing here all by yourself?"

The little girl looked up. "Do you know how to play Chinese jump rope? No one will play with me."

She held out her hand and showed Lindsey a long chain of interconnected rubberbands that she had looped together and tied at the ends. Stepping on one end and pulling on it, she demonstrated its elasticity and smiled. Lindsey was happily surprised. She hadn't seen a Chinese jump rope since she herself was in grade school.

"Of course, I know how to play," Lindsey said, then added, "But I don't think I should. I'm, you know, an adult."

The girl jumped up and down and pleaded for Lindsey to join her in a game. Eventually she just ignored Lindsey's protests and proceeded to wind the stretchy rope across Lindsey's ankles. Then she hooked the other end to a couple of sprinkler heads on the rectory's landscaped border. She hopped around for a while and performed the expected maneuvers, stepping on different sections of the rubber rope, then twisting it around and hopping over and through it until one of her spindly legs became entangled.

"It's your turn now," the girl said, but as Lindsey tried to step out, the entwined rubberbands tangled and became snagged on the buckles of her shoes. Soon enough, Lindsey's legs were hopelessly caught in a mass of rubber loops and knots.

"Hey, let's tie you up!" the girl laughed and began to wind her Chinese jumprope around Lindsey until she was bound up to her knees.

"Quit it!" Lindsey said.

She couldn't move. By the time she got the girl to stop, there was no way they were able to unravel it.

"Uh-oh," the girl said.

Lindsey sighed. "We're going to need to cut it." She looked across the yard and realized it would be really far for her to hop all the way past two basketball games, the handball courts, the hopscotch area, and the tetherball courts just to get back to her office and retrieve a pair of scissors.

"I know!" the girl yelped, then darted toward the rectory door.

"Wait!" Lindsey protested.

Still running, the girl called behind, "It's okay, I saw him leave!" She pushed through the door and disappeared.

Standing there with her legs tightly wound with the Chinese jump rope, Lindsey looked around to see if anyone was witness to her predicament. All the kids were at the other end of the schoolyard and she didn't see anyone watching. Both feet together, she jumped up the steps of the rectory and followed the girl inside.

"Hello?" she called. "Is anyone here? Excuse us, but we were just hoping to borrow a pair of scissors."

There was no answer. Lindsey stood in the entryway and noticed the furniture had not changed in twenty years. She saw the same couch, and the familiar set of hi-ball glasses. There was a new television with a cable box, and for some reason, a portrait of Monsignor Rathburn with George Bush, Sr.

"Come here, come here!" Lindsey heard the little girl calling from somewhere beyond a small kitchenette.

She found her in the study, directly across from a bedroom.

"There's gotta be scissors in this drawer but I can't open it," the girl said. Lindsey jiggled it, but it was indeed locked.

"We have to get out of here," Lindsey said, her shins struggling against the rubber lasso that bound her legs. She tugged at the loops of elastic bands, but they had become even more tightly wound by all her jumping and wriggling.

Lindsey heard some noises by the front door, and sure enough, the screen door popped open. Just beyond the dinette set she saw Monsignor Rathburn enter. Horrified, she pulled herself back into the study and grabbed the girl as well. They inched out of sight and the girl opened a closet door and got in. Lindsey hopped over and, squishing the girl under a row of black pants, managed to smash herself against a garment bag. She pulled the door shut, leaving it open just a crack.

"I can't see nothing!" the girl said in a muffled whisper. Lindsey shushed her and held her hand.

They were stuck there. Lindsey couldn't very well explain that she just came in to chat about Bruno Magli, Johnny Walker, and scissors. Oh, and she also just happened to have a spare kindergartner with her. She could say the girl was her little sister. No, that would be stupid. It wouldn't even make any sense.

She peeked out. Monsignor Rathburn fixed a tuna sandwich and mixed himself what looked to be a White Russian. After ten minutes of holding the girl's hand, Lindsey's palm was beginning to get sweaty.

"We have to get out of here," Lindsey whispered. "But we have to wait for the right time. Just stay quiet."

There was a window in the study where Lindsey thought they might be able to climb down to the bushes. But just as she was about to push open the closet door and make a move toward the window, she heard the monsignor's footsteps in the hallway. She froze, and grabbed the girl's hand again. She squeezed it to tell her to stay still, and the girl complied.

Monsignor Rathburn went to the bedroom and took off his white collar. Lindsey had a clear view of him. He pulled down the blinds and slid open the door to a wardrobe. He reached deep inside, then his arm emerged holding what looked like a floppy, suede purse.

He sat down on a plush armchair and held the leather bag in his lap. He unzipped it and flipped his hand through, talking quietly to himself. Lindsey strained to hear him, and eventually made out his voice across the quiet hallway. He was counting.

"Six hundred, seven hundred, eight hundred . . ."

Monsignor Rathburn was directly facing the doorway. There was no way he wouldn't see two Chinese people springing out of his den. Lindsey wondered what they would do. They couldn't stay there for much longer. To make matters worse, her legs were starting to cramp.

She peered out the closet door and examined the window that now seemed their only chance of escape. It had a crank handle and looked as if the glass opened outward. It would be an easy jump down to the landscaped area if only they could make it two steps out of the closet without being spotted.

She looked back at the monsignor. He was sitting in the chair with the suede bag still on his lap. She watched as he scooted down and fiddled with his trousers. She wondered if he had eaten too much tuna and needed to loosen his belt a notch. Maybe he would take a nap. Her plan was to make sure he was asleep before they made their break to safety.

"Just a few minutes more," she whispered to the girl. Hearing a faint rendition of "Row, Row, Row Your Boat," she added, "Stop singing."

They waited in the closet. Monsignor Rathburn wasn't falling asleep. Not only that, but what *was* he doing? His eyes were closed but he was moving a little and making low moaning noises. Lindsey grimaced and turned away when she realized he was rubbing the bag of money against his crotch in an effort at self-stimulation.

Oh, God. This was something Lindsey did not want to see. Nor did she want the little girl to catch a glimpse of what was going on. No doubt they'd both be scarred for life.

As Monsignor Rathburn's moans became louder, Lindsey decided she had to take action. She inched herself out of the closet and pulled the little girl out from behind the rows of musty pants. Grabbing the girl by the shoulders, she quietly pushed her toward the window. They cranked it open, and as the noises from the opposite bedroom increased, the girl turned to look but Lindsey pulled her away and held her with her forearm. Unable to hoist a leg over the windowsill, she leaned them both backwards like they were scuba divers somersaulting off the edge of a rowboat. At the moment they hit the dirt and tumbled into some groundcover, up through the window Lindsey heard Monsignor Rathburn exclaim in convulsed rapture, "Sweet Jesus!"

Lindsey and the girl lay disheveled atop several bushes of night-blooming jasmine. After she caught her breath, Lindsey managed to say, "What's your name, anyway?"

"Jilan?"

The voice did not come from the little girl. Although the first syllable of the well-enunciated name was high and possibly childlike, the last part was uttered with a throaty suggestion of menace.

She recognized the voice. It was Ms. Abilene's.

Lindsey slumped back into the jasmine and had the sensation of shrinking. She felt as if she were back in seventh grade. Looking up at Ms. Abilene, she couldn't make out her features for the sun, but was suddenly reminded of the look on Nelson Fong's face as he awaited his Rio Grande ass-whupping. Lindsey couldn't help but think she was about to find out exactly what happened to Nelson. She braced herself for a generous, down-home helping of corporal punishment served with pleasure by the Texas she-devil.

Ms. Abilene spoke. She said, "Jilan, I'll deal with you later."

The girl scrambled up and ran away. There was a moment of silence, then Lindsey stammered, "Wha-what are you going to do?"

Ms. Abilene folded her arms over her chest and said, "Something I should've done a long time ago."

Reaching into her pants-suit pocket, Ms. Abilene produced a slim penknife and raised it dramatically in her fist, the blade gleaming in the sunlight. In one swift motion she slashed through the Chinese jumprope that bound Lindsey's legs. She then beckoned for her to follow. Lindsey dusted herself off, rubbed her sore calves, and followed Ms. Abilene across the now-empty schoolyard. The heat of the day rose up from the asphalt and added to her profuse sweating. She was certain that serious pain awaited her inside the cool walls of St. Maude's.

Reaching the building, they walked through the foyer and Lindsey glanced back pleadingly at the portrait of Mary. They headed down the stairway to the basement.

"I'm doomed," Lindsey thought.

Down they went, switching back and forth down the polished steps. They took the exact path that Lindsey had taken the day she went snooping for the Permanent Record. Now she feared she was going to become a permanent resident, buried in an unmarked crypt or beneath a headstone that read, "Here lies a cheeky, cheeky girl." Perhaps she would be shackled to a dungeon wall, only to be found hundreds of years from now by a future Indiana Jones.

At the end of a quiet hallway, Ms. Abilene stopped and turned to Lindsey.

"I know you were looking at the old class pictures."

Lindsey said nothing. Ms. Abilene used a passkey and opened a door.

"Goodbye, cruel world," Lindsey said to herself and closed her eyes.

Click! She heard a light go on, and instead of a ravenous beast ready to devour her, she opened her eyes to find a room full of filing cabinets. Ms. Abilene walked to the far wall and rifled through one of the drawers. Lindsey waited patiently and considered that she might be receiving her walking papers. After about five minutes, Ms. Abilene exclaimed, "Aha!" and pulled out a manila folder. She held it out for Lindsey.

Hesitating for a moment, Lindsey took the envelope from Ms. Abilene and opened it. Reaching inside, she carefully pulled out about ten photos, all black and white, and all of the same girl. *The* girl. The girl from 1928 that looked exactly like Lindsey. Pictures of the girl sewing, playing with other girls, standing at a chalkboard and copying down lessons.

Lindsey raised her chin and looked at Ms. Abilene who, up until a second ago, she had considered her enemy.

Ms. Abilene smiled and said, "I've thought for a long time that you should have those. I'm not really supposed to, but . . . well, they're not doing anyone a bit of good down here."

Lindsey looked through the pictures again. Yep. Same eyebrows, same nose, same . . . arms.

Ms. Abilene slammed the file cabinet shut and Lindsey jumped. Sounding matter-of-fact yet chipper, Ms. Abilene added, "Seeing as how they're pictures of your grandmother, I figured they really belong to your family, not the school."

As they walked back up the steps, Lindsey seemed calm, but her mind was racing. Who knew that Lindsey and her grandmother had looked so much alike as teenagers? More urgently, though, she could not even begin to digest the insane knowledge that Yun Yun had been a student here. If St. Maude's had previously been a rescue mission, where had Yun Yun been rescued *from*?

At the top of the stairs, Ms. Abilene turned to Lindsey, then paused to flip her hair from her face, stopping for a millisecond to scratch the inside of her nostril. She said, "See, I'm not all bad."

Then she slowly smiled, turned, and clip-clopped down the hall.

Opalescent

Lindsey knew what she had to do. In a moment of absolute clarity, she resolved to get to Chinatown and find Yeh Yeh in his store. She would make him tell her everything.

She hopped on the Muni, then got off before the bus route diverted toward Union Square. On the cobblestones of Commercial Alley, she detected the aromas of a nearby bakery, and ventured a quick sniff only to experience, a second later, the pungent odor of rancid fish. She should have known better than to have inhaled so deeply while walking through Chinatown. But no matter. She was on a mission.

Zigzagging her way toward Jackson Street, she passed the black and turquoise tiles of the jewelry shop on Clay, then the orange and green ones of the souvenir place on Washington. She tried to remember if Yeh Yeh's storefront was marked with purple or yellow tiles.

As she walked, she remembered back to childhood when her family used to spend Saturdays in Chinatown. Her mom used to get her hair done on Stockton Street while her dad ran errands, buying Chinese beef jerky or fresh chow fun noodles. Meanwhile, Kevin and Lindsey were free to roam around, conveniently using Yeh Yeh's store as a home base for their tomfoolery.

Yeh Yeh's grocery store had been the first "American" grocery store in Chinatown that sold Chef Boyardee and Nabisco brands alongside fermented tofu and pickled bamboo shoots in jars. In the refrigerated section there was orange Fanta next to soy milk, and root beer alongside imported mango drinks from Hong Kong. Lindsey and Kevin ran up and down the cramped aisles, imitating maneuvers they'd seen in *Shaolin Mantis*, poking holes in packages of fruit pies and Zingers to render them unsellable so Yeh Yeh would let them eat them. On several occasions when their grandmother was in the store, she caught them smashing packages of Oreos and Fig Newtons and ejected them from the premises, driving them out with a litany of growling curses.

Kevin and Lindsey didn't care. There was plenty of mischief waiting for them between Powell and Kearny, Columbus and Bush. They made their rounds to various kid-friendly landmarks like the ice-cream shop, comic-book store, and the Sun Sing movie theater, where they gazed up at the photographs pinned outside under glass. The pictures showed stills from current and coming attractions; on the left side were scenes of warriors performing kung fu kicks and on the right were soft-focus pictures from the late-night nudie movies. After exhausting their possibilities for mischief on Grant Avenue, they walked down to the A-1 Cafe for greasy hamburgers wrapped in yellow-gold wax paper.

Sometimes they would head to the park at Portsmouth Square. At seven and nine years old respectively, Lindsey and Kevin went to watch the old Chinese men play chess and feed the pigeons. As an added bonus, occasionally they learned dirty words in Cantonese.

Over in the sandy area, they would scramble up and down

the metal slides. Once Kevin found a butane lighter, and they took turns flicking it on and off. A group of other kids came over while Kevin was showing off, trying to get the flame to grow really big. After accidentally setting fire to one kid's shorts, they all laughed, even the kid whose rump was burning. Kevin pulled off the boy's shorts just in time, but in his haste he also yanked off the boy's *dai foo*, and they all played catch with the underpants as the bottomless boy chased them.

Lindsey chuckled at the memory as she kept walking toward Yeh Yeh's store. Still reminiscing about Portsmouth Square, she wondered if the old guy with the huge goiter was still alive. She hadn't seen him in years. She and Kevin used to spy on him, and marveled at the bulbous growth on his neck that was as wobbly as a water balloon, and resembled a papaya attached to the man's eggplant-shaped noggin. The cumbersome goiter hung alongside his throat like the slightly smaller head of an undeveloped Siamese twin. As Kevin and Lindsey watched him they whispered their speculations to each other, debating whether the obscene deformity looked more like a butternut squash or a Walla Walla sweet onion. They pondered its consistency, wondering if it was soft or hard, and imagined that the thing talked to the man at night.

Passing the dressmaking shops and import stores, Lindsey gazed at the bolts of red silk fabric and big gaudy vases. She remembered how she and her brother used to push past adults' pantlegs and argued about who was the best fighter in the kung fu movies—Ti Lung, Wang Yu, or Fu Sheng. Getting closer to the grocery store, she stopped and peered into the comic-book shop where she and Kevin used to peruse the Ultraman books. She could see the same posters still pinned to the walls, now tattered, depicting Mothra, Rodan, and Johnny Sako's Amazing Robot.

Moving on, she dipped below Grant Avenue at Jackson Street, and finally spotted the purple tiles of her grandpa's store.

A bell tinkled as she pushed open the door, but she didn't see anyone. She recognized the low freezer with the Coca-Cola logo, and took in the combined smells of dried cuttlefish, rat poison, and candy. She hoped that Yeh Yeh was at the store today, and she peered down the cramped aisles for any sign of his greengrocer's smock.

Glad to be out of the sun, she loitered by the cash register and cooled her hand against the heavy jars on the counter. Through the glass she could see wax wrappers with Chinese writing, and noted that each container was filled with a different kind of *mui*. The crinkly white paper with the twisted ends suggested chocolate bonbons, but inside the wrappers were salted plums and other varieties of preserved fruit. *Mui* could be either wet or dry, sweet or salty, slimy or shriveled. She had seen old men gnaw on them with satisfaction until their tongues bled, but she found the flavors off-putting: tangy, syrupy, and encrusted with salt. The pits of the fruit were at once stringy, meaty, and slippery, and she wondered how the old Chinese ladies could work pieces of *mui* in their jowls for hours.

Just then, Lindsey heard someone singing "Superfreak."

Uncle Elmore came dancing down the aisle. He walked over and grabbed Lindsey's hand, then spun her around and bent her backward in a dip so low her hair touched the floor, which grossed her out. As he hoisted her back up, she gagged in a cloud of Brut by Fabergé.

"Watching the store today?" Lindsey asked.

Uncle Elmore didn't seem to be listening. He placed his hand around Lindsey's waist and danced a few more steps, twirling her around a revolving rack of wasabi crackers and dried squid snacks.

Uncle Elmore was like a Chinese Tony Manero from *Saturday Night Fever* who worked in a Chinese grocery instead of a hardware store. She could just picture him strutting down Jackson Street carrying a bucket of tofu to the rhythm of "Stayin' Alive" by the Bee Gees.

"I'm just here for a minute while Dad's out," he said, letting her go. He whipped a banana comb out of his back pocket and quickly spruced up his feathered hairdo. After checking out his reflection in the mirrored I-Ching octagon at the front door, he went to the cash register and hit a few buttons until the till popped open. Pocketing three twenties, he said, "Hey, you don't mind staying up here for a minute, do ya? Dad'll be right up. I gotsa go." He slapped his thigh twice and made a pistol with his thumb and forefinger, shooting at Lindsey as he backed out of the store like he was Leather Tuscadero from *Happy Days*.

Lindsey stood at the register and waved goodbye. After about five minutes, Yeh Yeh still hadn't shown up, so she flipped the "closed" sign and made her way to the back of the store. At the end of the refrigerated aisle that held fresh chunks of coconut and spiky durian fruit in yellow nylon netting, Lindsey pushed open a swinging door that led to a back room and called out a hello. She walked down a few steps into the dark space and felt the empty silence. A subterranean chill wafted through the room, and she shuddered.

"Hello?" she said again.

The back room was as scary as she remembered. It was a dirty, sunken place where Lindsey once imagined Fu Manchu might get her. She maneuvered around a stack of musty boxes with Chinese writing on the sides, and she peered down a dark cellar door, spotting a conveyor belt where deliveries came up.

She was afraid of rats and suspected raccoon-sized ones lurked down there. At a lamplit desk she found piles of receipts impaled on a rusty spike, accounting binders stacked beneath a pile of coupons, copious amounts of junk mail, and strangely, a Magic 8 Ball.

She picked up the plastic toy and shook it. She tried to think of something to ask the black ball, and finally ventured the question, "Am I really ready to get married?"

Flipping over the plastic sphere, she waited for the answer to appear. The cloud of purple ink swished from side to side until an answer floated to the surface:

UNCLEAR AT THIS TIME.

She shook the black toy again. "If I kiss Dustin Lee just once, will my life be ruined?"

She spun the magic ball and shook it vigorously. After a moment an answer appeared:

ALL SIGNS POINT TO YES.

Lindsey sighed. She looked up to the low-ceilinged loft. "Yeh Yeh?" she called.

Climbing the precarious ladder, she poked her head up above the platform. As she reached the top, there was barely enough headroom to stand as she surveyed the humble space with its narrow cot, several crates lined up for a makeshift table, and cigar boxes on the sloping floor of warped linoleum.

Curiosity got the better of her. Being careful where she stepped, she searched for sinister Chinese things that she had seen in movies and cartoons: torture devices, opium pipes, or other drug paraphernalia. She was anxious to think she might find a hatchet, knives with blood, or magic potions.

After several minutes of snooping, she didn't find anything other than a tube of denture glue and a Duncan butterfly yo-yo. She looped her finger through the string and gave it a few

spins. A minute later, she heard the front doorbell chime
faintly. She scrambled back down the ladder and flew out the
door and down the aisle toward the front counter.

"*Hai?*"

It was Yeh Yeh. He unwrapped two Styrofoam soup containers from orange plastic bags and said, "I go out to get
lunch, where is El-more?"

Lindsey grabbed a container before it spilled. "He said he
had to leave."

Yeh Yeh tossed her a plastic spoon. "You come visit. Fine,
fine. *Wonton mein. Sik la . . .*"

Lindsey slurped some noodles in duck broth, then tried to
pinch a wonton with her chopsticks, but it kept slipping from
the tips. She finally skewered it against the wall of the Styrofoam container. Chewing, she said, "I have some photos I'd
like to show you." Pulling the manila envelope from her shoulder bag, she emptied the pictures on the counter, flipped them
all right-side up, and lined them in a straight row.

Yeh Yeh moved slowly at first, but she could tell he was in-
trigued. He wiped his mouth with a napkin, picked up a couple
of photos, and held them up to the light, scrutinizing them. As
she chewed, Lindsey watched him. He didn't ask her where she
got them or what she knew. While he examined the rest of the
pictures, for a second Lindsey thought she saw his eyes get
teary with emotion, but she wasn't quite sure. As she slurped
soup and worked her mouth around slices of duck, she spit out
parts that were too bony or too fatty. Eventually, she couldn't
take the suspense.

"Well?" she said.

Yeh Yeh whispered, "Is it Pearl or Opal?"

Lindsey had no idea what he was talking about. "They're
pictures of Yun Yun," she said.

He replied, "Of course, of course," then placed the pictures back on the counter and resumed eating, shoving some more noodles in his mouth.

"Who are Pearl and Opal?" she asked.

"Your Yun Yun, American name is Minnie, but long time ago we call her Pearl. I just forget, sorry."

Lindsey nodded, confused all over again about Chinese people choosing American names, then picking up nicknames as well. Then her mind snagged on a weird thought: Pearl, Minnie . . . Minnie Pearl. Wasn't that some old country singer? She forgot to ask who Opal was.

When they were finished eating, Yeh Yeh cleaned off the counter and threw the Styrofoam containers into the trash. Then, to Lindsey's surprise, he took a pint of whiskey from behind the cash register, poured some into a paper cup, and nonchalantly began to sip it like it was tea.

Yeh Yeh picked up one of the photos again and placed it back down quickly. They sat quietly for a while as Lindsey bided her time. In her experience, aggressive questioning usually made sources retreat. Her tactic was to let the speaker say anything he or she wanted. She would vacuum up all the hints, hearsay, and memories and piece them together later, eventually fitting them onto her Frankenstein creature of family history. She waited silently and hoped he would continue.

After a customer came in and bought a pack of cigarettes and some Mentos, Yeh Yeh absentmindedly began to dust the *mui* canisters with a rag. Lindsey sat still and waited some more. When she first headed down here she was so determined to shake information out of Yeh Yeh like pears from a tree, but now that they were actually together, she didn't know how to force him to talk. She swallowed and tried to think of a way to get the conversation going. After a moment, she ventured, "I guess Yun Yun has always been a little bit shy."

Taking another sip from his paper cup, her grandfather said, "Not so much shy. Just worrywart." His eyes crinkled a little and they shared a smile.

But then the smile disappeared. He stared out into space, as if transfixed by the cuttlefish snacks hanging from the pegs in the aisle.

"I didn't know your Yun Yun back then, only met her later. Were these taken at orphanage?"

Lindsey nodded her head. So, it seemed, Yeh Yeh did know a few things after all about Yun Yun's past. She listened as he went on,

"I didn't meet your grandma until she was older. I was cook in a big house and she was the upstairs cleaning girl. Back then, there were many wealthy houses that had Chinese people running the show. Yeah, you think I joke? It is true! And I was very happy to see her. First few week she there, I only see her when she come out back to wash and fold laundry, but one day I talk to her. In Tze Yap I ask her name, and she tell me in English that the white ladies call her Mary, but her name is Pearl. Now people call her Minnie. See, you think your Yun Yun is just Yun Yun, but she have life before!"

Lindsey nodded.

"I was the only Chinese person, especially man, that she saw most every day. I bring her things. Special piece of food I save for her, or pretty vegetable I carve and leave in laundry basket for her to find. See, I show you."

Fairly animated now, Yeh Yeh went out from behind the counter, retrieved a radish from the small, refrigerated section, and returned to his seat. He pulled out a pocket knife and, as Lindsey watched him, proceeded to deftly whittle the root vegetable into the shape of a rose. She never suspected her grandfather had such hidden talents.

"See?" He handed it to her, and she admired the carved,

translucent flower, its vibrant red coloring the edges of the "petals."

Yeh Yeh stared into the cuttlefish snacks again. He said, "I like her very much, but also, Chinese people very practical. She Chinese. I Chinese, so we decide to get marry. But when we move to Locke, I don't think she like it too much."

Lindsey could almost picture Yeh Yeh as a young man taking his new bride up the Sacramento River to Locke by ferry. Her father had told her about the dirt-floor barracks that all the fruitpickers shared, and about how later the family moved into a makeshift building where the only insulation that separated the plank walls from the outside was tacked-up newspapers. They shingled the roof with the tops of tin cans that they'd saved.

Lindsey's dad had also once mentioned to her that in the evenings they ran a gambling hall. She wondered how Yun Yun must have fared in such an environment. Mulling over what Yeh Yeh had just said about Chinese people being practical, she wondered if, over the years of orchard work and hosting crews of gamblers, did Yun Yun have any affection at all for her husband? Had they desperately wanted children, or were her dad, Auntie Geraldine, and Uncle Elmore just the results of a matter of course?

Yeh Yeh started to talk again. "I was born in Locke, but moved to San Fran when I was small boy. Went to school here and everything, right in North Beach at Francisco Middle School. Then moved back to Locke with Yun Yun. By the time your dad was college-age we come back again to the city. And you know what? I was very content to be back. This place, no other place like it, you know?"

Lindsey did know, and smiled at Yeh Yeh.

She gathered up her photos and slipped them back into their folder. Before she could say goodbye, Yeh Yeh shuffled out from behind the counter and began to rearrange some cans of Campbell's soup, his back turned to her. As she called out a goodbye, he did not respond but she could hear him singing "San Francisco" again.

Where's the Beef Chow Fun?

That night, after a Top Ramen dinner and a Reese's peanut butter cup for dessert, Lindsey dug through her bureau drawer until she found her vine and pressed charcoals. She retrieved her sketchbook, turned to a clean page, and sat down on the floor to start a drawing. Holding the brittle, black stick in her hand, she hesitated for a moment, then touched the charcoal to the paper and tentatively made a mark on the white surface.

Every drawing began with a single line. A lonely, amateur smudge on the vast, empty space that looked so naked and humiliating. After hours of working the surface, perhaps the drawing would start to look like something—a still life with fruit, leaves on the trees outside, or the curve of the sofa—but the first few lines were always the hardest and required that she screw up her courage and assure herself that no one was looking, so it was okay.

Using a snapshot of Michael she'd taken a while ago when he'd been asleep, she tried now to do his image justice. With indecisive lines and lousy shading, she created contours where there shouldn't have been any. After twenty minutes, she was already fighting the urge to give up and tear the paper to shreds, but she went on.

By nine o' clock she'd spent an hour fixing one area, only to find that she accidentally ruined the best part of the drawing. As she worked into the night, she felt the emptiness of the apartment. Missing Michael, she tried to will the phone to ring, and to her surprise, around ten o'clock, it did.

"Hello?" she said, wiping her hands on a dishtowel.

There was a pause, and then, "What are you wearing?"

It was not Michael. Lindsey knew full well who it was, and said, "You are a pervert and I'm hanging up."

Dustin laughed. "You're up late, Miss Goody Two Shoes. What are you doing?"

She would've died if he made fun of her artistic aspirations, so she said, "Um, I'm getting ready for bed."

"Really? Then let's get back to my original question. What do you wear when you go to sleep?"

"Darling, that's not for you to know."

"Hmm. 'Darling.' I like that. Is that what you call . . . him?"

Lindsey walked into the bedroom and flopped onto the bed. "That's none of your business," she said. In spite of herself, she was enjoying this conversation.

"You don't sound very sleepy," Dustin said. "And I think you might be thirsty. Want to meet?"

Lindsey thought for a moment. She was already in her jammies and her fuzzy slippers.

"Hmm," Dustin added, "I can tell that you want to. Come on, just one drink. We'll meet in a public place so you can be sure I won't put the moves on you. I'll even come to your neighborhood. I'll be in that place on the corner from you in, like, fifteen minutes. Okay?"

He hung up before she could answer, so now she felt like she had to go. Deep down inside she was glad to have the decision made for her so she didn't quite have to admit to herself that she did, in fact, want to meet him. She kicked off her slippers excitedly, and quickly changed her clothes.

As she walked to the corner bar, she kept her eyes peeled in case she might get mugged. She realized that it had been a while since she had to be so wary. Other than walking to work, if she ever went anywhere it was usually with Michael. Plus, they mostly stayed at home. When had she gotten so used to having a guy around that now she felt vulnerable without him? When she was single she used to walk around alone all the time and didn't feel like such a scaredy-cat. When did she become such a chicken?

Standing outside the bar, she hesitated before going in. She and Michael hardly ever went out to bars anymore, but instead bought liquor at Beverages and More or Trader Joe's and made their own drinks in the kitchen. The festive string of lights and the laughter from within the bar reminded her of being single. Even the smell of stale beer made her feel kind of thrilled to be out, faced with an evening of possibilities ahead. She went inside.

Dustin was sitting at the bar with a sleazy, road-dog kind of gal slobbering all over him. She was leaning on his shoulder in her skanky, purposely ripped tank top when Dustin saw Lindsey come in. He turned to the boozehound and said, "Sorry, honey. My wife just got here."

He picked up two drinks from the bar and led Lindsey to a table in the corner.

"Here," he said, handing her a blended margarita with salt on the glass edge. "I figured you liked girlie drinks. It's mango."

"Thanks," she said, and sat down. She looked around the place as she took off her coat, and without looking at Dustin, she knew his eyes were on her.

"We're the only Asians in here," he said, scanning the room

confidently. "Where do all the twentysomething Chinese kids hang out, anyway?"

She raised an eyebrow. "You're asking *me?*"

Dustin took a sip of his drink. "Well you must have *some* Asian friends."

She gave him a deadpan stare. After a moment he said, "Yeah, me neither," and they both laughed.

"Actually," she said, "I have one friend, Mimi. But she's in Europe, hanging out with her boyfriend, Duan. He's touring with his Van Halen cover band."

"Oh-kaay," Dustin replied, raising his eyebrows at the concept of such a thing. After another moment he said, "So. If we were two Chinese people looking to hang out with other Chinese people . . . where would we go?"

Lindsey thought for a second, then replied, "There's some Korean nightclubs. Also, I think there's, like, a whole circuit of Asian parties, and once you get invited to one of them, you get invited to all of them. My brother, Kevin, goes to them sometimes."

"How come you don't go?"

"Well . . . no one ever asked me. And Kevin certainly doesn't want his baby sister hanging around. God forbid I see him smoking, which he thinks is a big secret, but he always reeks of smoke, so much that even my parents know."

"What, are they, like, house parties?"

"No, they're like organized, moving clubs, I think. Sometimes they're in bars. I think there's even a cover charge."

Dustin finished his drink and was now twirling the glass in his hand. She caught herself staring at his smooth skin, and looked away. Sneaking another peek at his perfectly symmetrical features, she wondered if he waxed his eyebrows.

"Well," he said, "other than those parties, where do they meet?"

"What do you mean 'they'? We're two Chinese people and we're here. How does anyone meet?"

"Um, hello? We met in sixth grade. I'm talking about regular Chinese people. Ones who don't like Kraftwerk or go around hitting other kids with their lunchboxes . . . people who have regular jobs, not just freeloaders who hang out at esoteric motorcycle shows or spend their days refilling holy water decanters in their former third-grade classrooms."

Lindsey was aware that she was smiling at Dustin. She couldn't help it. Something about him made her feel simultaneously at ease, but also a little giddy. She hated that she found him so handsome that she could barely keep her eyes off him. Her own behavior was embarrassing. Wasn't she a decent person who should be above ogling? For a second she imagined what it must be like to be a respectable man who suddenly found himself drooling over a picture of Lindsay Lohan. As she scolded herself in her head, she was shaken from her own thoughts when Dustin said something.

"What?" she said, not hearing him.

Dustin laughed at her. "I said, 'You're staring.' "

She felt her face flush. Quickly recovering, she said, "What were we talking about?"

He looked at her with a bemused expression. "I don't remember. All I can think about is how you might look . . . with your clothes . . . off."

She wasn't sure if she should act offended or fire back a snappy comment. Once again, Dustin had her tongue-tied.

Finally, she said, "We've had our one drink. I guess it's time to go."

As Dustin walked Lindsey back to her apartment, she felt all at once nervous, sneaky, and excited. It had been a while since she'd been around such blatant flirting as Dustin's, and she felt both flattered and guilty to be the recipient of it.

It was all harmless fun. It's not like she was going to ask him inside or do anything with him. She told herself this thing with Dustin was just a silly trifle between friends. It had no bearing on her status as a fiancée. She reminded herself that Michael had recently gone to the DMV to register her car for her so she didn't have to stand in line with anyone scuzzy. Now *that* was true love.

At her door, she held out her hand for Dustin to shake. Slipping his smooth fingers around hers, he shook her hand and gave her a quick peck on the cheek.

She was pleasantly surprised. He was going to act like a gentleman, after all. But then, his hand still on hers, he stepped close and pressed his mouth against her ear. His hot breath against her neck, he whispered, "Think of me when you take your clothes off tonight." And with that, he turned away and did not look back.

The Electric Shirley Temple Acid Test

The last day of school at St. Maude's was always reserved for a field trip to the natural history museum. Lindsey had skipped breakfast that morning because she was running behind, and later, in the school office, she was organizing permission slips when Sister Constance approached her desk.

"Lindsey, we're short one chaperone for today's excursion. Would you mind taking half the third-grade class? Oh, and we are certainly hoping that you will be bringing your grandmother to this year's summer jubilee."

She agreed to chaperone the field trip, then asked, "What jubilee?"

"No one has told you? We are organizing an alumni reunion to celebrate the two-hundredth anniversary of St. Maude's being torn to pieces by a pack of wild dogs. Also, we're taking this great opportunity to welcome back any lapsed Catholics to show them how progressive the church is now. We now advocate only lenient corporal punishment in the classroom. Also, the school is currently voting on whether to allow pepperoni pizza on Fridays during Lent. With enrollment down and the Sunday pews empty, we want to entice the wayward sheep back to the flock, and maybe their children will join us too. Which reminds me, we'll need your help with the food, and I do have names for you to call from our list of missing Chinese alumni. Can't hunt them down anywhere. Everyone who's ever been a student here is invited to the jubilee, so it would be a pity if they weren't included. Which is why you must bring your grandmother. She'll be a distinguished guest as one of the oldest survivors—I mean, graduates—from the missionary era."

Sister Constance reminded her to meet the third graders by the foyer in ten minutes, at oh-nine-hundred-hours, and then she squeaked away in her small-footed nun shoes.

Rubber-banding the last of the permission slips, Lindsey broke out into a sweat. *Everyone who's ever been a student here is invited to the jubilee*. That meant Yun Yun. That meant the Lost Chinese Children. That meant Dustin. She thought to herself, "It's been fifteen years since sixth grade. Now I'm helping to organize a reunion where I'll be expected to publicly kowtow to Sister Constance, make my grandmother proud, tend to the needs of Beethoven, the autistic guinea pig, and keep my hands off Dustin Lee. All righty."

It was not going to be pretty.

At 9:30 A.M., Lindsey was shepherding a gaggle of munchkins across Oak Street. The city was still enduring its heatwave, and Lindsey could feel her clothes already sticking to her as she shielded her eyes from the sunlight bouncing off the shiny leaves of the trees that lined the Panhandle. Hurrying the giddy students through the intersection, her stomach growled as she anticipated a day of chasing kids, breaking up shoving matches, and cleaning peanut butter from gooey fingers.

Ahead of her group were the second and first graders, and far in the distance she could see the kindergartners, led by Sister Boniface, clearly visible as she waved an Irish flag as a marker for the teachers who were bringing up the rear. At the entrance of the museum she spotted hundreds of students from various other schools lined up for what must have been a free admission day. As the St. Maude's contingent clustered by the handicap ramp, the black-cloaked nuns kept everyone together, performing their round-up job like a cranky band of nipping border collies.

After some instructions from Sister Constance, Lindsey gathered her half of the third graders from the ramp and led them inside the museum. The students were excited to be in "free dress" today, but Lindsey worried about how she would keep track of them all without their uniforms to remind her which kids belonged to St. Maude's. She made them all hold hands, then ushered them into the planetarium.

As the lights dimmed, Lindsey shushed some loudmouths and warned others about kicking the backs of the seats in front of them. Once they settled down, they all sank into a state of wonder as the night sky materialized above them and the volunteer at the lectern talked them through the southern constellations. Lindsey enjoyed the show as much as the kids did, and when the presentation ended and the lights gradually brought them back to daylight, they all filed out of the auditorium more mellow than when they entered.

She then led the students through the other exhibits. They stopped to visit the monitor lizard and the statue-still crocodiles that snoozed in the pool bordered by the tarnished seahorse fence. Past the mosaic tile wall, she corraled them through a tunnel of blue, glowing glass tanks that held yellow-eyed gars and spiky angelfish, and she allowed them to linger amongst the displays of anemones, coral, and crabs. For fifteen minutes or so, they all stood enthralled by the antics of a particularly spunky pufferfish with its tiny fins propelling its bulbous body around a miniature sunken treasure chest.

Pushing through a glass door, they crossed the courtyard of marble and granite animal sculptures. Lindsey instructed the kids to sit around the fountain while they ate their lunches, and as they pulled sandwiches, cookies, and sodas from their bags, Lindsey was disappointed to discover that in her morning haste she had forgotten to bring a lunch. She sat and watched the kids as they finished up, making sure they threw all their trash in the proper receptacles. Through another set of doors, she then led them to the endangered-species wing, which was connected to the safari exhibit.

Time flew by. It was already one thirty by the time they reached the dioramas of the African animals. They spent twenty minutes lingering among the antelopes and ibis, and enjoyed looking out at the painted savannah and backlit horizon of thin pastel clouds outlined by the red setting sun. The faux trees and piped-in sounds of chirping birds relaxed everyone. They moved along the brass railing and gazed at the resin pools of fake water and rested their eyes on the thick-furred lions relaxing on the African veldt.

Lindsey read to them from a plaque about nyalas, zebras, and klipspringers, then let the kids explore the adjacent exhibits on their own as she kept an eye on them from beneath the watchful gaze of California's last grizzly bear, who stood, stuffed and preserved, by the women's bathrooms.

It was then that she remembered her favorite exhibit from when she was small. With a running hop she turned the corner to find the prehistoric, saber-toothed marmot with the miniature rhino horn growing out of its stubby head. She laughed out loud at the absurd sight. Partially submerged in its dirt hill, the comical animal peeked out with stern consternation, looking as threatening and dangerous as an overgrown chipmunk with a big bump on its head. "Hah!" Lindsey thought to herself, "no wonder you're extinct."

She was surveying the animal's tiny claws when suddenly she heard a voice say, "If you like taxidermy, you'd *love* my house."

She turned and saw her little Chinese friend, Jilan. She almost didn't recognize the girl without her uniform; moreover, her "free dress" attire was downright bizarre. She wore saddle shoes, an argyle vest, and blue and orange Madras-print pants. Standing bowlegged with her oxford shirtsleeves rolled above the elbows, she resembled Gene Kelly in *Singin' in the Rain*.

Jilan repeated her statement about her home being a haven for taxidermy, and then added, "I think you'd really like it."

Lindsey wasn't exactly sure how to reply, so she said the only thing that came to mind: "Do you know whose carpool you're supposed to go home in?"

The girl nodded, then pulled out a yo-yo. She tossed it down and reeled it back up a couple of times. Lindsey scanned the hall and made a mental tally of the third graders.

"Okay," she called out to the kids who were milling around. "Everyone, it's time to meet back out in front and join your carpools."

They all went outside and scattered to their respective rides. Lindsey watched her charges scramble into parents' cars. Then, satisfied that her job was done, she convened with Sister Constance before heading down the steps and pondering which route to walk home. She zigzagged between double-parked cars and dodged kids who were running every which way, and she eventually detoured down a secluded path strewn with fallen eucalyptus leaves. Water from a poorly aimed sprinkler spigot ran in rivulets along the sidewalk, and as it evaporated, it released the pleasant summer scent of grass and damp concrete.

Turning a corner, she came upon something that she could only imagine was sinister. She spotted Jilan, so recognizable in her mini-Gene Kelly garb, and Ms. Abilene walking alone in the distance. They were headed to an old, bronze-colored Corvair parked near a Parisian sculpture of men working a cider press. Ms. Abilene's hand rested on the back of the girl's neck, and Lindsey wondered if everything was okay. It suddenly occurred to her that Jilan might need saving from uncertain punishment for some minor infraction of school rules. She still didn't trust Ms. Abilene, and ran across the concourse to catch up with them.

"Hey, wait a minute!" Lindsey called out just as Ms. Abilene was scooting Jilan into the car. Seeing Lindsey, the little girl smiled, revealing babyish teeth.

"I can take her home," Lindsey offered.

"Are you sure?" Ms. Abilene said, eyeing Lindsey with a raised eyebrow. Lindsey nodded, as did Jilan excitedly. "Well, I do have some papers to grade back at school."

"No problem," Lindsey assured Ms. Abilene, then took Jilan's small hand in hers, convinced she had just saved the girl from certain harm.

Ms. Abilene got into her Corvair and tore out of her parking space like a banshee in a demolition derby. As Lindsey and Jilan watched the wheels of the car kick up dust, Ms. Abilene did not look back.

"She wanted to take away my yo-yo, but I hid it," Jilan said, pulling out her toy and grinning triumphantly.

The friendly lilt of the girl's voice, her casual attitude regarding the weirdness of her clothes, and the silly look of her chatterbox crackerjack teeth made Lindsey feel as if she herself were back in third grade and this girl was her regular after-school buddy.

"I don't live too far from here. We can walk," the girl said. Just then her yo-yo got away from her, spun out of control and hit the ground. She scrambled after it, looped the string over her finger and wound it around the center groove.

"C'mon," Lindsey said. "I'll show you how to 'walk the dog.'"

Exiting the park, the two companions snaked past Sharon Meadow and back out toward the Panhandle. The bright sunshine beat down on them. As they walked block after block, Lindsey figured it must have been at least eighty-five degrees. She began to wish they would come upon a corner store so she could get a bottled water.

"Are you hot?" she asked, but Jilan shook her head. With a museum brochure Lindsey shielded the sunlight from her eyes and scanned the sidewalk ahead for some shade.

They didn't talk much, except when Jilan wiggled her loose front tooth, saying it was about to fall out and she wanted at least fifty cents for it. They crossed the street and Lindsey gazed up at the hundred-year-old canary palms that shaded them from above like giant, feathered fans. It occurred to her that they were only about eight blocks from her apartment. As she stared up at the buildings' peeling paint and curved windows she absentmindedly wondered what was in the fridge at home. She definitely needed to eat something.

"We're here," Jilan said, stopping in front of an enormous Queen Anne that sat behind a massive concrete retaining wall overgrown with wildflowers and weeds. It was a huge, crumbling pink mansion that Lindsey had noticed before. Creeping rosemary spilled topsy-turvy like a shaggy, topiary waterfall onto the stairs, and above, wisteria grew over the windows like a fox-fur stole around an old lady's shoulders.

Lindsey glanced up at the plaster casts of lions' heads on the third-floor balcony. In their mouths they clenched several feet of rusted chain which supported a faux drawbridge bustling with a few raggle-taggle pigeons.

"You're coming in, aren't you?" Jilan asked. Lindsey didn't really want to, but agreed when the girl mentioned she could get a glass of water.

Crumbling on the corner roof-tiles, gargoyles smiled. Lindsey followed Jilan up the staircase, feeling like she was in a Hitchcock movie. Stepping onto the marble landing, she took a deep breath and waited a fraction of a second before following her small hostess. With a key from around her neck, Jilan opened the lock, pushed open a heavy door, and held it open. With a beckoning patty-cake hand, she motioned for Lindsey to step inside.

Lindsey placed her hand on the tiger-maple door, stepped inside, and shut it behind her. As her eyes adjusted to the dark space, she noted that it was cool inside and quiet, except for the hum of silence and machinery echoing from somewhere.

While the shabby, gothic exterior had been made somewhat cheery by the pinkish paint job, the interior of Jilan's house was downright macabre. A huge portrait of a menacing Russian wolfhound was perched above the fireplace, and the foyer and front rooms were filled with cloudy mirrors, their silver backings dissolving in flakes. Garish wall-to-wall crimson carpeting clashed with silver-and-green-flocked wallpaper.

The walls were lined with oil paintings of crying clowns, and in between each gold frame were fist-sized pottery faces of craggy sailors and grimacing leprechauns. In addition, every inch of floor space was covered by life-sized ceramic animals: coyotes and muskrats snarled from beneath tabletops, carousel horses frolicked by the front window, and a flock of majolica cockatoos dangled from ceiling-chain perches.

And Jilan hadn't lied about the taxidermy. A cheetah, its fangs bared, appeared ready to pounce on the gazelle behind the high-backed peach velvet sofa. Various oxen heads jutted from the wall, and stuffed finches and parakeets perched atop the windowsill above chiffon curtains.

Lindsey trailed Jilan into a room dominated by an enormous ebony desk. At first she did not see the small person who sat behind it. When she did notice the woman, she gave a startled little shriek. The lady looked like a wax figure, like an old granny-under-glass in the tell-your-fortune booth at a carnival. Her face resembled a spent narcissus blossom, thin and papery as onion skin, looking as if it might crumple in the slightest breeze.

Lindsey knew who she was. She was the neighborhood woman who had been watching her. The one who seemed to be following her, spying on her at every turn. In the past weeks, Lindsey had seen her at the corner store, silently staring at her from behind trees and peering out from behind mailboxes. Today she was cloaked in her familiar periwinkle shawl.

Lindsey looked up to a coiled cobra mounted on the wall. It was arranged to appear as if it was about to strike, with its venomous fangs ready to kill. Looking into its beady eyes, she felt suddenly lightheaded. She blinked and saw the woman's lavender eyes gazing deeply into her.

Lindsey took a deep breath, but before she knew it, the cobra was moving in a spiral motion. The silver and green walls were spinning, too. White light encroached on her field of vision, and then, suddenly, everything went black.

Lindsey awoke on a moth-eaten settee covered in blue velvet. Disoriented, she did not immediately remember the events of the day or what had brought her to such a place. She sat up.

Having never dropped acid, Lindsey wondered if she was indeed experiencing some kind of drug-induced hallucination. She focused her eyes on a ceramic Buddha that resembled an albino Jabba the Hutt, and beyond the statue she regarded a pair of taxidermied mountain sheep prancing by the fireplace. A murder of stuffed crows looked down from their perch atop a high armoire.

Spotting a pitcher of ice water sitting on a mirrored end table, Lindsey slowly reached out to pour herself a glass. She shakily lifted a tumbler from the tray, and accidentally knocked a crystal picture frame to the carpet. Bending down on one knee to retrieve it, she picked up the photo and stared in confusion. It was a picture of Ms. Abilene.

Just as she was wondering if she was dead, in hell, or on drugs, in waltzed Jilan in her kooky outfit. Mr. Magoo in drag trailed behind.

"This heat is something fierce for San Francisco," the old woman said.

"Did I faint?" Lindsey asked.

"Mmm-hmm. Appears so."

Lindsey remembered where she was now, but still wondered if she might be on drugs, since she had no explanation as to the connection between Jilan, this talking mannequin-granny, and Ms. Abilene.

The old lady held out the very tips of her fingers so Lindsey could grasp them in greeting.

"Let us get acquainted," she said. "Some refreshments, Jilan."

The small girl bounded out of the room as Lindsey propped herself up on the sofa and looked around. On shelves behind the old woman's wispy, pumpkin-shaped hairdo were skulls of small animals, a stuffed mongoose, a withered python skin and a turkey-sized tortoise shell. The cobra stared down menacingly from above.

After a moment the old woman said, "Would you kindly accompany me down the hall?"

Lindsey stood up and followed the woman across a plush, florid carpet, past a staircase with balustrades like ivory ladies' legs.

"Let's sit in this cooler room where you'll no doubt be more comfortable," she said, leading her to a mustard-colored chaise with a carved armrest in the shape of a sea serpent. Green-glazed stools sat stolidly between fake citrus trees planted in chipped pots, and all around them stood every kind of Chinese fu dog—yellow, tan, and green ones, some lying flat with wagging tails, and some balancing brown-edged ferns atop their ceramic heads.

Lindsey's eyes traveled from the top of a chinoiserie cabinet to a teak table with cinnabar candy dishes. Red silk pillows embroidered with dragons and phoenixes accented a Chinese wedding bed in the corner. *Ah so.* She had stumbled upon the Lair of a Hoarder Lady.

Just then Jilan came in carrying a tray with beverages on ice. She placed the drinks atop a garden seat, then scurried back into the hall only to return wheeling a bamboo cart containing an entire miniature bar, complete with cornichons, pearl onions, and sugar-pickled cherries. It was as if Jilan and the old woman were accustomed to some antiquated way of life that prompted them to keep cocktail refreshments on hand at all times, where peach cordials and candied apricot cubes dusted in confectioner's sugar required vigilant replenishing.

The woman took a sip of her drink, keeping one still, sparkling eye trained on Lindsey. She rattled the ice cubes in her glass and Lindsey, nervous, mistook the sound for her own chattering bones. Nervously, she reached for the red concoction on the tray in front of her and tasted it. It was a grenadine Shirley Temple.

Lindsey waited for the woman to tell her something extraordinary, like she was actually 280 years old, or a time traveler. She imagined seeing the old woman's likeness in an old documentary, perhaps in some film footage about Hearst Castle, where she would have easily fit in playing tennis with Charlie Chaplin and Oona O'Neill.

Lindsey gulped her drink. She knew there had to be an "only in San Francisco" kind of story going on in this decrepit house filled with such terrifying junk.

She waited in silence as her eyes darted around the room, noticing a collection of scorpion-under-glass paperweights and a stuffed emperor penguin in the corner. Jilan had run off, leaving Lindsey and the old woman alone, sipping their beverages until finally, the woman spoke.

"My name is Mrs. Clemens. I was raised by Chinese, right here in this house," she said. "My daughter too, before she moved to Abilene, Texas, and changed her name. Now she teaches at your school, has been teaching some years. Didn't talk to me for a long while. Had things all figured out. Didn't want nothing to do with this family, or this house. But now she's not so tough. She adopted a girl from China. That's Jilan, who, as you can see, lives with me now."

Lindsey's inner monologue took off. *I am at Ms. Abilene's house. I should have figured she was raised in a haunted mansion filled with snarling, dead animals. No wonder she's nuts. And Jilan is her kid? I've got to get out of here immediately and call Child Protective Services. What weird shit goes on here? And . . . why am I here?*

Lindsey actually blurted this last question out loud. The old woman sat back and sipped her drink for a moment longer.

The woman's head jiggled around like a bobblehead on a dashboard. Finally, she answered carefully, "Let's just say . . . someone asked me to keep an eye on you."

For all Lindsey knew, this old lady was one of Michael's octogenarian fans. He was always attracting elderly gals who needed help, just like at the grocery store. Perhaps the old woman had seen him on the street one day and asked him to help her get across. Or maybe he was walking by and she asked him to help bury a body for her in the backyard. Who knows. But why would Michael have asked the old woman to keep an eye on her?

Before Lindsey could inquire further, Mrs. Clemens said,

"Was a time, all good San Francisco homes had Chinese. Cooking, cleaning, raising the children."

Lindsey interrupted, "Yeah, but wasn't that back in the eighteen hundreds? How old are you, anyway?"

She knew her question was rude, but it just popped out. She started to apologize, but the old woman let out a whooping holler, a screaming kind of merriment that bordered on a howling wail of insanity, like Laughing Sal at the Museé Mechanique.

"Well, ain't we all big for our britches!"

Lindsey nodded, wondering when her acid trip was going to fizzle out. She sipped her drink down to the bottom of the ice and placed her empty glass on the silver tray.

"Let's back up," Mrs. Clemens said, smiling now. "What else would you like to ask me?"

Lindsey was still digesting the Jilan/old lady/Ms. Abilene connection. She said, "Where did all these dead—I mean, stuffed—animals come from?"

The woman patted her pompadour. "Ain't they something? My family's been in San Francisco a long time. My Granny Mae was in the *entertainment* business, shall we say. She was an old friend to Mr. Adolph Sutro—you hearda him—and when his home out by the ocean shut down in thirty-nine, she inherited most of this stuff. Made our house famous for its décor. Mae's Menagerie, is what the men used to call it."

Lindsey wasn't quite sure what the woman was trying to tell her, but had a pretty fair idea.

Mrs. Clemens looked at Lindsey with a twinkle in her eye. She said, "But really. Call it what you want. It was a long time ago, and the house hasn't been that sorta thing around here since way before you was born. But still. It was a good business for a while and someone had to do it. Did you know there used to be upwards of five hundred whorehouses in the San Francisco city limits? Cornichon?"

"No thank you."

The old woman popped a pickled nub in her mouth, then munched on some cocktail onions.

"Our décor made things a little more memorable. Sally Stanford, Mabel Malotte—you hearda them? They were good gals. Sometimes I think about opening up this place as a museum, but reputations, you never know . . ."

Lindsey felt nauseous from the syrupy drink. "I think I should go now," she said, abruptly standing up.

The woman looked at her with amused eyes.

"Is that so? Well, there's plenty more I gots to tell you, so when you feel better, you come and see me."

Lindsey took a few steps toward the door, then ran out of the room and catapulted herself toward the hallway banister. Careening down the stairs, she reached the bottom of the landing and heard Jilan's high-pitched, sweet goodbye float over her head. Either the portrait of the wolfhound or the shutting of the heavy door made a *whoofing* sound as she escaped the cavernous house. Stepping out into the sunlight, she headed home.

Slowly She Turned, Step by Step, Inch by Inch

A few days later, Lindsey was still flipped out about having met Ms. Abilene's mom. She tried to call Michael at the Psychic Food Ashram several times, but there was only a recording with space music playing in the background. She didn't want to blow his cover, so all she could do was leave a series of hang-ups and hope he psychically got the message to call home.

Meanwhile, she was getting lonely. One balmy evening after work, she found herself walking down the street with Dustin. They had decided to meet spontaneously, and were strolling down the street near her house, eating ice-cream cones.

Dustin was like Niagara Falls. She had read recently that the awe-inspiring majesty of the site somehow inspired fairly happy, well-adjusted people to jump into the rushing water and end it all. Dustin had the same effect on her. Something about him just sucked her in. As they walked in the last light of dusk, Lindsey glanced sideways every few moments to check him out, and the sight of his pink tongue against the drippy vanilla made her feel tingly. Down there.

Between licks, Dustin said, "So, have you given it any more thought?"

"What?" Lindsey asked, biting into her sugar cone.

"Marrying me."

She figured he was just taunting her to get her all riled up. "Aw, shut up," she said.

"Don't you like the idea that I'd be your first Chinese boyfriend and you'd be my first Chinese girlfriend? And besides, we wouldn't have to get engaged right away," he said. Giving her a little shove, he added, "I'd have to get in your panties before I really decided if I like you."

"What part of 'I'm already engaged' do you not understand? And hello, I thought friends aren't supposed to give each other ultimatums."

Dustin stopped walking and reached out to touch her arm. He brought his face so close to hers that the tips of their noses almost touched. He said, "I don't want to be just friends."

Lindsey felt her stomach drop. She twisted away from him and kept moving without saying anything. Her mind began to race.

Dustin satisfied a certain part of her that had been dormant for a while. It was a side of herself she'd abandoned in college, and he made her feel more like her younger, more carefree, more stupid self. Being with him reminded her how entire relationships could be forged and sustained with well-aimed putdowns that sparked an inflammation that started in the ego and traveled down to the groin. She missed competitive flirting, and had to admit it had been a while since she felt this nervous around Michael.

In a lot of ways, Dustin was no better than a Hoarder of All Things Asian who fetishized her because she was Chinese. He was constantly talking about how he'd only ever dated white girls. In fact, his pride in this "achievement" suggested that he might be some kind of Hoarder-in-reverse.

All of these variables confused her, compounded by the fact that she couldn't deny that she liked the way he moved. No Chinese guy had ever liked her before, and that, in itself, was a novelty. Was she no better than he, curious to know what it would be like to do the nasty with a Chinese person? Was it even possible to fetishize your own race?

Just then they stepped into the intersection and a middle-aged, Chinese woman in a convertible Mercedes-Benz slowed to a stop. She waited for them to pass, smiled and watched them for a long second before slowly accelerating. Lindsey briefly wondered if she knew the woman. She was fairly certain that she didn't.

Another block later, Lindsey was still thinking of the Chinese woman in the Mercedes. The eye contact between them had lasted only a moment, but something about the exchange was more than just a motorist allowing pedestrians to pass. Something in the way the woman looked at them, smiling and nodding with appreciation, made Lindsey feel slightly uncomfortable. Her uneasiness had everything to do with Dustin.

When Lindsey was with him, she never noticed strangers giving them hostile looks, the kind she sometimes got when she was with Michael. Rather, walking side by side with Dustin, she noticed subtle nods of approval, and not just from old Chinese people. In the course of the ten blocks they walked from the ice-cream parlor, complete strangers—white, black, Asian, and Latino—had taken one look at Dustin and Lindsey together and not blinked an eye. Maybe she imagined it, but she could have sworn that some of them had sent barely detectable messages of approval with their split-second glances and adjustments in body language. The few smiles and looks they received in just a few short blocks made her feel a little freaked out and tapped one of her deepest insecurities. It was something that no one had ever come right out and said, but it loomed over her anyway, all her life. Even if it wasn't an absolute law, she knew that deep down inside people thought it but didn't necessarily say it: *A Chinese should be with a Chinese.*

In contrast, when Lindsey was with Michael, passersby talked all kind of smack, right to their faces. It happened more often than she liked to admit. Although Michael was a quarter Chinese, his appearance never struck anyone as anything but white, and their pairing of races seemed to push people's buttons like a passing motorcycle setting off car alarms. Jerks hung out of cars and called out, "Hey geisha," and once, "Go back to Korea!" Even hipsters jokingly called them "John and Yoko."

She hadn't ever mentioned it to Michael, but a couple of times when he had stepped away from her for a second, to go into a store or to pay for gas, strangers had approached her and said, "What are you trying to prove?" and "What, Asian guys aren't good enough for you?" She had gotten it from both sides, white people and Asians alike. It was simultaneously weird and tiresome to be at the grocery store, in the car, or on the sidewalk and, at any given moment, have someone say something or give a look that made her feel forced to defend her relationship. Michael and Lindsey didn't consider their union an aggressive political statement. But people all over, at any given time, felt free to offer their commentary. One time a lady walked up to them in a Chinese restaurant and said, "Good for you," and a homeless guy had once said, "Love is color-blind! Got a quarter?"

Not that she had spent that much time with Dustin, but so far, nothing like that had happened. Moreover, she began to wonder, hypothetically speaking, if she did marry Dustin, maybe some things might be easier. If they were a couple she wouldn't have to explain certain customs to his family as she sometimes had to with Michael's, and she could revel in a certain level of Chinese acceptance that she would inevitably garner from her relatives. Yeah, her family loved Michael, but that marry-a-Chinese vibe was so strong and ran so deep, she still felt a twinge of guilt, as if by marrying Michael she would always undoubtedly be disappointing one ancestor or another, even dead ones she never knew and didn't care about.

Funnily enough, in several ways—except in looks—Michael was far more Chinese than Dustin could ever be. Michael had come a long way since she had first met him, and now he even knew more about Chinese food and customs than she did. When using his chopsticks and selecting from a shared plate, he knew to turn them over and use the clean ends. He was an expert at cracking pumpkin seeds between his teeth, and loved *mui*. He had even learned a few phrases in Chinese, and in his spare time read books about Chinese history. He was more kind, helpful, and respectful to Lindsey's parents than she or Kevin had ever been.

Dustin, on the other hand, was nothing like the usual Chinese Number-One Son. He called his parents "workaholic assholes," but lived off their money while acting as if his motorcycle, cool clothes, and slacker lifestyle made him better than they were. Although his family owned the second-largest chain of Chinese fast food restaurants in the United States, he sometimes made fun of it. He had said, "I don't eat any of that msg shit," and was unapologetic about knowing hardly any Chinese words. He even pronounced food names like white people did—*chow mein* as *chow* "mane" and *won ton* like it rhymed with "Juan" instead of "one."

And talk about a hollow bamboo—Dustin was the *jook-sing-*

iest ABC she had ever met. He looked unmistakably Chinese on the outside, but he didn't know anything about Chinese customs, and didn't even hang out with his relatives or cele-brate Chinese New Year. Also, his over-the-top preppie style suggested that he was always trying a little too hard. His Aber-crombie & Fitchiness was somewhat repellent.

And also attractive. Maybe because he was so damn white-washed and unabashedly proud of it she didn't feel so bad about herself. She too, had once claimed not to like Chinese food, but that was back in the nineties. Dustin's lack of cul-tural acceptance struck her as *so* 1999, but maybe she liked feel-ing superior to him for that.

She had to admit that his saying he didn't relate to Chinese people and things made her feel less alone. She was on her own path to accepting her Chinese self, and maybe Dustin was just a couple of changes behind her. In any case, it was comforting to know that he could relate to the feelings she had been work-ing through, and because of that, she was beginning to feel more than fond of him in spite of herself.

Lost in thought for several blocks now, she realized they had finally reached her doorstep.

"It's early," Dustin said. "Eight o'clock. Gonna invite me in this time?"

"Um, I don't have air-conditioning."

"This ain't Dallas. It's not even that hot. Come on, open up."

She opened the door and they went up the stairs. Dustin walked in like he owned the place. Running ahead a little, Lindsey shut the bedroom and bathroom door, then met up with Dustin in the living room, where he had taken the liberty of sprawling out on the sofa.

"Would you like something to drink?" she asked.

"Glass of water, thanks."

In the kitchen she listened for the sounds of Dustin rustling through any of her stuff, but instead she heard him turn on the television.

"You got cable?" he called out.

"Yeah, it's the silver remote, not the black one."

"Got it."

She came out with two glasses of water and stopped dead in her tracks when she saw what Dustin was watching. The actress who played Cherry Valance in *The Outsiders* was humping some unshaven guy in a bathroom stall.

"*Unfaithful*," Dustin said, taking his glass of water from her hand and placing it on the coffee table.

Mercifully, the sex scene ended, and she sat down next to him, leaving a safe distance between them.

After ten minutes of awkward movie-watching, Dustin said, "So . . . what do you think?"

Lindsey sipped her water. "I think there's no way Diane Lane and Richard Gere could have a kid that funny-looking."

"I'm not talking about the movie."

"Then I don't know what you're talking about." She shifted uneasily.

"You and me," Dustin said, bouncing closer to her. He put his arm around her and gave her a teasing look. "Don't you want to show me some of your *Kama Sutra* moves?"

She laughed. "The *Kama Sutra* isn't even Chinese, Dummy."

"Aren't you even curious about me? C'mon, I'm *La Bete Jaune*."

She pushed away from him, but his hand still touched her shoulder.

"Then what does that make me?"

"I don't know," he said, laughing. The fact that he didn't seem nervous or serious made her unsure if he was really putting the move on her or just joking around. She actually felt fairly comfortable, sitting there on the couch with him. That is, until he suddenly leaned over and tried to kiss her.

She blocked his face with a pillow.

He laughed, and snatched it from her grasp. After she pushed him away, he shoved her back a little too hard, and sent her flying off the couch with her legs in the air.

"Don't look at my underwear!" she yelped, scrambling upright.

Dustin laughed. "I already did. They're pink."

She straightened her clothes and said, "It's time for you to go, Loverboy. You're gonna get me in trouble."

"Oh, come on. Let's just do it and get it over with."

Just then, the telephone rang.

"Go ahead," Dustin said. "I'll wait."

Lindsey could hear the phone's muffled ringing from underneath a sofa cushion.

"Hello?"

"Hi, Babyface." It was Michael. "Whatcha up to?"

Lindsey hesitated. On the TV set, Cherry Valance had resumed screwing her lover. Since the sound was on mute, Lindsey was aware that Dustin would overhear anything she might say.

"Just watching a movie," she said, neglecting to mention that she wasn't alone.

"I miss you, Baby," Michael said with a sigh. "What did you do today? I want to hear all the details. Even the mundane ones, so I feel like I'm at home with you."

Lindsey nervously glanced at Dustin who was watching the on-screen humpage. She could hardly think. "Uh . . . I went grocery shopping after work."

"What did you buy?"

Dustin turned and glanced back at her, but she looked at the wall and tried to concentrate on talking to Michael.

"Um . . . garbage bags, laundry detergent, and toilet paper . . ."

"What kind?"

"The quilted kind with the flowers."

"Just don't get that brand that dissolves and turns into dingle fuzz . . ."

Dustin was making faces at her now, and she was afraid she'd start to laugh. She said to Michael, "Sweetie, I'm really tired. Can you call me back tomorrow?"

"Oh, sorry. Okay," he replied, sounding a little disappointed. "I love you, Baby."

"Yeah, me too," she said, and hung up quickly.

No sooner had she pressed the "end" button did Dustin blurt out,

"Boy, that was the sexiest conversation ever. You two are separated for weeks and all you can talk about is toilet paper. Could you get any more boring?"

He really enjoyed egging her on. "Hey, let's jump on my Norton. I'll take you down to Auto Row and we'll find a minivan showroom so you can pick something out. You're gonna need an extra-roomy model to fit that thirty-six pack of toilet paper."

"You're really asking for it," she said, feeling the electricity between them.

"Yes," Dustin replied with a flirting challenge. "I certainly am."

The next thing Lindsey knew, they were out on the street, walking back to the ice-cream place, where he'd parked his motorcycle. The air was warm, and she felt strangely free.

"Wanna go for a ride?" Dustin said.

Lindsey knew she should go back home. She should brush and floss, get into her nightgown, and if she wasn't sleepy, the best use of her time would be to go online and browse wedding websites.

But spontaneity seized her. Without further thought, she threw her leg over the seat, and she and Dustin zoomed off toward downtown.

Speeding past the trees, cars, apartments, and houses, Lindsey watched the city go by. Looking up into the darkened windows, she imagined couples already asleep, tucked in safe and thinking about bills, taxes, and potluck dinners. On Van Ness Avenue, they flew past the auto showrooms. At one point, Dustin threw out his arm to point out a Ford Winstar, and she was fairly certain he was laughing at her under his helmet. She considered pinching him when suddenly he cut across a lane and barely missed colliding into the side of a parked Volvo. Her heart skipped. Nearly getting creamed on the back of Dustin's motorcycle was definitely thrilling.

In the Marina District, Dustin careened through the winding streets until they finally stopped in front of a modern, glass-fronted house with sleek, clean lines. Lindsey hopped off the back and pryed the helmet from her head. Dustin, already at the front door, called over to her, "If we get married, this is where you'll live."

"Do I get my own servant?" she quipped.

"No, but you could be mine. I've got a French maid's outfit that would fit you just right."

Walking through a stainless steel gate, they passed a stand of bamboo and went up some steps. He unlocked the door and touched a panel that set off a chain reaction of lights in the house.

"Check it out," he said. "Everything is automatic. As soon as I come in, even the stereo and TV go on."

Lindsey stepped inside the bachelor pad extraordinaire. Everything looked straight out of *Metropolitan Home*—brand-new, and designed within an inch of its life. She recognized tables by Eames, and Le Corbusier armchairs upholstered in pony hide. She walked over to a zinc-topped bar and watched an angelfish as it floated within a wall-sized aquarium.

"Hey," he said, beckoning her over to the stereo. He reached up to a shelf and handed her a CD.

"Here, I burned this for you," he said. "Eighties classics."

She took it and smiled. "Don't you think I know what it means when a guy makes a tape or burns a CD for a girl? It's a serious get-in-your-pants maneuver."

"That's what I'm talkin' about," he said. "Do you want a tour of the bedroom?"

Lindsey was suddenly nervous. It was one thing to be in public places with Dustin, or even at her own house where she felt in control. But being at his place was totally different.

"I should probably go," she said, turning around. Just then, the state-of-the-art, plasma-screen television hanging off the wall caught her attention. It was hard not to miss. In all its 52-inch glory, a pornographic movie was playing.

The images were so big, they were almost abstract. Unable to stop staring, she finally made sense of what she was seeing. It was a close-up shot of a woman's hands clutching a guy's butt and spreading his ass-cheeks. Horrified, she continued to look, and could see little flecks of toilet paper stuck in the porno guy's butt. Earlier that evening she hadn't been sure what Michael meant when he mentioned "dingle fuzz," but now she knew. The TV's picture was remarkably clear and sharp.

"Oh, oops . . ." Dustin said, searching around the room and fumbling desperately for the remote control.

Lindsey was aghast. Without thinking any further, she walked straight out the door and down the steps. Amazingly, as she reached the sidewalk, a taxicab was dropping off a couple next door and she ran into the street to catch it. Hopping in, she slammed the door and told the driver her address.

"Don't go!" Dustin called, running after her.

But she was already safe inside the cab, thinking about flossing, brushing, and getting into bed.

The Family Jewels

Lindsey woke up the next morning feeling sick. Walking into the kitchen and sitting at the table, she decided to skip having coffee. Her insides felt twisted in knots. She told herself she might be coming down with a touch of the flu, but she knew she was just kidding herself. She knew what her problem was.

She replayed the events of the previous night in her head and felt her stomach churn. Hanging around Dustin was turning her into a nervous, flinchy mess. She felt like barfing all the time. As calm and cool as she was trying to act, he was definitely getting under her skin. She imagined she was slowly being poisoned with some kind of hormonal arsenic which was causing dementia. Why else would she be thinking about Kraftwerk Boy when she should have been dreaming about Michael, picking out china patterns, and reading *Here Comes the Guide*?

But she couldn't get Dustin out of her mind. She went to the bathroom to brush her teeth, and by the time she rinsed, she was actually considering calling him to go to the beach. She rationalized that they would just be two friends drowsily soaking up the sun, chatting about current events and rubbing oil into each other's lightly freckled, supple skin.

Hah. What a lie. In her heart of hearts she just wanted to see him half naked. Standing in front of the medicine cabinet mirror, she said to her reflection out loud, "You're going to be married, idiot. Keep it in your pants!"

She finished washing up, and a few minutes later she was back in the kitchen wondering what she should eat. She was used to Michael cooking her breakfast, and he had been gone for several weeks now. At a loss for what to do, she got a bowl and some milk and proceeded to inhale an entire box of Cocoa Krispies.

About an hour later she was standing with the phone in one hand and Dustin's phone number in the other. She dialed the first three digits, then hung up. Before she could get any more bright ideas, she ran to the bedroom and threw on her clothes. She was going to hop on a bus that would take her to Chinatown. She figured nothing would take her mind off Dustin's exquisitely oiled torso better than hanging out in a dusty grocery store with her grandfather.

Climbing on the 21 Hayes, she knew immediately that she was doing the right thing. Nothing was as unsexy as riding the Muni on a hot day. Watching a ratty, Haight-Street girl color in her toenails with a black Sharpie marker squelched any inclination she had regarding extracurricular romance.

A little while later she was walking down the street, passing wrinkly faced ladies and solemn Chinese men trudging uphill, clutching pink plastic sacks of vegetables. As they silently strolled by, Lindsey contemplated the disparity between what the old Chinese folks knew and what they seemed willing to tell.

She supposed she didn't blame them. After all, who wanted to remember the days when they tilled rice paddies in China or cleaned garbage cans in Stockton? Now that everyone's kitchens were remodeled with marble countertops and windowboxes for raising orchids, who wanted to remember the old shacks with ill-fitted planks for stairs?

As Lindsey walked, she thought about Yun Yun. She had once asked her grandmother, "What did your parents do to make a living?"

With her tightly clamped, Jason Robards mouth, Yun Yun had grumbled, "None your business."

Perhaps her grandmother thought she was protecting her from some terrible knowledge. But it all just added to Lindsey's frustration. She knew that *not* telling was how stories evaporated, facts were forgotten, and history was lost.

Lindsey initiated many such conversations and was consistently stonewalled. Sometimes her determination fizzled out. That is, until the next time she got a bee in her bonnet. The farthest she ever got with Yun Yun was when she once asked her about her childhood and her grandmother had replied, "Why do I want to remember?"

But Lindsey felt that she, her brother, and cousins had a right to know their family's history. It just didn't seem right that they had all reached their late twenties and thirties and still knew so little.

Which is why she was going to see Yeh Yeh. With nothing to do all day except sit at the cash register and sell the occasional box of Nabisco crackers or pint of whiskey, he was ripe to talk, she figured.

She passed the Chinese sausage shop with the meat hooks and shriveled, smoked ducks in the window, and continued down Washington Street until she cut over on Grant Avenue and down to Jackson Street. When she entered Yeh Yeh's store, the sensor let out a ring and he looked up from his newspaper.

"Eh, you again?" he said, then gestured for her to help herself to some *mui*. She shook her head, but thanked him anyway.

Pulling up a crate, she listened as Yeh Yeh made small talk about a sale on two-liter bottles of 7-Up and strawberries at Safeway.

"What have you got there?" her grandfather asked, pointing to the sketchbook peeking out of her bag. She'd brought it on the off chance she might stop at Portsmouth Square to sketch the pigeons.

"Nothing, just my drawing book," she said.

"Give me see," Yeh Yeh said, holding out his hand.

A little embarrassed, she handed it over and watched as her grandfather flipped through the pages. She knew her drawings weren't that great, but still hoped for a small sign of encouragement.

After a moment, Yeh Yeh handed back the sketchbook and said, "Okay, you can put back."

Well, Lindsey thought, *at least he didn't laugh.*

Her grandfather unwrapped a piece of *mui* and popped it into his mouth. After a few minutes of silence, he asked Lindsey if she wanted to run some errands with him and she said okay. Removing his green smock, he pulled a heavy, London Fog overcoat out from under the counter and put it on, along with a wool cap and gloves. Lindsey headed for the door in her skirt and shirtsleeves into the hazy sunshine.

"Bring umbrella in case of rain," Yeh Yeh said, grabbing a portable one from a paint bucket by the front door before locking up.

Yeh Yeh wanted to get *gai mai bows* and buy a lottery ticket at Wonder Bakery. They walked up to Waverly Place and turned into the alley.

Inside the small space was crammed wall-to-wall with Chinese men sitting at tiny tables, socializing and playing keno. Yeh Yeh ordered from the counter and Lindsey watched as the server wielded her stainless-steel tongs to retrieve the buns, then plopped them into a white paper bag.

"Your grandma not like too many things, but like these pastry," Yeh Yeh said. As they walked out, they passed a countertop with lottery slips and pencils. "Lottery very good. In Locke, I used to collect the cardboard ticket for all the old men, then run around to find winner. One time big winner gave me ten dollar. No kidding! Everybody gamble, those days. Mostly small potato, but Som Goong, he carried pistol just in case. Never use it, though. Some places down the street more serious—one thousand, five thousand jackpot. Had machine gun on top of balcony. You surprise? I'm not pulling your legs."

Lindsey stood and waited as Yeh Yeh took his wallet back out and disgarded some old lottery slips. Trying to reorganize the rest of the contents, he shook his head and said, "Too many things inside!" He sifted through the billfold, but his fingers slipped and suddenly the entire wallet and its myriad of contents fell to the floor.

"Oh!" he exclaimed, bending over to collect his things.

Lindsey knelt down to help her grandfather, and as she picked up his Safeway discount card and his Muni fast pass in its plastic sleeve, she came across a tiny black-and-white photo of a Chinese girl that she recognized as Yun Yun.

The picture was not unlike the photos that Ms. Abilene had given her, but appeared to be from an earlier period. In the St. Maude's pictures, Yun Yun was probably about sixteen, but in this photo she appeared to be about twelve. She held it up and looked at it closely before holding it out to Yeh Yeh so he could put it back inside his wallet along with the other items.

As they made their way past the tourist stores, the incense-and-funeral-papers shop, and the place with the good *don-don mein*, Lindsey thought for a moment.

"Yeh Yeh?" she said. "I thought you told me last time that you didn't know Yun Yun before you met her at the fancy house where you both worked."

"That's right," he replied, shuffling along.

"But what about that picture in your wallet?"

The old man pulled his cap farther down over his matted gray hair as he kept walking. By the time they reached the corner, Lindsey was about to repeat her question, but Yeh Yeh said, "I hear you, I hear you. You wait till we go inside store."

They walked back to the grocery store without talking. Once inside, Yeh Yeh flipped the Open sign and resumed his perch on his yellow stepstool. He opened a pack of bubblegum and offered it to Lindsey, who took a piece and chewed it as she bided her time. A construction worker came in, bought a carton of cigarettes, and left. Yeh Yeh looked around to check that the store was empty, then began,

"That not Pearl. That Opal."

He retrieved his wallet from his pocket and removed the fragile picture, handling it carefully.

"Opal was my grammar-school sweetheart. I tell you I went to Francisco Middle School? She was there, too. Five and six grade. We never even hold hands, but we talk, and I walk her to school. We both live in Chinatown. Her family and mines live cross street in Waverly Alley, not too far from where you and I just buy *gai mai bow*. I watch her from my window, second story. She live in basement apartment down below. I watch her come and go with brothers and sisters, mother and *baba*."

"What happened to her?" Lindsey asked.

Yeh Yeh sighed. "She move away, after six grade. I was very depress see her go. I finish at Francisco, then go to high school, but not ever forget her. You believe me? Most boy think of catching frog, chase thing, blow stuff up. But not me. I have romantic feeling with this girl, just too young to know what to do." He chuckled at his own words, and Lindsey offered a smile.

Then, animatedly, he went on, "After school I went to work

selling vegetable, and after a while get my job in the kitchen at the big house. Can you imagine my amazement when I saw upstairs cleaning girl? She was my Opal! First thing I say when I see her is, 'Opal, what you doing here? Your family all move back? I so happy to see you!'

"She look at me like I crazy. She say, 'I am not Opal.' Then she walk away fast. All I know is I am very confused. Then I remember. All those times I look out window and watch Opal's family across street, I remember she have a twin sister. I always wonder why this sister not go to school with us, just stay at home and cook or cleaning, or what, I don't know. Maybe the parents think no use send two girl to school. Who knows? Back then very different from now.

"Anyway, so I think, maybe this girl is Opal's sister. And you know what? I was right. After she and I get to know each other a little, talk to each other here and there, she tell me she was born on Pike Street. That's what Waverly was called long time ago. And she tell me before work at this house, she lived in a white-lady orphanage. It probably hard for you to understand these days, but back then family move, get split up. Was very common. Too many mouth to feed."

He continued, "We work together for one year before get married. Since I was from Locke, I figure we move there for a while. I hope moving could take her mind off things. We were very busy picking fruit, white asparagus, you name it. Not too much time for fun, especially for Yun Yun. But she have one friend in Locke, a girl who also used to live on Pike Street, and her family move to Locke, too. That was Mabel Ahchuck, her old-time friend. You remember we went to her son's house for big party? Anyway, Yun Yun never like the country. She was city girl. After about twenty year in Locke, we move back to San Francisco again. We buy Thirty-Eighth-Avenue place and settle here."

Lindsey was still thinking about Opal. She said, "When did you tell Yun Yun that you knew her sister in school?"

Yeh Yeh sighed again. "I never tell her. After the first time when I mention Opal's name, I never say it again. I figure if she want to talk, she would tell me. But years go by and she never say anything."

Lindsey reflected for a moment, then asked, "Did you ever find out what happened to Opal and the rest of the family?"

Yeh Yeh shook his head. "One time, after we been married for a while, I want to take a trip to Vancouver. 'Supposed to be nice place,' I say. 'Let's go on vacation.' But your Yun Yun throw big tantrum. At first I don't know why. Then she say, 'No way I going to Vancouver. They leave me here and all go there. Why I want to visit?' She scream her head off. So I figure that's where her family move."

Lindsey's mind was reeling. Her imagination was conjuring so many scenarios. She pictured the scene from *Grease* when John Travolta yelled, "Sandy, what are you doing here?" and Olivia Newton-John exclaimed happily, "We had a change of plans!" As she visualized the moment, Lindsey substituted her grandparents for the actors in the movie, but in Yeh Yeh's case, when he exclaimed, "Opal!" it turned out she wasn't the girl he knew at all.

Then the movie in her mind turned to Alfred Hitchcock's *Vertigo*. She pictured her grandfather as Jimmy Stewart realizing this girl wasn't his old flame, but an exact look-alike. She imagined Yeh Yeh getting all obsessed, just like Scottie Ferguson. Her brain jumbled the disparate scenes from the two movies together. At the same time, she tried to picture her grandparents as younger people.

Finally, she ventured, "But . . . how could you forget Opal and . . . marry her sister . . . and then never talk about it?"

"I never forget Opal. But she is gone, and Pearl is there. If you have someone right there, you cannot keep hoping for someone else. The old phrase is, 'The grass is always green on other side,' but cannot go living like sixth grade forever. Know what I saying?"

"Uh-huh," was all she managed to say.

"I know what I know, and Yun Yun know that I know. But still, she never want to talk. Maybe too painful. Maybe she want to forget. If that's what she want, I figure, okey-dokey. I let her forget."

Yeh Yeh trailed off into his own thoughts as Lindsey digested everything. After a while, he slid off his stool and gestured to the back room. "You want Chef Boyardee ravioli? I heat up in microwave."

"No thanks," Lindsey said, her head about to explode with all this newfound knowledge. She wanted to go home and write everything down before she forgot anything. She said, "I think I'd better get going."

"Suit yourself," Yeh Yeh said. As he shuffled down the aisle, Lindsey tried to think of something poignant to say. She wanted to acknowledge that she and her grandfather had just shared a landmark moment by finally breaking through their family's wall of silence. But it was too late. Yeh Yeh had disappeared into the back room. Slowly, she turned and walked out of the store, with only the tinkling bell of the motion sensor to bid her goodbye.

Altoids, Androids, and Tofoysters

The next night at the museum, Lindsey was meticulously cleaning the fur-lined teacups. As she was explaining to a couple of Junior-League-set, Tipper Gore types that Meret Oppenheim's 1936 original had been a triumph of surrealism, she spotted Dustin skulking around. When he made a little kiss noise to get her attention, the preppies turned around and giggled. Lindsey tried to ignore him as the girls twirled their hair and glanced back toward Dustin, making doe-eyes his way.

Lindsey placed the *Breakfast in Fur* mini-sculpture back on the shelf, then proceeded to mark down all the Jeff Koons merchandise that hadn't been selling. The Junior Leaguers moved a few feet away and began trying on the Warhol wigs, periodically glancing Dustin's way. Their flirtatious behavior plucked Lindsey's jealousy nerve. She wanted to brag to them that she knew Dustin way before he was a cool cat with a suede jacket and a kick-ass Norton parked outside. She knew him when he imitated androids and endured lapsits with a horndog nun.

She snuck a peek at Dustin and noted that somehow, in his cowboy boots, he came off as rugged and sexy instead of just totally gay. He caught her staring at him and winked. His batted eyelash made her feel immediately less lonely, but also like a devious two-timer. She didn't like having feelings she couldn't control.

As the minutes passed, Dustin didn't budge from the artist monograph section, but snuck glances at Lindsey every few seconds, making obscene gestures at her with his tongue when he thought no one was looking. She wanted to tell him to stop, but at the same time, like a petty high schooler, she reveled in the fact that the cutest boy was actually paying attention to her. Hanging around Dustin made her feel, by association, all at once more popular, daring, and glamorous.

Over the past two weeks, she had seen Dustin shoplift a candy bar, smoke a joint on the street in broad daylight, and badger a teenage employee at the ice-cream parlor into giving them their cones for free. Being in such close proximity to bad behavior had given her a certain thrill.

Of course, she knew her behavior was getting more and more inappropriate. Just the other night they'd shared a Mexican dinner of chicken smothered in molé sauce and sexual innuendo. For every hand brushed against a shoulder, mouth closer than a distance of six inches, or word turned tawdry with a salacious glance, she knew in her heart that she was being a worm.

She was *acting the maggot*.

They hadn't done anything yet, and that's why she had to stop hanging out with him. Even if she rationalized that her actions could be construed as innocent, she reminded herself how, in movies, cheaters always claimed they didn't mean to hurt anyone. Naturally, they always said this *after* the fact. They only expressed remorse after they were caught red-handed in a naked, post-coital heap with a lover. Meanwhile, the unsuspecting spouse was left with only razor-slashed lower intestines and a decimated bank account.

Lindsey thought about how she and Dustin had bantered and flirted. They had even sipped from the same straw. At the time, she told herself it was all just innocent, clean fun. But now she felt sick with guilt.

Tidying up Zone Four, she waited until Dustin wasn't looking and then ducked behind the jewelry counter. He was no doubt waiting for her to get off her shift, so she snuck out the back door that led to the employee offices. Finding the assistant manager, she told her that she had a personal emergency and had to leave early. Racing out the back door and through the lobby, she ran across the sidewalk and hopped on a bus that had just pulled to the curb. She flopped on a seat and felt relieved. She was glad to have potentially saved herself from an evening of tongue wrestling with someone other than her betrothed.

But she couldn't stop thinking about Dustin. He appealed to some animal part of her and she felt cornered. This crush had somehow snuck up on her and pounced, and although she wanted to break free, her intellect and will couldn't seem to help her. Desire had taken her totally by surprise. It was like a trap that, in one swift motion, had clamped down on her. As the bus lurched past the familiar streets, she told herself that when she got home she needed to research which types of animals were known to get caught in hunters' snares and gnawed off their own limbs to free themselves.

The worst part of her crush was not telling Michael. Last night on the phone he had casually asked her what she had been up to and she neglected to tell him anything about Dustin. Maybe that was her problem. The things she and Dustin had done were not terrible in themselves, but her own secretive attitude followed by remorse was the bad part. If she just told Michael that she had been hanging out with an old school chum, he probably would have just said, "Oh?" and not given it a second thought. He trusted her.

But *was* she trustworthy? She certainly wanted to be.

Hopping off the bus, she walked the remaining distance home. She trotted up the stairs, went inside, and after changing out of her clothes, pryed open a bottle of Anchor Steam. She was on her second beer when the phone rang.

"Hello?"

"Hey. It's me. Sorry I haven't called, but I'm being watched all the time. I miss you so much . . ."

As Michael quickly regaled her with tales of the ashram's rutabaga exfoliating scrubs and kundalini-boosting diet of "Tofoysters," Lindsey suddenly felt the urgent need to get Dustin off her chest.

"Michael?" she interrupted.

"Yeah?"

"Did I ever tell you about my friend Dustin Lee? He's back in town and we've been hanging out."

"So?"

"I dunno. I just wanted to tell you. The other day you asked me what I've been up to, and he and I went to dinner a couple of times, had drinks . . ." She started to blather, telling too many details, like what Dustin had been wearing and how cool his socks were. At the end of her fashion report she said, "I just wanted you to know that you can trust me."

In the background she could hear someone harassing Michael for being on the phone. He held his hand over the mouthpiece but she could hear him say that he would be off in a minute. Although she thought her admission had gone all right and she was already feeling better, her little confession elicited a response she didn't expect.

Michael turned his attention back to her. Annoyance in his

voice, he said, "Well, that's just great. I'm glad I can trust you, seeing as how we're getting married. You can trust me, too. You think I'm down here romancing protein-deficient waifs and having tantric sex with the *owsla* who are constantly searching my room for Flaming Cheetos?"

He paused but she didn't say anything. He went on, "At night I'm not even sleeping. I'm sneaking around like a store detective trying to snag samples of the pesticides and pork hormones they're using to dose the supposedly organic vegetables. And all the while I'm running out of excuses to get out of the celery-stalk, butt-flushing enemas and the only thing I get to eat is, like, three chickpeas a day. Meanwhile, you're eating porterhouse steaks and throwing back gimlets with some guy? I'm so glad you're *dating* in your spare time . . ."

Amidst the jumble of his words, she could hear the *owsla* wrestling the phone away from Michael.

"I didn't mean it like that . . ." she yelled into the receiver.

The line went dead and she listened to the phone silence for a while. Hmm. That hadn't gone so well.

Teletubbies in the Fog

Standing on the driveway of her grandparents' house, Lindsey held an invitation to the St. Maude's jubilee addressed to her grandmother but couldn't stop staring at the taxidermied jackrabbit with deer antlers affixed to its head.

"What the hell is that?" she said aloud, giving the inanimate monstrosity a wide berth, but no one was around to answer. She called out a hello through the open garage door. A moment passed before she heard her dad's voice. He yelled, "Come help me drag out some more stuff for the donation pick-up!"

She had come by just to drop the invitation into the mail slot and planned a quick departure, but now she wandered inside the dark garage and found her dad immersed in a huge cleaning project.

"It's about time we clean out all this old junk," he said. "There's fifty years of stuff here, and your Auntie Geraldine and Uncle Elmore can't clean worth a dang. Give me a hand."

She slipped the invitation into her coat pocket, and helped him drag out a laundry basket filled with moldy shoes. After heaving a few more bags of old clothes to the sidewalk, she helped him move a few boxes of miscellaneous housewares.

Stopping to catch her breath, Lindsey figured this might be a good time to ask her dad what he knew about Yun Yun. She didn't want to bust right out and ask him about her twin sister, Opal, so instead, she thought of something more innocuous. She said, "Dad, when you decided to send us to St. Maude's, did it have anything to do with Yun Yun?"

Her father kicked a few more dusty boxes out to the driveway and said, "No, why would it?"

Lindsey sat down on a broken garden table. "Well, I found out that . . . that Yun Yun went there a long time ago."

"Oh, yeah?"

Her dad, stacking chairs, seemed nonplussed by this bit of news. Lindsey wondered whether he already knew and was feigning disinterest, or simply didn't care.

"Yeah," she said. "In fact, St. Maude's is having this big reunion and I'm supposed to give Yun Yun this invitation."

Her dad wiped his brow with his sleeve. He said, "Well, she's upstairs."

Before she could ask him anything else, her dad disappeared into the depths of the garage. Lindsey dusted herself off and thought about following him inside to question him further, but instead, she hesitantly headed up the back stairs. She thought about sliding the invitation under the bedroom door, but knew that that would have been chickenshit of her. She was going to give the invitation to Yun Yun herself. The woman was just her grandmother, for heaven's sake, not some ogre. Why was it so hard just to talk? She was determined to thwart the insidious silence that had settled around her family like Sunset District fog.

Having no idea what she was going to say to her grandmother, she ascended the steps. For a half-second she considered turning around, leaving, and just sending the invitation through the mail. She told herself to get a grip.

Screwing up her courage, she emerged from the stairwell,

stepped across the hallway, and knocked on her grandmother's bedroom door.

Taking a breath, she listened for a reply.

"Eh?"

Lindsey pushed open the door.

"Hello Tinky Winky, hello La-La . . ."

For some reason her grandmother was watching *Teletubbies*. Lindsey said, "I'm helping my dad clean downstairs. And I brought you some mail."

Yun Yun sipped a cup of tea. After a moment she said, "Do you know the red one is Chinese?"

Confused, Lindsey glanced at the television and watched as the red Teletubby counted, "*Yut, yee, som* . . ."

Yun Yun was actually smiling. Lindsey had never seen her grandmother so amused. After watching her for a moment, Lindsey handed the invitation to her without saying anything.

Yun Yun sliced open the envelope with the pinky-nail she kept extra long for ear scratching. As her grandmother read the card, Lindsey stood in silence. For what seemed like a long while, neither of them said anything, just watched the television screen as Tinky Winky and Dipsy rubbed bellies and repeatedly exclaimed, "Eh-oh!"

As Lindsey awaited a response, she could hear Yeh Yeh shuffling around in the adjacent bedroom, presumably getting ready to head to Chinatown and open his store. She could see him through the open door, pulling on galoshes and a rain slicker. He didn't seem to notice her standing in Yun Yun's bedroom. After a minute, he made his way through the hallway and headed down the front stairs.

Lindsey turned toward Yun Yun and found her still captivated by the Chinese Teletubby. Lindsey cleared her throat and was about to back out of the room, but as she turned, her grandmother said,

"Yeh Yeh say you go and visit him down in Chinatown. Two, maybe three times?"

"Um . . . something like that," Lindsey answered with trepidation.

Yun Yun stared at the television screen as she talked. "He say you been asking questions about me."

Lindsey waited to get yelled at, but her grandmother went silent again. Not knowing quite what to do, Lindsey made a motion toward the door.

"He say you been asking questions," Yun Yun repeated. She slowly nodded her head as if mulling over something in her mind, and then added two little words that packed a wollop.

"Is okay," she said.

Lindsey tried not to smile, but inside she felt a small triumph. Maybe Yun Yun didn't think she was such a scurvy dog after all. It occurred to Lindsey that even if her grandmother wanted to forget, maybe she didn't want to be forgotten.

And just then, Yun Yun lifted her hand and held up the invitation. Still looking at the television, she said, "You going to drive me?"

Stunned, Lindsey got a hold of herself. "Yes," she said. "Sure, I will."

Yun Yun turned up the volume and Lindsey took that as a signal for her to leave. Closing the bedroom door behind her and bounding down the front steps, she felt the strange optimism that came from finding an easy resolution to an anticipated difficulty. The brief exchange with her grandmother had been the most positive interaction they had had for as long as Lindsey could recall.

As she walked through the gate, she found Yeh Yeh and her dad arguing on the sidewalk.

"It's about time we throw out all these old things," her dad was saying.

"No, no, no. I need these," Yeh Yeh replied emphatically, gathering up a loose collection of his miniature knives, fondue forks, and other tiny tools. "Perfectly new screwdriver kit! How can throw away?"

"But you have ten sets. How about giving three to charity?"

Lindsey watched as Yeh Yeh scowled at her dad. "You . . . kids," he muttered disapprovingly.

Lindsey smiled to herself. It was the first time she had ever witnessed anyone calling her dad a kid, treating him like a foolish whippersnapper who was driving the older generation nuts. Up to this point, she'd thought she'd cornered the market on youthful disrespect in her family. It was funny to get a glimpse of her dad as a son.

"*Ai-ya!*" Yeh Yeh suddenly exclaimed, running up to the driveway.

"What, you crazy? Cannot throw out my jackalope! It once belong to Mayor Sutro!"

He snatched up the taxidermied rabbit by its antlers, and as he cradled the thing safely in his arms, he dusted off its muzzle with his sleeve.

Her dad sighed with exasperation, then went back inside the garage to place the screwdriver kits back in their rightful place.

Lindsey approached her grandpa.

"Yeh Yeh," she said, pointing to the treasure in his arms, "where did you get that?"

The old man got a faraway look in his eyes and said, "It was gift when I leave my employ at the big house, Mae's Menagerie. A big pink house filled with animals!"

Yeh Yeh's words jarred Lindsey's brain. She thought hard for a moment. A pink house filled with *animals*? She thought about the day she took Jilan home. *Mae's Menagerie*? Isn't that what Mrs. Clemens said her "establishment" had been called?

Just as Lindsey was about to open her mouth, Yeh Yeh

looked up to the rising hill in the distance and beyond to the sky. Suddenly his eyes became wide. Before Lindsey could ask him anything, her grandfather suddenly thrust the jackalope into her arms. He said, "Fast! You put back. Here come my bus!"

Her dad wandered back out onto the driveway and together they watched with amazement as Yeh Yeh's spry, ninety-year-old legs pattered down the sidewalk to the corner just as the 66 Quintara came careening to a stop. Yeh Yeh climbed aboard, and the bus lurched out in front of a motorcycle that whizzed by in a blur of gleaming chrome. Lindsey's dad shook his head. He scoffed, "Crazy Chinese drivers!"

China Mary, Why Ya Buggin'?

Lindsey approached the imposing pink mansion surrounded by blooming camellia trees. Set back behind a row of canary palms, the house, just south of Alamo Square, reminded her of a Victorian wedding cake with frosting sagging at its sides.

She had never taken a long look at the building, but now that she studied it, she was fascinated. While the other houses on the block had been updated to include modern patios and added garages for Subaru Foresters, this grand Painted Lady was an untouched relic. With its high widow's-walk tiara and crumbling stone lions carved into the pillars, it seemed like the kind of place that would have been destroyed years ago either by earthquake or corrupt developers, but somehow the old gal miraculously managed to survive the decades. A black cast-iron fence encircled the property with rusted fleur-de-lis and quatrefoils. She was undeterred by the fence's fanglike appearance, and climbed the rotted, wooden stairs.

Looking up to the darkened windows, she imagined eyes staring down at her from somewhere behind the gossamer fabric. She ducked beneath the thick, overgrown curtain of wisteria and rang the bell. A few moments passed before she heard the sound of small feet running, and soon enough, the door flew open, revealing Jilan in a polka-dotted bathing suit and white cowboy boots.

"Where have *you* been?" the girl said.

"Um, I dunno. Around. Is your . . . grandmother here?"

"Yeah, yeah. She said you'd come back sooner or later. We got a kiddie pool out back. Did you bring your suit?"

Jilan left the door open and walked back through the dark hallway as Lindsey followed her in. Passing the portrait of the wolfhound and the parlor filled with tufted furniture and trophy heads of animals, Lindsey made her way through the dimly lit house by feeling along the wainscoting. She turned a corner and came to a high-ceilinged room that opened onto a massive garden enclosed by topiary walls.

While the interior of the house resembled something out of *The Rocky Horror Picture Show*, the backyard was strewn with plastic kiddie toys—which relieved Lindsey, assuring her that Jilan had a certain degree of normalcy to her childhood. She watched the girl fill up her inflatable swimming pool with a hose and again asked her the whereabouts of her grandmother. Jilan pointed to an oval-shaped stained glass window high up in a mansard gable. She said, "Try the Bengali room."

Lindsey didn't know where the Bengali Room was or why it was called that, but she traced her way back through the hall and started up a steep stairway, running her hand along the curving oak banister. She recognized the dizzying, harlequin-diamond wallpaper from her previous visit, and as she climbed farther up, she kept her eyes off the florid carpet pattern to avoid vertigo. Reaching the third floor, she made her way down a hall where an uncurtained window let in a wash of sunlight that illuminated the slow-motion, swirling patterns of dust, like a projector beam in the darkness of a movie theater.

Beyond, she could see an open door and inside, a wall decorated in the pattern of tiger stripes.

"Come in, dear."

"Hello, Mrs. Clemens."

Lindsey stood at a polite distance. Having been to the house once before, this time she was not so taken aback by the room's macabre adornments. But she did notice Mrs. Clemens's clothes, which struck her as even stranger than her usual "madam" garb. The old woman was wearing tweed trousers and an unseasonal Christmas sweater with an appliquéd Santa Claus.

Lindsey said, "Sorry to barge in on you like this."

"Nonsense. Truthfully, been a little worried about you. Haven't seen you and your boyfriend walking to the park much lately. Have a seat."

Lindsey sat herself down on a chair upholstered with saffron-colored fur of unknown animal origin. At her feet grazed ceramic peacocks atop a real zebra-skin rug. Lindsey rested her elbows against deer-hoof armrests. She settled in and relaxed like she was in the most natural setting in the world.

Mrs. Clemens noticed Lindsey taking in her surroundings. She said, "I know some things don't quite go right in this room, but, well, at my age you can't go around moving things from place to place. Besides, you move around these old animals and you never know if a beak or an eyeball might pop off, and then what?"

Lindsey smiled politely, then said, "Mae's Menagerie?"

The old woman plucked a glass paperweight from her desktop and gazed at the blue-black scorpion inside. "Yep," she said, "we was the longest running house in the city. Went back to the old days of Tessie Wall, back before the earthquake, and when she and every other place went belly up, we still survived. It was the animals that kept things interesting. And the girls, of course. My Grandma Mae, she had a way with folks, and she liked to collect things. We got some stuffed pelicans left over from the Pan-Pacific Exposition in 1915, and like I said before, the stuff from Sutro's old place before they tore that down."

Lindsey shifted in her seat. "My grandfather has a stuffed jackrabbit with antlers. He says he used to work here."

The old woman let out a world-weary cackle. "Christamighty! He still has that old thing? I gave that to Johnny years ago." She leaned her pointy chin on her hand and laughed to herself.

Lindsey had never heard her grandfather called "Johnny." She thought his American name was "Joe," or at least that's what the old guys at the Family Association had called him. She wondered if Mrs. Clemens's Johnny was indeed Yeh Yeh, but then she figured, hell, he had the jackalope to prove it, so it must be true.

After a moment of reverie, the old woman continued, "It was your grandpa who asked me to keep an eye on you. I was down on Grant Avenue buying my herbs for my arthritis when I ran into him. Boy, was he a sight! Looked exactly the same, so I recognized him right off. Anyways, he said his grand-daughter moved into a place near me. He said your phone number meant "roll over and die" in Chinese, so he was worried. I didn't know what kind of sense he was talking, but I promised I'd keep my eyes peeled for ya. Him and me go back a ways. Must have been back in the early thirties. I wasn't all but twenty even yet. My mother was running the house, and we was doing a steady business."

She stopped for a moment and opened a desk drawer. As she sifted through the contents, she went on, "Back in the old days, Chinese didn't have much choice about things. When they came to look for the gold, they was beaten up and left with only the areas other people had already mined out. Laws were made against them in using their nets for shrimping, and even for carrying their bundles using those poles. Everywhere they was discriminated against in work. But the Chinese, they resourceful. It's not like they had a natural propensity for laundry work or being house servants. They took the jobs no one else wanted. Eventually, they became a part of the everyday household. Time was, every house had a John Chinaman, and that's what we all called them, even though they had their own names in Chinese, I suppose. But that was their business and none of ours.

"Grannie Mae and Mother always said Chinese was the best servants, best cooks, everything. A Chinese vegetable seller came to the back door every day, another one brought fresh fish and crabs caught that same morning. They picked up our linens and brought them back fresh and clean. The house servants did all the cooking, cleaning and raised us kids. People like your grandfather—they was indispensable. I tell you, he sure dusted a lot of these animals. And that's why when he left, I saw fit that he should have that old jackrabbit. He always had a fondness for it."

Lindsey listened with a mixture of fascination and angst. She didn't quite feel comfortable hearing about Chinese history, let alone her family history, from a non-Chinese source. But at this point she was willing to take any information whichever way it came to her, even from a Hoarder Lady.

Mrs. Clemens tossed a few photos on top of the desk for Lindsey to see. They were old snapshots of the house, some of the exterior and one of the downstairs interior.

"See that picture taken in the parlor? Look through that door on the left. See? That skinny son of a gun is old Johnny, your granddaddy."

Lindsey scrutinized the photo and could just make out the face. She recognized his crooked grimace and low ears. He was dressed in a smock similar to the one he wore in his grocery store.

Mrs. Clemens continued, "Your grandpa was our cook and we were sore to lose him. We never thought that he and the upstairs cleaning girl would hit it off. She mostly kept to herself, but guess it makes sense. They was both Chinese, working in the house all day, bound to get together sooner or later. When he said they were going off and getting married, we all had a sip of wine in the kitchen before sending them off."

Mrs. Clemens frowned, briefly bringing all her wrinkles together and then releasing them, like the strings of a purse suddenly cinched and then loosened.

"Just like the John Chinamans, we called all the girls China Mary. She cleaned and changed the beds. Tell you what, she must have got an eyeful, seeing the things that gone on around here! No wonder she latched on to your grandpa and they beat it out of here to go God knows where."

"They went to Locke."

"Oh, yes, the Chinese town." Mrs. Clemens sifted through the photos on the desk, occasionally holding one up and studying it.

Lindsey said, "So they were in love? I always assumed their marriage was arranged."

The old lady shrugged. "Love? How should I know? Maybe they got on, but being on her own, maybe she figured she had to do something. Back then wasn't how it is now. A woman couldn't marry any fella she wanted, change her mind, then change it back again. And it was even more strict for a Chinese. There was laws to make sure a Chinese only wed another Chinese. Not repealed until the 1960s or something another."

Mrs. Clemens collected the pictures in a loose pile, then sifted around in her desk for some more. "Actually," she said,

"I don't know how they done it, but Mother's second cousin, Ella, married a Chinese man named Wong Sun Yue. Here's her photo right here. Look at my old, burly aunt in her Chinese dress and her Chinese husband selling earthquake relics in their Chinatown store. They was kind of famous. The novelty of them was a sight back then. But you see, Chinese and Caucasians been getting together for a while now."

The old woman handed the photo to Lindsey, who hadn't counted on plucking a page from the Annotated History of Hoarder Ladies. But here it was, firsthand. She put down the picture, then retrieved the photo with Yeh Yeh to study it again.

After a moment she looked up to see Mrs. Clemens gazing gently at her.

"Questions?"

Lindsey didn't know where to begin. She couldn't quite speak yet, due to a sudden case of cottonmouth. She swiveled her head toward the open doorway where she could see Jilan chasing a fluorescent ball down the stairway.

"Do you know anything about my grandmother's twin sister?"

Mrs. Clemens cinched her face again and squinted as she searched the microfiche of her mind.

She said, "I don't recall such a thing."

Lindsey nodded solemnly. Standing up to thank the old woman, Lindsey said, "If you ever need any help babysitting or anything, I don't live very far."

Lindsey turned to leave, but then Mrs. Clemens said, "Do you gots any experience cleaning animals? I'm trying to do right by the menagerie, but don't have the time to clean every single one of these critters. Think you could help sometime?"

Lindsey thought of the many hours she had logged cleaning the velvet mannequin limbs, Warhol wigs, and fur-lined teacups at the museum gift shop. She figured she was as qualified as anyone to spruce up the former bordello's bevy of one-eyed ocelots.

She nodded, and said, "I promise I'll come back."

A Bird in the Hand

It was the kind of night when even ugly people were having sex. The city was enduring a two-week heat wave that had reached temperatures unmatched since 1894, and when the sun-drenched days faded to azure evening skies, the city air crackled with the intoxicating possibility of animalistic rutting in the petal-soft breeze.

There was nothing quite as seductive as San Francisco on a warm, windy night. Above the skyscrapers and beyond Twin Peaks, stars flickered like bits of glass shining beneath a mermaid lagoon. The hot breath of summer rose through the night air, mixing with the earthy smell of dirt and trees. Inhaling the magical scent as she walked through the city, Lindsey saw San Franciscans laughing and flirting everywhere she went.

For her, it was one of those nights when anything could happen. She hadn't spoken to Michael since they'd quarreled, and she felt confused and adrift. It had been several weeks since she'd last seen him in the flesh and felt the comfort of his touch, and now she was irrationally beginning to think he'd never return.

In comparison, it had been just one week since she'd last seen Dustin. Hideous as it was to admit, she didn't know whose company she was wanting more, his or Michael's. She couldn't think straight, and not just because of her mounting loneliness and the strangely warm weather, but last week she'd also had the bright idea to give up all carbohydrates. She'd foolishly hoped the diet would give her more energy, but she was wrong. And tonight was the moment she just might crash. Nature seemed to be conspiring against her personally, and she was ready to surrender to her body's cravings for sweets, for Dustin, and for anything else bad that came with being bored and lonely.

When she counted in her head, it had actually only been six days since she'd sucked down a Twinkie or seen Dustin. And while she hadn't sprung for any Ding Dongs since, just yesterday she had congratulated herself on successfully ignoring Dustin's phone messages. But a few hours ago she had broken down and called him. Now here they were, standing together outside the museum at the end of her shift.

He waited at the back door for her, and when she spotted him he was holding a gardenia in his hand. By the look on his face and the warmth she felt surging up her thighs she could tell they were both thinking very bad thoughts.

"Seeing you makes my whole day better," he said. As she pinned the flower to her blouse, he added, "I had the kind of crummy day where I tried to get all my check-ups out of the way. Went to the doctor, the dentist, even had my eyes dilated."

"Is everything still all blurry?"

Dustin squinted. "Yeah, so I need you to hold on to me as we walk. Incidentally, now I can also see through your clothes."

She smiled and took his arm as they headed down the sidewalk.

As they ambled along, she quickly deduced that Dustin was one of those guys who instinctively knew how to turn on the charm when he suspected a girl's interest was waning. Like a lingering perfume spiraling through the air, his flirtatious behavior pulled her along until they walked for so many blocks that they finally ended up in Golden Gate Park. They meandered toward Sharon Meadow. The smell of leaves, dust, and nectar from a million bursting buds, from the rhododendron dell to the Shakespeare Garden, beckoned to them.

Darkness fell and a hot wind blew through San Francisco like someone had uncorked a vintage bottle of summer and let it rise through the air like liquid dandelions, its syrup pooling in the city's corners. Lindsey and Dustin walked along, their shoes making a soft, crunching noise.

Looking up at the creamy magnolia blossoms glowing in the last dim light of dusk, Lindsey wondered just what, exactly, she was doing. Kicking through a pile of leaves with her arm linked to the crook of Dustin's elbow, she knew she was acting at once daft, cheeky, and maggoty, while Michael was far away enduring hairy hippies and vegan Moonies.

She was sure of Michael's trust and faith in her even as she avoided admitting to herself that she was the one who had instigated this evening tryst with Dustin. The awareness of this deception rested like a ripped shred of paper tucked inside the mini-pocket of her slit skirt.

Amidst the billowing scents of the surrounding greenery and blossoms, like an animal, Lindsey caught a whiff of danger in the air. As she and Dustin strolled, she suddenly detected the smell everywhere—in the grass, behind the bushes, across a fallen eucalyptus log, and scattered between the limestone ruins from Hearst's disassembled Spanish temple, which lay in rubble behind the Arboretum's duckweed pond. She could smell it near the gazebo by the succulent garden, and behind a pillar at Portals of the Past. It was a summer scent, that of seasonal heat and animals mating and bodies thrown together everywhere across the city, the primal odor rising through the air and blowing hot and violent down to the Pacific where it tumbled in the waves and churned to the bottom of the salty ocean.

Every tree, plant, and flower seemed to be in bloom. As she and Dustin wandered the paths, pollen and tiny petals from the cherry trees fluttered through the air. Sharp scents from rosemary spears and manzanita bark swirled around them like cool currents. Rising hints of cedar and pine washed with calm confidence from the nearby Japanese Tea Garden.

Too bad Lindsey didn't have any Post-its with her. If she did, she would have written:

NOTE TO SELF: Do not take non-boyfriend to most romantic place on earth.

They walked through an underground tunnel where man-made stalactites "dripped" from the ceiling, a leftover bit of make-believe from a hundred-year-old city fair, when a miniature train had once chugged through the dark passage.

As they strolled along, Lindsey was keenly aware that Dustin was giving her The Look. It was that watery, doe-eyed, Bugs-Bunny-pleading-with-Witch-Hazel-Please-don't-kill-me kinda look. The Puss-in-Boots-pity-me look. The Let's-make-out kinda look. The look Richard Gere gave an actress before devouring her face. Lindsey told herself to stare straight ahead. She knew that any glance Dustin's way would ignite a certain recklessness on her part, the kind that might lead to Very Bad Acts.

While the evening heat amplified the traffic sounds on Crossover Drive, she wondered why she had led herself to this place in the park as the rest of the city went about its life. She imagined that somewhere, someone could see the Milky Way, and elsewhere, a person could hear the trickling sound of an underground stream. She took a deep breath and inhaled the fragrance of backyard lilacs mingling in the ocean air along with Nineteenth-Avenue gasoline. She caught the pleasant, charred smell of briquet embers, perhaps from a rickety balcony or porch nearby. Making a half wish, she suddenly imagined herself far away from Dustin, perhaps on a friend's back stair, somewhere safe and alone, not tempting fate and fidelity, but guiltlessly taking in a dazzling and streaky view of twilight heat waves smudging the glowing lights across the bay.

But she wasn't there. She was here, walking beside Dustin.

And where was Michael? In Santa Barbara, trusting her. She thought of Michael and felt him in her heart even as she contemplated what it would be like to let Dustin kiss her.

By now she was actually holding hands with him, not quite sure of how her fingers so effortlessly became entwined with his. They walked, seemingly without a destination, and without even looking at him or talking, she began to feel a buzzing sensation on her skin. It was like a bee hovering over her heart, thinking about stinging. A tiny, buzzing honeybee of her own imagining was asking her, "How could you take Dustin to Golden Gate Park *of all places?*"

The honeybee knew that this was *their* park—Michael and Lindsey's. They had picnicked, skipped stones, discovered night herons amongst the reeds, boated, canoed, chased, and kissed. They had fallen in love here. But where, exactly? Perhaps near the crumbling sphinxes that marked a long-forgotten, grand path, or by the carved panthers by the Eighth-Avenue gate. Maybe it was beneath the waterfall or beneath Stow Lake's turquoise-tiled Chinese pavilion, or behind the statue of Buddha in the Japanese Tea Garden. Maybe all these locations combined to make a perfume of places, an elixir of air and space and time. Their ghosts were everywhere in that park, and even as Michael and Lindsey went to work or shopped or ventured to other points in the city, a part of their spirits remained ever-present within the greenery there. Like ducklings or a single, snowy white swan, something of their love stayed in the park always, silently paddling in the mossy waters or wafting through the breeze between Saturday roller skaters. Love lingered, and theirs inhabited many places at once.

So what the hell was she doing here with Dustin? She shook her hand free from his and wrapped her arms around herself, suddenly chilled in the balmy wind. She looked across the path to the shadows in the underbrush, and at that moment, the park struck her for the first time as overwhelmingly spooky.

Why was she sharing her favorite location with someone who used to pretend he was Mork from Ork? Golden Gate Park was her most sacred place, she realized, and even birds in heat knew better than to shit where they slept.

This revelation caught her just in time. She and Dustin stopped walking and found themselves standing beneath the statue of the Spartan soldier. According to urban legend, the statue moved at midnight, and she cowered slightly at the sight of it. With his sword drawn, he appeared ready to pierce a heart or slay Medusa, she wasn't sure which.

The stars glimmered above, and she could see the twisting light from a homeless man's campfire on the concourse below. A gust of warm wind blew through the nearby eucalyptus, and she could almost hear the nostalgic melodies from a hundred Beach Boys' songs breezing through her tangled hair. It was a perfect summer moment, except that she was with the wrong guy.

Dustin grabbed her around the waist and pulled her closer. "Have you ever made love in the park?" he said.

To the tops of the swaying trees, through the spray of the nearby fountain, to the tip of the statue's sword, Lindsey felt the warm air all around. She recalled the shade-dappled strolls, the skipping of rocks across silty ponds, and the chases across the meadows she had shared with Michael. She thought of Michael and the way his face lit up when he saw squirrels. She loved that light in his eyes, that pure, innocent spark that showed that his amazement for living had not been squelched.

Despite the heat, her skin grew cold, and although it wasn't midnight, she could almost see the statue move. Did it dip its chin toward her and give her a solemn gaze?

Dustin pulled her even closer and whispered in her ear again, "Have you ever made love in the park?"

She pulled slightly away from him and stared into his eyes, all moist and adoring in a way most girls would have fallen for.

Lindsey caught the silhouette of an elegant heron floating overhead. She recognized the slow flap of its wings and its unmistakably long legs that peeked beneath the outline of the tailfeathers—details that Michael had shown her how to identify. Remembering him, her thoughts flashed to the sensation of holding a bird, cupping its fluttering heartbeat in her palm. She was suddenly, keenly aware that with a single, stray kiss, she could crush Michael's heart, as delicate as the bones of a parakeet. Just then she realized she didn't need to break Michael's heart to know she held it in her hand.

She wasn't interested in making a terrible, irreversible mistake. For years, more than anything she had wanted to feel another creature against her, one who would never flee her side, but stay. She wanted someone of whom she could be certain. And she was certain of Michael. The idea that she was untrustworthy was suddenly unbearable. She wasn't going to blow it.

"Thanks for the walk," she said. "But now I've got to go."

Velvet Hyacinth Sky

After weeks of sun, the fog finally rolled in and settled over the city, ominous clouds hovering over the bay. Lindsey took one look out the window and decided to sleep in, but around nine she awoke to the sensation of being squashed. Michael was lying on top of her.

"Hi Babykins," he said, touching her hair.

"Hi, Mister. What are you doing here?"

He traced the satin neckline of her nightgown with his finger. "I'm squishing you. Did you miss me?"

"Mmm-hmm," she said, grabbing his forearm and pulling it under her neck.

Michael kissed her tenderly on the head and rested his cheek against hers. He said, "So . . . who's this guy you've been hanging around?"

She scooted out from beneath him and rolled over.

"No one important."

Michael pulled the blanket over them both and pulled her toward him.

"Are you sure? See, if I have to break someone's legs I'd like to do it early, before it starts to rain and my shoes get wet while I'm kicking his ass."

She looked up at Michael, not quite sure if she should make a joke or spill her guts and explain how tempted she had been, how close she had come to screwing up everything. She remembered that loose lips sink ships. She decided to say nothing. She kissed him instead.

They rolled around in bed for a while until Michael suggested they go for a walk by the ocean. She agreed, and soon they were dressed and headed outside. Holding hands, they traipsed along the sidewalks, and she was glad to finally be together again.

After a mile or so, Lindsey wondered if Michael could tell that instead of moping around alone in his absence, she had been enjoying the company of another rooster who had been circling the henhouse. Michael kept looking at her sideways, playfully at first, but then with an expression she couldn't quite read. She wondered if he sensed a fraction of her affection gone astray or the accompanying guilt that covered her like greasy sunscreen.

In the distance, the dark sky bulged like a heavy hammock of water above the Golden Gate Bridge, its famous span and cables now the color of a ripe, purple plum. The wind was strangely warm, tropical and blustery as it rushed like a river through the trees. As Lindsey and Michael walked from the residential area toward the sandy bluff of Ocean Beach, they gazed at the water between the shadowed Marin Headlands and Angel Island. Staring ahead, Lindsey thought briefly of all the Chinese immigrants who had been detained there, and their collective, forgotten sadness seemed palpable as she stared off into the milky bay, an opaque powder blue that mirrored the moody sky.

Holding her hand, Michael tilted his head and gave her a

look that made her wonder if he suspected anything. Maybe it was her imagination, but she thought he looked a little unsure, as if he sensed she had drifted slightly away from him. She hoped that any whiff of deceit was hopefully covered up by the fragrant air, which smelled heavily of orange blossoms and impending rain.

Lindsey was aware that somehow her friendly flirtation with Dustin had crept into a corner of her heart, and had slithered into a pinhole where it now lodged. She had not completely ferreted out that wayward desire, but imagined dripping sealing wax over the tiny perforation where the delectable poison had pricked her skin. Walking, she felt a pain in her stomach. A lump of guilt rolled around the empty cavity of her belly like a marble, causing her a slight feeling of unbalance. The residual exhilaration of her flirtation with Dustin was still humming softly through her cells, but she could only hope that the once-jubilant fizz of infatuation might eventually fade, like carbonation in spring water that went flat over time.

Somewhere in the distance, crisply outlined skyscrapers met the static-crackly air with sleek angles and glassy facades. But as Lindsey and Michael made their way down the sidewalk within sight of the Pacific Ocean, she felt they could be in Hawaii. The temperate wind now carried a more pronounced scent of honeysuckle, and Lindsey imagined the blossoms in the trees imperceptibly opening their teardrop, eyecup petals to catch the rain that was about to come at any moment.

She and Michael stopped at a viewing wall and looked out to the water. With the Chagall-painted sky, today Lindsey could believe that the world was just a shoebox diorama in a schoolboy's lap. Could she kick through a dark blue cloud to find a cardboard backing? Was the swaying wind and jostling ocean simply a result of their creator tripping on a stone, skipping over a fence, or enduring a turbulent ride in a carpool?

She checked her watch and was surprised that, despite the early hour, the ominous storm was bringing night to the daytime. Lights flickered on across the hill, and little by little, San Francisco became a box of stars.

The landscape was all dark gray and white, drawn of alternately dull, charcoal smudges and gleaming, reflected light. The city seemed to be waiting, taking a deep breath before the rain dropped like a satin curtain, or silver fringe on a flapper's hem.

Down a ramp behind the Cliff House, they approached a modest shack with a blue-peaked stovepipe hat for a roof. The tiny shelter was painted to resemble a giant camera, and a plaque promised amazing sights within. Paying two dollars and walking inside behind black curtains, Lindsey and Michael entered the Camera Obscura.

As their eyes adjusted to the room's séance dimness, they could hear a *pit-pit-pat* against the roof—the rain, finally. Lindsey walked to the center of the room and approached a concave disk. It was a screen shaped like a horizontal satellite dish that reflected a rotating picture of the live ocean view below, optically cast by a periscope above. An invention of Leonardo da Vinci, the device illuminated the otherworldly reflection of the stormy waves outside, and as watery cascades drifted across the expanse, Lindsey hovered at the edge of the tumultuous ocean moon.

Michael came behind her and kissed her hair, the palms of his hands resting gently against her neck and shoulders. Lindsey could smell the faint scent of his shaving gel mixed with the sweat of his skin and ocean salt. Her face resting against his neck, with her cheek she could feel the tightening and release of his throat as he swallowed.

Holding her close, he whispered in her ear, "Is there anything you need to say before I say what I'm gonna say?"

The wind outside had picked up, and she could hear it howling like a roaring crowd. Playland at the Beach was gone, but Lindsey could almost sense the crushed memory of past revelers. Beyond the walls and through the rain, she heard a faint bicycle bell and she could almost pretend the tinkling chime was a distant carnival noise, a gentleman winning a stuffed toy for his sweetheart lover.

She turned to face Michael. "No," she said. After a moment, she added, "Except that . . . I love you."

Their breathing syncopated, she realized that his coming somewhat easily to her made her almost take his warmth for granted. She remembered that he once told her that as a child he suffered from night terrors, and as recently as last year he still used to wake up drenched in sweat and would sometimes sleepwalk, finding himself in the kitchen and wondering how he got there. He said he was never able to sleep through the night until he met her. He spent his twenties constantly moving from town to town, but when they met he knew San Francisco would be his home. Standing still now and hugging him, she could feel his heartbeat and was reminded that even a dirt-brown sparrow puts itself at risk to nest with another, settling in low brush where predators were never very far.

They exited the dark curtains into a ray of sepia-toned sunlight. It had momentarily stopped raining. The sounds of the city were muffled by the rolling cotton clouds overhead, and although the sky was dark and heavy, the air was strangely clear and crisp. Maybe it was the peculiar light or maybe the brief rain shower had cleansed the atmosphere, but looking out at the horizon, Lindsey could see details that weren't usually apparent. At the foot of the hills across the bay, she could just make out the lapping whitecaps and the curlicue eyelashes of saltwater following the ocean currents like metallic threads. She could see the stick-legs of shorebirds as they drifted in the distance. Down below on the sand, she watched a snowy plover as it bounced like a Ping Pong ball to meet up with its skittering flock, and for the first time in a long while, she felt calm.

A footpath led them through a maze of overgrown foliage and down to the ruins of the Sutro Baths. After descending, they climbed the twisting path steadily upward until they had trudged high up the face of the cliff. As the incline leveled off, they looked below to the pounding surf, swelling and crashing as the tide churned in and out. They walked onto a precarious cement platform on a rocky crag that jutted out over the Pacific and stepped to the safety rail. Holding each other tightly they watched as curling whitewater threw itself against the land, soaking the emerald iceplants that clung to the steep, sandy slope just below.

Michael smiled and when their eyes met, Lindsey recognized the look she loved. Not the least self-conscious, he rested his brown eyes upon her in a steady, soulful gaze, and his clear and bright expression conveyed his total affection and deep love for her. In his presence she felt guileless. His confident gaze made her feel forgiven for the things she hadn't done but had nonetheless thought about. His love made her feel stronger, and in that moment, her worries melted away.

"I think this is the perfect place to officially ask my girl the big question," he said. "Shut your eyes for a second, okay?"

Lindsey's heart soared. With her eyes shut, she was acutely aware of all the ocean sounds, and she listened attentively to the quiet sounds of Michael sifting through his jacket pockets. She could tell he was doing something elaborate as she could hear the incidental sounds of several objects being placed on the guardrail. She recognized a couple of electronic beeps as that of their camera, and opening her left eyelid ever so slightly, she could see that he was nimbly attempting to adjust the settings. She offered, "You have to remember to push the green button first."

"Stop looking!" he scolded. Then, over the sound of the crashing waves he said, "I'm setting up the remote so we'll have a photo to remember this moment." She heard him step a few paces away and assumed he was perching the camera somewhere and setting the timer.

Her eyes still closed, she was suddenly startled to hear his voice so close when he said, "Okay, open your eyes!" At the same moment, a huge wave whooshed up and sent seafoam flying overhead. She opened her eyes and stumbled back a bit, grabbing for the rail to catch her footing.

As she reached out her arm, she felt her hand brush against something, but as she balanced herself and looked to the ledge, nothing was there. Glancing over her shoulder she saw a quick, black dot bouncing down the rocks to the cliff below. She caught a look of sheer panic on Michael's face, and stood back, confused, as he lunged over the rail in a futile attempt to stop gravity.

Bombarded so suddenly with the sensation of almost falling, the spray of saltwater on her face, and then the sight of Michael's terrified expression, it took her a moment to realize she had inadvertently done something very wrong. Glancing from Michael's face back to the rocks and waves below, her eye managed to catch the black speck just as it blinked out of sight.

Michael grabbed his own face, his palm covering his mouth while his fingers gripped his cheek and jaw. It was something Lindsey had only seen him do a few times, like the time he failed to block the winning goal during a soccer match or once when they saw a humongous rat one morning on Kearny Street. Lindsey knew it was a gesture inspired only by instances of fairly severe anguish, as if he needed the grip of his hand over his face to forcibly keep himself from screaming like a girl. Hence, she knew that whatever just happened was bad.

The wind picked up and the clouds rushed in thick and dark above their heads. Michael was still staring down the cliff below with his hand across his face, but eventually managed to mumble, "That . . . was . . . the . . . ring."

A light sprinkling of rain speckled Lindsey's cheeks. She didn't know whether to cry for joy that Michael was so romantic, or cry because she just knocked an excruciatingly expensive rock into the Pacific Ocean. Suddenly, the rain began to fall in bigger drops. Their airspeed increased by the second until, moments later, it was pouring.

A short distance away, their camera flashed and caught their wrecked faces for posterity.

"What should we do?" she screamed. Looking below to the rocky cliff, she knew there was no way they could climb down.

"We'll have to climb down!" Michael said, as if the horrifying thought had floated directly out of her head and into his and then past his lips, the idea morphing from an impossibility into a necessity in the short process.

Michael wasted no time swinging himself under the railing and planting his feet on the nearest rock before helping Lindsey down. The hillside was muddy and slippery, and although they were slowly inching their way down the cliff, she still thought they were crazy to think they could find a ring box smaller than a cookie in this weather and on this terrain.

"I can't go any farther!" she yelled, the sandy soil giving way under her feet as she slid toward a rain-pelted boulder.

Michael yelled from ten feet below her, "Don't think too much. Just keep moving forward!"

Above, Lindsey stood for two minutes while feelings of despair swirled around her. Meanwhile, Michael scrambled down to an outcropping of iceplants where bright magenta flowers punctuated the green spears. Holding onto tree roots jutting from the rocks, he lowered himself down the steep incline. The rain was coming down hard now. Lindsey watched with utter fright as Michael briefly slipped on an unreliable foothold, then climbed from one grouping of weeds to a section of downtrodden wildflowers, finally pouncing on a patch that, from Lindsey's view, appeared indistinguishable from the other clumps of greenery.

Unbelievably, a minute later Michael exclaimed from below, "I see it!"

He scrambled sideways and headed toward a rocky area. A few seconds later, clutching the box in his hand, he held it up triumphantly for a brief second before attempting the treacherous ascent.

By the time he climbed up to where Lindsey was clinging to a boulder, the quick and heavy raindrops had dwindled to a light pattering. They gazed at each other and saw that they were both covered in mud, drenched to the skin. Gazing at Michael, Lindsey noted that he was the dirtiest she had ever seen him. His pants were smeared with mud, his shoes caked, and the heaviest rain from a moment ago was still trickling down his neck, disappearing under his jacket and shirt. His shoulders were streaked with particle matter from the shrubs and trees.

"Boy, are you filthy," she said, somewhat gleefully.

"No Handi Wipes are gonna help us now," he replied with a smile.

From above, the pattering gave way to a sprinkle, and in another second, the rain completely stopped. As if on cue, a sunbeam cut through the clouds, shining on them like a spotlight.

Michael managed to get down on one knee without falling off the cliff. He took Lindsey's hand, looked at her rain-streaked face, and said,

"Hey, Babykins. Wanna get married?"

Standing in the sunlight with Michael, her heart was no longer a flat rock skipping along the placid surface of a pond. Although she had always been afraid to swim in the ocean, with Michael she trusted they could plunge into cold water and find the warm currents. Together they would endure choppy waves, storms, and high seas, and where other lovers might be blindsided, she would be a stronghold for Michael as he would be hers. They would light the darkness for each other in the lowest depths, and protect each other like coral surrounding guppies.

She suspected there would be days when they would be like dolphins at play, and at other times, there would be days of bare survival. No matter the years, love was a vulnerable moon jelly of membrane. She was willing to bet that theirs would stretch with amazing elasticity and not break. She vowed to encircle Michael like a soft-bellied anemone, and through fresh, salt, or brackish water, she would stay with him however the tides in their particular ocean swayed.

Michael's marriage proposal still hanging sweetly in the air, Lindsey found she was all out of clever replies. Only one word came immediately to her mind and it rolled off her tongue and through her teeth with simplicity and mirth.

"Yes," she said.

Reaching down and gripping his collar, she pulled him close, never minding the fact that he looked dipped in dirt. She wrapped her arms around him as the rain suddenly began again, pelting them.

"Great!" he said. "Now let's get out of here!"

"Wait! Aren't we going to kiss?"

"I'll kiss you up there," he said sensibly. "Give me your hand."

Michael pulled her up and helped her steady her heel with each step on the slippery slope. They climbed slowly and delib-

erately until they eventually reached the top and she pulled herself up onto the other side of the safety rail. Michael hoisted
himself up as well, and once they were both on solid ground,
he pocketed the camera and grabbed her hand. They ran for
cover into a tunnel carved out of the cliffside.

Michael held the box out to her, the velvet sullied with mud.
A little out of breath, he said, "You said yes, but you haven't
even seen the ring yet."

"I know I'll like it," she said, brushing wet hair from her
forehead.

"I hope so." He teasingly rattled the box. Then with great
fanfare, he slowly lifted the lid.

She gasped. They both stared at the bright, bejeweled thing
nestled against a tiny cushion.

"You didn't have to," she said, not touching it.

"I wanted you to have exactly what you wanted," he said.

Lindsey couldn't take her eyes off the ring. It was a too-
brassy-to-be-real-gold Hello Kitty head encrusted with tiny
rhinestones and teensy-weensy fake-sapphire eyes.

"No, you *really* didn't have to."

Michael feigned devastation, then laughed. "Don't worry,"
he said. "The real one is below."

He lifted a false backing from the interior of the ring box.
Plucking the prize from behind a miniscule satin pillowcase, he
gently picked up her left hand. Onto her finger he slipped a
gold band delicately stamped with a pattern of interlocking
leaves surrounding a shockingly perfect, rose-cut ruby.

Lindsey stared in suspended amazement. Because she was
Chinese and descended from a long line of jewelry-obsessed
women, she instinctively recognized that the gem was something special. It was the kind of ruby one hardly saw in jewelry
stores. It gleamed with richness and depth like the eye of a mythical beast, its color at once clear and flawless, but thick as blood.

"It belonged to my grandmother," Michael said.

"Which? This one or the Hello Kitty ring?"

He grabbed her by the waist and yanked her into his arms. He said, "Awright, Sassypants. Just kiss me."

Feet on the Ground

The early summer storm had passed and the sun was shining bright on the morning of the St. Maude's reunion. Michael and Lindsey drove out to Thirty-eighth Avenue to pick up Yeh Yeh and Yun Yun, but when they arrived they faced a problem. Yun Yun had recently been having more difficulty walking and couldn't make it down the stairs.

"Just forget about me," Yun Yun said. "Leave me here. Too much trouble."

Lindsey noticed her grandmother was already dressed to go, her walker by the front door sporting extra-special, fluorescent pink tennis balls. She even had her hair done.

"We'll figure out a way," Lindsey said.

Yeh Yeh suggested tying a rope around her waist and lowering her out the window. Lindsey attempted holding Yun Yun on one side as she tried to descend the steps, but the old woman's legs simply wouldn't cooperate. Although Yun Yun explained nothing, Lindsey could see by her tentative movements that her grandmother couldn't quite feel her own feet touching the steps.

Michael said to Yun Yun, "If you wouldn't mind placing your arms around my neck, I think this might be easiest this way." Very slowly and gently, he leaned over and picked up Yun Yun as she hesitantly raised her arms.

For a split second Lindsey felt panicked, but Michael lifted Yun Yun with apparent ease. "Easy does it, here we go," he said as he maneuvered the curve of the steps. The way Michael held her it looked like she hardly weighed anything at all, as if her bones were hollow. It was strange to see anyone touching Yun Yun, let alone carrying her, let alone that person being Michael. It wasn't until he carefully set her down at the bottom landing that Lindsey could see Michael exhale with exertion. After setting Yun Yun down, he let her steady herself on his shoulder until she could feel her weight settle into her feet. Lindsey scrambled down with the walker and positioned it in front of her grandmother.

It took about ten minutes to get both Yeh Yeh and Yun Yun comfortably in the car, but Lindsey and Michael slowly and deliberately helped the old couple tuck in their legs and buckle their seat belts. Lindsey loaded the walker into the trunk, and soon they were off to St. Maude's.

Michael drove the car into the schoolyard so the old folks wouldn't have to walk far. He got out and helped them to a nearby bench while the caterers set up the tables.

Sister Constance suddenly appeared. After greeting Yun Yun she walked briskly over to Lindsey and said, "Can you drive out and pick up the *lumpia* donated by Mrs. Bantay?"

Michael sat with Yun Yun and Yeh Yeh and urged Lindsey to go ahead. "We'll be fine," he said. "Everybody else will be here soon enough, anyway," he added.

Lindsey slipped into the driver's seat, turned the car around and moved forward out of the schoolyard. Following the edge of the park, she turned onto Nineteenth Avenue, then onto the freeway toward Daly City.

Detouring through a residential neighborhood she drove past pink and green houses interspersed with *carnicerias* and *pupuserias*. A few blocks later she approached her destination, the Fil-Am Snack Shack.

Parking, she actually thought the run-down building was on fire because she saw huge clouds of smoke spewing from the roof, billowing so thick and heavy that it obscured the auto repair station next door. Opening the car door, she was immediately accosted by the intense odor of burning meat.

At the entrance, customers were crammed every which way. Waiting on the sidewalk, she noticed hundreds of wads of old, black gum that covered the cement like a hard, rubber carpeting of bubble gum paillard. Dodging past a Filipino man wearing dress slacks and a tucked-in Forty-Niner jersey with letters on the back that spelled BAD BOI, she finally nudged her way inside. She waited her turn near the front counter lined with cases of soy and fish sauce, boxed mango drinks, and netted bags of onions. Over the glass partition she watched men without hairnets grill hundreds of pieces of chicken and ribs.

Finally, she reached the front of the line and explained that she was there to pick up the pre-ordered *lumpia*. Two women speaking fast in Tagalog yelled back over their shoulders, and through a cloud of dark gray smoke Lindsey could see a cook smoking a cigarette over a wok filled with bubbling oil. The man used a gigantic, Flintstone-sized spoon to heap the piping-hot *lumpia* into several aluminum trays that were lined up on the scrap-covered floor. As Lindsey watched, she wished she had a cell phone to call the health department right then and there.

After several trips to and from her car, the trunk, back and front seat were loaded down with enough *lumpia* to build a small, deep-fried igloo. She drove back toward St. Maude's with the air-conditioner on because the heat from two thousand *lumpia* in the car was making her sweat.

Finally arriving back at the jubilee, she unloaded the *lumpia* at the food station, then headed across the schoolyard that had been transformed into a huge picnic area with rented tents and tables. A parquet floor had been assembled for dancing, but Lindsey couldn't take her eyes off the huge, overhead banner that read, "Welcome Back, Sheep!" Over by the hopscotch, an elderly woman from Catholic Services Abroad held up a sign that urged, PLEASE PRAY FOR A MISSIONARY POSITION.

Lindsey observed the crowd. People seemed to have naturally separated themselves into Italian, Irish, and Asian groupings. The benches on the east side of the schoolyard appeared to be a desegregated zone where a multicultural smattering of old ladies fanned themselves in the shade. Little kids in dress-up clothes lolled about, seeming not to know what to do with themselves. On the yard's west side, some thirtysomethings played basketball. Meanwhile, over by the rectory, Monsignor Rathburn glad-handed a few senior parishioners.

The whole mélange of St. Maude's past and present Marauders was a little overwhelming for Lindsey, and she hadn't even spotted her family yet. Sister Constance caught her standing by the water fountain doing nothing and said, "Are you daft, lazing about here? Go assist the name-tag table."

Lindsey was glad to be assigned a specific task with which to busy herself while her mind conjured an endless number of potential disasters that might befall her. She wondered how she would respond if she saw any of the Lost Chinese Children, and she hoped Yun Yun wouldn't say anything too embarrassing. Since current students were also invited, she wondered if Mrs. Clemens would show up with Jilan, and if so, would either Yun Yun or Yeh Yeh recognize the old lady?

And lastly, if Dustin actually showed up, what would she do if and when he and Michael came face to face?

Lindsey organized the name tags in neat little rows and helped alumni and their spouses as they approached the table. Some attendees gave either their married or maiden names, which resulted in brief confusion, and as Lindsey sifted through the alphabetized labels, she couldn't help but notice the peculiar results of a few of the Chinese hyphenated names. There was Dixie Dang-Long and Fanny Fat-Chin in the first row, and farther down the line, someone named Willemina Wang-Goo and then, unbelieveably, Virginia Poon-Tang.

As she separated the labels from their backings, her friend Franklin Ng approached.

"Hey Lindsey, why are you stuck here working?" he said. "Come over to my table. I'm sitting with all our old classmates." He pointed to the near distance and everyone looked over and waved. Grabbing her by the arm, he dragged her over, assuring her that people could find their own name tags.

Stumbling toward the picnic table she saw them all. They were grown up now, and although some were fat, some were prematurely gray, and some bald, they looked staggeringly the same. But instead of blue plaid uniforms, the clothes of regular, everyday people made them look, well, like regular people.

Nelson Fong, a.k.a. "The Shitter," was a genial lad who was a computer programmer now. John Goon, a.k.a. "The Barfer," was a banker with a pretty wife. Jefferson Lee showed everyone the scar on his head from where he smacked his skull on the water fountain. Nellie had plumped up quite a bit since the second grade, and Gina Fang introduced herself as Gina Wilson now, clutching the arm of her Caucasian husband with white knuckles as if she desperately feared that one of them would at any second utter her schoolyard nickname, Vagina Fangs.

Lindsey was relieved that none of her Chinese brethren and sistren had been killed by the nuns or turned into guinea pigs after all. (Hmm . . . but then again, she didn't see Beethoven anywhere.) Spotting her parents a few tables away, she quickly excused herself from her former classmates and made her way toward her family.

"Hey everybody," she said. She touched Michael's arm as he helped Yun Yun move from her walker to a chair. Yun Yun was wearing a polyester leisure outfit, an extra-long visor strapped to her head, and wraparound shades. Lindsey kissed her grandmother's cheek and received an acknowledging grunt for her effort, which was a better reaction than she usually got.

Yeh Yeh, as usual, was dressed for a blizzard. He sat stock-still in his plastic chair, so different from the fairly animated person Lindsey had visited in the Jackson Street grocery store. She stared at him for a moment, and just as she was about to look away, he gave her a little wink and she smiled.

"Save some chairs for Elmore and Geraldine," her dad said. "I invited them, and they should be here pretty soon."

As Lindsey placed some extra napkins on the table, her mom reached out and grabbed her wrist, admiring the ruby engagement ring for the fifth time that morning. She said, "Hey Lindsey, are they going to make an announcement about you getting married? Wouldn't that be nice?"

Kevin cracked, "There won't be time after the extensive lecture about the missionary position."

A while later at the buffet table, everyone was pleased to find an array of food choices, some provided by caterers and others potluck items brought by alumni with their names and years of graduation proudly affixed to the dishes. Platters of eggplant parmesan sat next to trays of tomato-beef chow mein, homemade chow fun, and fried chicken. There was Greek salad, olives, and moussaka, and a whole section of Mexican food with

a placard that read, HELENA IBARRA (CLASS OF 1977) GUARAN-
TEES NO FAT! ONE-HUNDRED PERCENT LARD. Directing people
toward the dessert table, Lindsey's mouth watered when she
saw that a classmate had brought his mother's famous short-
bread cookies shaped like Jesus heads with halos.

Halfway through the meal, music began to play and some
people got up to dance. While the speakers blared "Achy,
Breaky Heart," Lindsey looked over at the makeshift dance
floor and her eyes rested on the surreal image of Uncle Elmore
and Ms. Abilene dancing the Electric Slide. Leaning over,
Lindsey pointed out the bizarre coupling to Michael.

"It's best not to think about anything too disturbing," he
advised.

Kevin sauntered over with two buddies from his class whom
Lindsey recognized as Scott Fukuda and Scott Kuriyama.
Kevin reached into his jacket pocket and handed Lindsey his silver flask, saying, "Hold this for me. Actually you look like you
might need it."

"Where are you going?"

"Basketball. Hey Michael, come over when you're done. We
play China versus Japan, and I need you to help me take down
Fukuda and Furry Mama."

"Okay," Michael said as he and Lindsey scooted over to
make room for Auntie Geraldine. She plopped down with
two plates stacked with food, removed an entire roll of foil
from her gigantic purse, and proceeded to wrap up several
items.

Although Lindsey couldn't see Yun Yun's eyes behind her
shades, she saw her lip curl into a tiny sneer as she looked
Geraldine's way.

"*Gum Fay!*" her grandmother chided, calling her a fatso.
Lindsey watched Auntie Geraldine crumple slightly before sitting up defiantly and proceeding to inhale several deviled eggs.

"Lindsey," her dad called across the table. "Do you have an extra sweater? I think Yun Yun is getting a little chilly."

Yeh Yeh piped up, "I told you might rain!"

Lindsey thought for a second, and said she might have something in the office cloakroom upstairs. She sprang up from her seat and headed for the main building. Halfway across the schoolyard she ran into Jilan, or rather, Jilan smashed into her on purpose.

"Boo!" she screeched.

"Hi. Is your grandmother here with you?" Lindsey asked, patting down the girl's tousled bangs.

"No, I came with my mom."

"I see you have on your Gene Kelly outfit again."

"Huh?"

"Never mind. See you later, okay?"

Lindsey continued on her way, and Jilan ran off. When she finally reached the double doors that led up to the mezzanine, she lurched back before colliding with Dustin.

"Hey, do you know if they have 'updog' here?" he asked.

"What's 'updog'?"

Dustin slapped her on the shoulder. "Nothing, Dog! What's up with you?"

She had to smile, and after a moment of awkward hesitation, hugged him in the most sexless way she could muster.

Dustin said, "To heal my psyche, I figured I had to come back to the scene of the crime."

Sitting down on one of the benches where she used to eat her Del Monte chocolate pudding cup every day at recess, she said, "Which crime are you talking about, the rat-eater incident or the death of Mork?"

Dustin sat down next to her and stretched out his legs. "Both, I guess. I don't necessarily feel better being here, though. I didn't come here to relive the horrors of sixth grade in 3-D Technicolor."

"Why are you here then?"

"I guess I wanted to make sure you're not mad at me. Are you?"

She shook her head.

They looked at each other for a moment. There was nothing between them except what could have been, and that sure was a lot. But for now they seemed to have reached some kind of truce. It was as if they had each imagined doing it with the other person so many times that they may as well have dated, and now they were in the imaginary break-up phase which was much more painless than the real thing since, after all, nothing had physically happened. As an acknowledging gesture of their just-friends status, Dustin reached over and lightly punched Lindsey in the shoulder as if she were his cousin. He said, "Oh, by the way, I wanted to tell you that . . . I met someone. A Chinese someone."

"Really? Where?"

"She crashed into my shopping cart at Ranch 99—"

"That's *so* Asian!"

"Yeah, isn't it?"

Just then, Sister Constance burst from the double doors and stopped dead in her tracks. She spotted them sitting there and seemed to recognize Dustin immediately. Blinking a couple of times, she trained her gaze at him with her beady, Doggie Diner eyeballs. After a discombobulated moment she looked like she thought she was dreaming, but then, with a gooselike honk she called out, "Boy, is that you?"

Lindsey and Dustin both stood up as Sister Constance approached. Lindsey watched as Dustin braced himself for an attack, but it was Lindsey's arm that the gray-haired woman grabbed. The withered nun turned to Lindsey and said, "If I may say so, I do remember what a schoolboy's crush your young friend had on me!"

Turning to Dustin she released Lindsey's arm and pinched his face. "I tell you! Such a cheeky, cheeky boy!"

With a light slap to his face, the nun pivoted on her low heel, but then stopped and swiftly cupped Dustin's ass before walking off.

Lindsey laughed out loud. "Did she just . . ."

"I'm going to pretend that didn't just happen. And now . . . I'm leaving. Before I really need therapy."

Lindsey began to protest, "Wait, you have to meet—"

A hand came out of nowhere and offered Dustin a handshake. "Michael Cartier."

Dustin introduced himself and the two shook hands. Michael smiled warmly, but Dustin gave him that half-second, sizing-up thing that guys often did.

Lindsey felt like shrinking into nothingness, but she held her ground. Reaching down, she interlocked her fingers with Michael's and squeezed his hand. Dustin flashed his killer smile that struck Lindsey as slightly less dazzling now, and she listened as he told Michael how smart he always thought she was in school. The way he said it, he ambiguously implied something negative, like she was a know-it-all or stuck up, but Michael took the comment in the best way possible and proceeded to enumerate a handful of Lindsey's good qualities. Affectionately pulling her closer to him, he said, "Thanks for looking out for my girl while I was gone."

Michael seemed unaware that Lindsey and Dustin had come close to doing the bone dance. She didn't know if he was suppressing his suspicions or just being his gracious self, but it was probably the latter. Relaxed, yet animated, he curiously asked

Dustin questions about himself, all the while continuing to treat him like a friend instead of an interloper.

Lindsey leaned in to Michael and admired his aplomb. Although the three of them were only engaged in small talk, she soaked in Michael's chocolate-voiced kindness and marveled at his open-hearted nature. She was relieved to have never marred that elusive and rare quality. Standing there a few feet from the dodgeball court, she felt she truly had dodged a bullet by not allowing her infatuation with Dustin to get the better of her. *May I always deserve Michael's trust*, she thought.

Whatever potential for tension that may have existed never materialized as Michael and Dustin displayed a spontaneous semblance of male friendship. Over the ensuing minutes, they all exchanged pleasantries, which dissolved any outline of a love triangle among the three and simultaneously reset the spatial parameters between them. Lindsey's hand in Michael's suggested their positions were fixed closely together on the same axis, while the distance she stood from Dustin signified that her relationship to him would henceforth never exist in the same quadrant. As they continued to talk, their designated positions, marked in invisible space, seemed to crystallize into a shape they could all agree with, and by the end of the conversation, Michael again thanked Dustin for being such a good friend to Lindsey.

Lindsey knew then that everything would be fine. When guys were mad, they just brawled and got their shit out of the way instead of stewing for years like girls, so she figured that if Michael wasn't pummeling Dustin by now, things were okay.

She said goodbye to Dustin, kissed Michael, and bounded up the stairwell to retrieve the sweater for Yun Yun. Before ducking into the office, she looked out the mezzanine window and watched her fiancé and her old school friend as they headed toward Kevin's basketball game. She felt someone's gaze on her and she looked over her shoulder. She saw the portrait of Mary, and smiled.

Walking over to the painting, she stared at Mary's sapphire blue cloak and wondered how many students over the years had also found solace and comfort standing in this same spot. She thought about Yun Yun and wondered if her grandmother ever prayed—to Mary, or Buddha, or anyone.

Standing there, Lindsey's mind conjured the past:

Before Yun Yun was ever called "grandmother," she was a baby girl born crying to a midwife down two flights of stairs on Pike Street, now Waverly Place in San Francisco. Directly before or after she entered the world, her twin had arrived, perhaps more robust, heavier, and with a happier disposition. Had her family decided right then and there to give her away? Maybe they reasoned that no one needed two infant girls. Perhaps her parents saw her as another mouth to feed instead of a tiny person who needed the sense of touch and the scent of her mother's breath to know that love was nearby.

Lindsey wondered if Yun Yun remembered anything of her family—their faces, their personalities, or the fact that they always loved her sister, Opal, more. Maybe the girls cried and held each other before she left her home for good.

Arriving at St. Maude's, perhaps there were no friends. Yun Yun probably learned the Bible, did her chores, went to sleep, and started the next day all over again exactly the same. Lindsey couldn't begin to imagine how the girl who was her grandmother must have felt. Desolate and angry, Yun Yun most likely had to steel herself against her own emotions just to make it past her loneliness. Lindsey was finally beginning to understand why her grandmother might want to forget. Perhaps the burden of memory was too heavy to bear.

Still standing in front of the portrait of Mary, Lindsey reflected on the past few weeks. She had found out more than she expected about both her grandparents. Although there was still a lot she didn't know, looking now into Mary's compassionate eyes, she wondered if she would ever know the whole truth, or even if she had the right to.

Her grandparents were living people, and to dig up what did not want digging up now struck her as disrespectful. "Why stir up trouble?" so many Chinese people always seemed to say, and now Lindsey, too, began to wonder why she should. Was compelling curiosity reason enough to further discomfit those who had already experienced so much hardship? She was no longer certain her own needs superseded others'.

She walked to the office and retrieved the blue sweater she had left behind last week. Although the weather had been warm for a while now, in terms of days and months, spring was finally just now giving way to summer. Leave it to Yun Yun to need a sweater even though it was seventy-five degrees outside. However, Lindsey did think she detected a slight thawing in Yun Yun's behavior. And in turn, she, too, felt the iceberg between them melting. She bounded down the stairs and back to the table where her family all sat in the breezy sunshine.

She approached Yun Yun, who had temporarily taken off her wraparound shades. Lindsey noticed the prominent puffiness beneath Yun Yun's eye sockets, and the dour mouth that kept so much unspoken. She could see haunted disappointment etched in her grandmother's worn-out face.

Lindsey stepped close and draped the blue sweater around Yun Yun's weary shoulders. She noticed the beginnings of a wan smile on her grandmother's lips, but it disappeared before it had a chance to fully form. Lindsey pulled the ends of the sweater's collar together to warm her grandmother's neck, and as she fastened the pearl button, a bony hand reached up and touched hers. Yun Yun pressed the flesh of Lindsey's hand with her soft, raisinlike fingertips.

A creaky voice like the noise from an un-oiled hinge caught Lindsey unaware. "I'm glad you're here," Yun Yun said.

Taking a seat between her grandmother and Michael, Lindsey stared across the table at the faces of her parents, brother, aunt, uncle, and Yeh Yeh. She contemplated the words her grandmother had finally said to her, words she had never heard before from the matriarch. It was a simple, straightforward statement that belied the complicated relationship she and Yun Yun had always shared. Lindsey realized it might be the best that she was ever going to get from her. Over the years she had waited for an eloquent pronouncement of grandmotherly affection, but this sentence, uttered softly and without pretense, was fine for now. Lindsey realized she had, in fact, waited a long time to hear it, and today it was finally enough.

"I'm glad you're here, too," Lindsey said, and meant it.

Buddha Baby Got Back

Lindsey Owyang was sitting in a minivan. She and Michael had rented it and were driving up Highway 160 with her parents and grandparents. They were on their way to the quiet town of Locke.

By the time they'd passed Vacaville, all the chitchat had fizzled away and they now rode in silence. Thank goodness the mild-mannered commentary of a baseball game on the radio could be counted on to interject noise into the dead air. Squeezed into the backseat between her mother and Yun Yun, Lindsey stared out the window and wondered if organizing this trip was a good idea after all. She hadn't expected witticisms to be ricocheting back and forth among them all, but a little pleasant conversation at periodic intervals wouldn't have been bad. For the past forty-five minutes she'd made as many comments about Costco as were humanly possible, and now she was a little tired of trying to think of things to say. She looked at each person out of the corner of her eye and wondered what they were thinking. Finally, to no one in particular, she said, "Will it be hard to remember which building was ours?"

"Right on Main Street," her dad replied. "Calvin Ahchuck's mother still lives in town. She's going to meet us."

Yun Yun let out a little huff. "That old lady?" she said.

Lindsey's mother took up the conversation. "Michael," she called over the back of the seat, "You two better hurry up and figure out where you're going to have the wedding. Places book up a year and a half in advance." She turned to Lindsey. "And you better start dieting now, if you're going to lose ten pounds."

Lindsey was about to tell her mother flat out that she was not overweight. But before she could summon the gumption, she heard Yun Yun mutter, "Not so bad."

Waiting for the punch line, Lindsey was certain Yun Yun was going to make further comment about the current state of fat in the backseat. Several seconds passed but miraculously no insult came Lindsey's way. She was quietly absorbing her grandmother's attitude adjustment when Yeh Yeh piped up, "River looks low for this time of year! But you never know, flash flood very dangerous."

Lindsey's dad humored Yeh Yeh. He said, "Is that so, Pop?"

When Michael eventually made the turnoff to Locke, they drove right onto Main Street and found a ramshackle block of rain-beaten, sun-bleached shacks. The wooden planks of the buildings' walls all leaned as if huddling together to keep each other company during the lonely afternoons.

Lindsey's dad hopped out of the front passenger's seat and opened the back door. As it slid open, it made a satisfying *ka-chunk* sound. Inside the air-conditioned vehicle, Lindsey, her mother, and grandparents had been shielded from the rising valley temperature, but now with the side door open, the air enveloped them like heat from an oven.

Yeh Yeh sniffed. "Peat," he said. "And firecrackers. Must be some kids here joking around."

"There's Mabel Ahchuck," Lindsey's dad said.

Lindsey looked across the street and saw a tiny Chinese woman with a frizzy perm and strange, amber-colored dye job. She was wearing an orange apron over a housedress that made her look like she'd just gotten off work at Home Depot. Squinting in the sunlight, she looked like a kind, blind orangutan.

"Welcome!" she called. And then, "Is that you, Pearlie?"

Michael had just lifted Yun Yun down from the backseat, and Lindsey ran to the back of the van to help her dad unfold the wheelchair for her grandmother.

"I don't need that thing," Yun Yun said. She walked very slowly toward Mrs. Ahchuck with outstretched arms, and exclaimed, "Look at you, Mabel, you're an old lady!"

Lindsey realized Yun Yun hadn't been *complaining* about the old lady in the car. Rather, it seemed she'd been looking forward to seeing an old friend.

The two ladies linked arms like schoolgirls and walked a short distance. Anticipating that Yun Yun would eventually get tired, Lindsey unfolded the wheelchair and followed behind, pushing it around empty. After about five minutes, Yun Yun slowed to a stop and did not protest when Lindsey offered the wheelchair. She grabbed Lindsey's arm and sat down with matter-of-fact dignity. Lindsey then arranged her grandmother's legs and feet into comfortable positions, then got up and resumed pushing the chair while everyone else walked alongside them.

They all strolled down Main Street, and when Lindsey's mom threw out questions regarding ceremony plans, Michael intercepted them. Lindsey was trying to listen in on the old ladies' conversation.

"Expected to see you at your boy's anniversary party," Yun Yun said.

Mrs. Ahchuck shook her head, "Too much trouble. Pick up, drive back, *ai-ya* . . . rather stay here. Guess I'm used to quiet place like this. Not too much hustle and bustle like Waverly Street, eh?"

While everyone else dispersed along the empty street to look around, Lindsey was still walking directly behind Yun Yun, pushing the wheelchair. Meanwhile, Mrs. Ahchuck strolled right alongside. The old women talked, seemingly oblivious to Lindsey's presence even though she was as close to either of them as they were to each other.

"Remember how we played Chinese jump rope in the street?" Mabel asked. "I remember you could jump higher than anyone else."

"Except Opal," Yun Yun replied. "She was always very good at that game."

Even though Yun Yun's back was to her, Lindsey couldn't help but feel that her grandmother meant for her to overhear what she was saying.

Yun Yun continued, "We known each other a long time. First you live across the street when I was small, then I was very lucky your family moved to Locke, too. After I marry and come here, you are the only one who know me from before. I was happy that you remember me after all that time."

Mrs. Ahchuck rested an arm on Yun Yun's shoulder. "You my old friend, how can I forget you? But now . . . we are old ladies. The difference between remember and forget is not so big. We only think about whether our feet hurt today, am I right?"

Yun Yun interjected, "Remember when I first come here, you and I still not bad-looking back then. You wanted to be chosen Asparagus Queen—"

Mrs. Ahchuck hooted. "In all delta region, we not know they always pick a blonde for the festival parade. We were naïve!" The old woman laughed until tears formed in the corner of her eyes. Yun Yun reached into her sleeve for a tissue and held it up for her friend to take.

Then Yun Yun pointed to Yeh Yeh up ahead and said, "When his parents die in flash flood and we move back to San Fran, I missed you very much. You more like sister than my sister. Sorry I haven't come back to see you in so long."

Mrs. Ahchuck nodded her head. "Is all right, Pearlie."

Lindsey pushed the wheelchair forward slowly and steadily, which was no easy feat considering how lopsided the sidewalk planks were. She tried not to jostle her grandmother too much, and kept her eyes trained ahead on the upcoming path.

Mrs. Ahchuck said, "This town used to be so busy with so many people. Year after year, every one of us picking cherries, asparagus, grapes. But this place is like us now. All dried up. Hardly anyone comes to visit, not even my grandchildren. Pretty soon no one will remember you and me."

About ten feet ahead, Lindsey could see Yeh Yeh peering inside a door. As they approached him, Mrs. Ahchuck stopped and called everyone over. Lindsey stepped out from behind the wheelchair, and gave Yun Yun a small smile. Her grandmother's face was as impassive as she'd always known it. They waited together as everyone gathered around.

Mrs. Ahchuck led everybody inside a newly painted space that was furnished in a straightforward and functional way. She offered them tea and almond cookies from a pastry box and said, "Look familiar? Can you believe this is the same gambling room where we used to run the *pai gow* poker game? Newly refurbish to be a tourist center next year."

Mrs. Ahchuck was pretty steady on her feet, and took to slowly wheeling around Yun Yun. Lindsey's dad said, "Hey look, the cashier's cage is still in the back."

Lindsey felt the lopsided floor beneath her shoes and noticed the old tongue-and-groove walls. Wandering around the room, she quietly noted that the new paint couldn't quite cover up all the cracks and blemishes, and she liked that.

Lost in thought, she stopped to admire two framed banners written in Chinese calligraphy. Yeh Yeh suddenly sidled up behind her. She was slightly startled when she noticed him suddenly by her side. Studying the banners as well, he said, "My *baba*, your great-grandpa, was a calligraphy artist. He never made any money from it, but he had passion in his heart. Drove my mother crazy. *Amah* always wanted him to stop dreaming and make money, but he was always seeing things a different way, observing, and listening. More important things than making money. Am I right? He was like you. An artist."

He patted her lightly on the shoulder, then headed for the cookies.

Like you. An artist. Her grandfather's words were still floating in her ears when she spotted Michael through the doorway, standing out in the middle of the sunny street. After quickly checking to see that both Yun Yun and Yeh Yeh were sitting down and comfortably sipping tea, she went outside.

Catching up with Michael, she said, "Since your exposé was a success, now do you get to take some time off?"

Michael shook his head. "Nope," he said, "this week I start working on a story about a meatless bratwurst company from Germany called Gluten-Taag."

She twirled her ruby ring around her wedding finger and held it up to the sunlight. On her other hand, she wore her *bague de Hello Kitty* with equal pride.

"Hey," she said. "How did you manage to get your hands on these jewels while you were down at the Psychic Food Ashram?"

Michael put his arm around her and pulled her close. "I had my mom send them to my cousin in Santa Cruz, then I picked them up on the way."

"You thought of everything," she said, then got on her tiptoes to peck him on the cheek.

Across the street was an old joss house from which Lindsey detected the strong smell of Chinese incense. The scent reminded her of childhood days in Chinatown, and they went inside.

In the darkened room, they approached a statue surrounded by fruit offerings and flowers.

"Look," Lindsey said, "this Buddha looks friendly."

She picked up a few magenta- and mustard-colored joss sticks and lit them. She placed them into the sand beneath the Buddha's toes.

Michael added, "I think he looks like a big, healthy baby."

He reached for her hand, and they gazed at each other for a while. Turning around, they noticed that her parents and grandparents were outside, now standing in the middle of the street, enjoying the sunshine.

Facing the altar again, Lindsey and Michael each bowed to the statue of Buddha. From the dark, cool room they looked out from the temple doorway, then slowly turned and walked toward their family.

Want More?

Turn the page to enter
Avon's Little Black Book —

the dish, the scoop and the
cherry on top from
KIM WONG KELTNER

Scenes from the Cutting Room Floor of *Buddha Baby*

As a writer, I spend a lot of time in my head thinking about the backgrounds and idiosyncrasies of my characters. Sometimes it's hard to decide which details to leave to the readers' imaginations and what to include. Believe me, I could go on for several chapters about germphobia, but it's got to stop somewhere. (Note to reader: When staying at a hotel, always spray the remote control with Lysol before touching it.)

In this book I really wanted to show the closeness between Lindsey and Michael, and how they sometimes got into little fights. But I eventually realized the following scenes needed to be filed under T.M.I.—too much information. So sit back down and enjoy a live broadcast from the cutting-room floor, starring Lindsey Owyang and Michael Cartier in these original deleted scenes:

Love Means Never Having to Say You Smell Like Miracle Whip

Monday morning, Lindsey awoke to discover that Michael smelled like pepperoni. She was spooning him in bed and had her cheek against his shoulder when, barely awake, she detected the fine aroma of something kinda spicy, kinda meaty. She leaned in for another sniff. Yep, definitely something porky going on there.

Now, Lindsey was familiar with the notion that white people had a different smell from Chinese people. Michael was a quarter Chinese on his mother's side, but maybe in the olfactory category that other three fourths just dominated. She detected the faintest whiff of something else, perhaps mayonnaise. She tugged the sheet down and smelled his shoulder. Hmm. Bologna?

Perhaps she was confusing her affection for Michael with her undeniable enthusiasm for pork products, but these discoveries were what a person risked for domestic bliss. No one could smell like CK One all the time. She'd heard that Eskimos had more than a hundred names to describe snow, and as she took a couple more sniffs of her sleeping boyfriend, she wondered if the Chinese language had different words to describe the various ways white people smelled.

"What are you doing?" Michael said, then turned over.

Lindsey looked at him, startled. "Nothing. Um, you smell like Miracle Whip."

"What?" he said, rubbing sleep from his eyes.

"Maybe it's more like Spam," she said, sniffing his face.

"Get off me," he said, pushing her away.

"I don't think it's a matter of what you ate for lunch or dinner. It's just a white-people thing," she said.

Michael looked at her like she was nuts.

She continued, "Don't be too offended. Some Chinese people seem to smell naturally of mothballs."

"Just because you have no scent at all, doesn't mean you can pick on everybody else," he said.

Lindsey Is Germ-phobic and Sometimes Michael Is a Grumphead

Michael got out of bed and pulled a T-shirt over his head. He glanced at some of Lindsey's socks that were strewn on the floor. Picking them up, he said, "Have you worn these? Are they clean or dirty? Why don't you put them away?" He tossed them on top of the dresser. "Your clothes are everywhere," he grumbled.

As Michael went into the bathroom to brush his teeth, Lind-

sey scampered after him. She tried to explain: "I have different stacks of clothes around the bedroom according to their
level of cleanliness: just-out-of-the-washer clean, worn-once
clean, clean-enough-but-only-to-wear-outside-the-house, and
not-dirty-enough-to-wash-but-okay-to ride-on-the-bus clean."

Michael said, "Whatever, Howard Hughes," then got into
the shower.

Lindsey crawled back into bed and wondered just how irritated Michael was. She felt bad. Maybe she was crazy, or
maybe it was a Chinese thing, this germ concern. Lying there,
she thought about the fourteen-year-old Chinese girls she saw
spitting by the high school. Who taught them to do that? They
acted like spitting was as natural as smoking. Why did Chinese people spit everywhere? For a moment she wondered if,
in some twisted way, spitting was considered sanitary. God
forbid those germs were actually *in your mouth*. Of course you
had to spit them out! And not in a handkerchief, but on the
street. In China there were laws against spitting on the sidewalk because the blobs froze and pedestrians slipped on them.
There weren't laws against spitting because *it was disgusting*
but because people slipped.

Michael was out of the shower in a quick three minutes,
then back in the bedroom getting dressed for work.

Lindsey sat up. "I'm sorry I said that you smell like Spam."

Grabbing his keys, Michael headed for the door.

"Wait!" she called.

"What?"

She hesitated, then launched into a more extensive apology,
"I'm a freak, I know. But I'm working on it. See, I could have
told you I noticed you're leaving the house without going to
the bathroom, and you know how I feel about public toilets. So
many hideous possibilities: no toilet paper, backsplash, gross
smells. But see, I didn't mention it because I'm trying not to
be such a freak. And last night, before you got into bed, I
didn't even ask if you had used a public toilet, and if you did,
I didn't ask if you made sure to cover the seat with the protective paper shield. I didn't say anything. I just let you get into
bed. See? I'm getting better—"

"I HAVE TO GO!" Michael said, then ran down the steps.
Lindsey ran to the window and was about to yell out that
she loved him. He stopped and turned on the sidewalk to see if
she was there, and seeing that she was, blew her a kiss.

*I used to have recurring nightmares about being back in
school even though I was already grown up. Unlike Lindsey, I never took a job at my grammar school, but I did,
in fact, work at my old high school for one year. Incidentally, the dreams stopped immediately. Life, however, had
become surreal. I just didn't feel quite right about calling
Mr. Simon and Madame Donalds "Steve" and "Midge."
I couldn't walk up to the headmaster and be like, "Yo, Al,
wanna get some coffee?" No, no, no.*

*The following scene was supposed to be near the end,
but didn't make the final cut:*

From the Mixed-Up Files of Mrs. Basil E. Grupico

Monday morning at work, Lindsey alleviated her feelings of
loneliness by getting high off the fumes from the ink of the
ditto machine. Who knew why, after all these years, the nuns
still used the mimeograph instead of the digital copier? Maybe
wielding the hand-crank of the old contraption kept their slap-
ping arms in top form and brought a little extra-credit suffering to daily life.

At St. Maude's, outdated technology was somehow regarded as more pious than state-of-the-art machinery. Actually, Lindsey had a theory that the nuns kept their old ways
because they, too, were addicted to the pleasant, incidental
highs that could be had in an antiquated workplace. Who
needed colorless, odorless glue, when rubber cement did the
job and gave off those soothing, stress-reducing fumes? Noting the office was strangely quiet, Lindsey imagined all the
penguins huddled in the infirmary sniffing Liquid Paper and
doing shots of Robitussin.

Lindsey held a couple of loose-leaf pages to her nose and
inhaled deeply. As she enjoyed the astringent vapors that rose

off the damp sheets of paper, she read Sister Constance's instructions for the day. The jubilee was fast approaching, and it was up to Lindsey to locate hundreds of missing alumni.

Glancing over the long list of names, she wondered how Sister Constance could expect her to track down all of them. Some addresses and phone numbers hadn't been updated for ten to twenty years, and she didn't have the slightest idea how long it would take to find the ones with such common names, like "Mark Wong." It was going to take a lot of legwork on her part to dig up the hiding places of her fellow Marauders, and it seemed like a lot of trouble just to invite them to the school's Welcome-Back-We-Still-Think-You're-Sinners-but-Now-Desperately-Need-Your-Money jubilee.

Lindsey, Mrs. Grupico, and Mrs. Mann were all sharing the task of finding the wayward alums. Lindsey was not privy to how the lists were divided, but Mrs. Grupico seemed to have laid claim to tracking down all the Italians, while Mrs. Mann took on the Irish and occasional Portuguese. As for Lindsey, she supposed it made some sense, but she was still a bit annoyed that she was assigned the list of Chinese names, as if her non-fluency in both Cantonese and Mandarin could possibly come in handy.

Working from a mimeographed list with random updates from sporadic years scrawled in the margins, she cross-checked addresses and phone numbers with Internet directories and the telephone book. As she plodded through the tedious work, the only thing that kept her from going nuts was listening to the *Hits of the Eighties* compilation CD that Dustin had given her.

88 Lines About 44 Chinese Kids

In *The Dim Sum of All Things,* I mentioned that Lindsey was really into music from the eighties. One song that really captured that era was *88 Lines About 44 Women* by The Nails. I imagined that this was one of the tunes on the CD that Dustin burned for her, and I pictured Lindsey toiling away at work while the song became etched on her brain with repeated listenings. With so many people to call about the reunion, to help remember who was who, she wrote her notes in the same format as the song:

Nelson was a dirty boy
He took a crap then disappeared
Glenn Wong was gone after lunch
Murdered by nuns, everyone feared
Franklin was a gay guy
Was always stylish, avoided perms
Johnny barfed in the yard
Spaghetti-Os like chewed-up worms

Jeff Lee was a round-head boy
He cracked his melon on the sink
Debbie looked like a baboon
Kids used to call her "missing link"
Nellie had a skin disease
Left little flecks atop her desk
Hoover ate paste at recess
His fingers bled, left a mess

Darren split, moved to L.A.
His mom gave no address or phone
Yong was eating chicken wings
Heard him gnawing on a bone
Arthur was a busy dad
Babies crying in the background
Dirk was a heavy breather
Wouldn't talk, he made no sound

Lindsey called all these people and caught them at odd
moments. She talked to mouth-breathers, people who were
eating, and others who felt free to tell her the most random
information:

Ruthie worked at Safeway now
She was the store's fastest checker
Humphrey Chang was a bus driver
Now he drove a double-decker
Garren Chew was another boy
Worked in TV, won an Emmy
Arnold had a funny face
Like a Chinese Steve Buscemi

Horatio raced motorbikes
Smashed his leg up in a crash
His friend, Rob, was not so lucky
Died young, cremated into ash
May was a social butterfly
Her Call Waiting beeped, said goodbye
Jackson said he'd try to come
If only time would heal his sty

Vincent was a rich film mogul
Tried to call back from his plane
Lincoln was an edgy artist
Thought reunions were mundane
Jasmine's voice was a monotone
Just like talking to a wall

Anselm Chin was one bad-ass mo-fo
He didn't take no shit at all
(Uh-uh. Not Anselm.)

Melvin had moved to Chicago
Would fly back to see the gang
Oliver would donate some food
From his restaurant, House of Wang
Helmond was a stoner surfer
On the phone he fell asleep
Tiffany was overtly shy
Didn't utter a single peep

Ingrid was a renowned doctor
Busy at UCSF
Raymond, always good at sports
Worked for the NBA as a ref
Alex had a wife named Jing
Who spoke no English—please call back
Pam bragged about her boob job
Couldn't wait to show off her rack

Kelvin Toy was so excited, said
Sure, he'd be there in a jiffy
William sounded oh-so-snobby
When called "Bill" he got miffy
Ulysses was way more friendly
Said he'd make it if he could
Clarence was a total pervert
Said right now he had stiff wood

Lonnie worked the graveyard shift
Voice mail said, "Call back at nine"
Jimmy was like Uncle Elmore
Said, "Don't jive me, what's your sign?"
Sergio couldn't talk now
A baby slept in his lap
Morris was an angry man

Had no time for this crap
Oi's name was always mispronounced
Was half Chinese, and also Hmong
Dan was a couch potato
Heard him sucking from a bong
Nathan moved to O-hi-o
Sourdough bread was what he missed . . .
Dustin Lee, where's that kiss?
You're the last to end this list

88 Lines about 44 Chinese Kids

A Guided Tour Through Lindsey Owyang's San Francisco

I think of the City of San Francisco as one of the main characters in the book. I was always thinking of specific places and also certain times in the city's history, and tried to weave them together with the past and present stories of Lindsey and her family.

Golden Gate Park: Anyone who grew up in San Francisco probably has great memories of Steinhart Aquarium and the African Hall, and Lindsey is no exception. She would have gone to these places at least once a year on school field trips, so when she chaperones the third grade, it's another trip down memory lane. As for those places now, they've been demolished. After writing the scenes that took place there, I trekked over to the park on a fact-checking mission and found the places were gone, and won't be the same ever again, even though they were unchanged for, like, fifty years. (Anyone who wants to take a peek at how these places looked in the past can catch glimpses of them in two disparate movies, *The Lady from Shanghai* and *Howard the Duck*.)

    The stalactites in the underground walkways had been around since the 1894 Midwinter Fair, but I think they are mostly gone now, too. Thankfully, those sphinxes with the huge boobs near the DeYoung Museum are still there. Where did they come from, and how did they survive while so many other parts of the park got the wrecking ball? I'm convinced it's all about the boobs. If those sphinxes didn't have those mysterious D-cups, I'm sure they'd have been demolished long ago.

Lastly, there really was a crazy heat wave a few years back, and there was this one week when you could simultaneously smell the ocean, peppery freesia, jasmine, and gasoline. And ugly people were having sex. I'm sure of it.

Mrs. Clemens's House: With Mrs. Clemens, I wanted to create a link between Old San Francisco and the present. When I was in high school, I actually did meet an old woman who lived in a crazy house like hers, and I found out many years later that she supposedly had run a brothel. I have no idea if this woman is still around, but the memory of her has always fascinated me.

The Western Addition is a great setting because it's a moody neighborhood where there are hardly any shoppers, just old houses and empty sidewalks. In 1906 the city took great pains to save it from the fire that accompanied the earthquake, so there's a high concentration of old mansions with really ornate facades and architectural embellishments. To help me conjure the look of her house, I walked the neighborhood and took pictures of an angel with a third eye, flowery plasterwork, and twisted, cast-iron gates. The end result was that the outside of Mrs. Clemens's house is a mishmash of parts from actual places. For anyone, including myself, who's ever wished they could be invited into one of these old places to have a look around, we can all live vicariously through Lindsey as she wanders through Mrs. Clemens's crumbling Victorian, which is like a closed museum that nobody gets to see.

I mentioned that Mrs. Clemens was related to a lady named Ella. Not long ago I saw a postcard from the early 1900s of a Caucasian woman posing with her Chinese husband in front of their Grant Avenue shop. They sold "earthquake relics," which was basically broken stuff they'd saved after the 1906 disaster. Old San Francisco wasn't even that old yet, but they already had an inkling that nostalgia and memories were alluring. There was another postcard, too, that displayed their mixed-race daughter, Ah-Yoko, in the shop window. The fact that they were semi-famous in their day and that someone had made souvenir postcards of them proved to me that even at the turn of that century, the Asian-American combo was fascinating and compelling to people.

Chinatown: In describing the Chinatown of Lindsey's childhood I rely heavily on my own memories. Some readers are very familiar with the streets, stores, and restaurants I describe, but some know just a little, and it's hard to balance writing for both audiences. Some people might say, "Oh yeah, that old man with the goiter. I used to see him in Portsmouth Square every day." Others have no idea why I'm going on about this guy, but he really was a fixture for years.

Where would Lindsey go in Chinatown? She and Michael would probably eat at this hole-in-the-wall restaurant on Washington Street called Lucky Creation, and she'd shop at Suey Chong, which is a deluxe shop that's every Hoarder Lady's dream come true. Farther down Grant Avenue is Eastern Bakery, where they sell all sorts of Chinese pastries, but I imagine Lindsey is addicted to the glazed donuts there.

What's Real and What's Not

People ask me a lot what's real and what's made up. They want to know if this story is about my life. I tell them it's not necessarily my family, but somewhere, sometime, these feelings and situations were true for someone. And sometimes, yes, true for me.

Was my grandmother born in a basement on Waverly Place? No, but someone's grandmother was. I don't know how, but their story is in my brain . . . or maybe it's a Chinese thing, and these details are just slightly different for all of us, but we all carry around the blood-soaked feelings and memories of hardship that our families share.

I see many Lindseys walking around San Francisco. Sometimes she is across the street, or sometimes wearing my shoes. Sometimes I recognize her in a thirteen-year-old girl walking home from school, other times she is the actual age she is in the book, but driving a different car from what I might expect. I see her at the movies with her friends, or sometimes waiting at the bus stop. Sometimes she's me, but other times I just see her around, living her San Francisco life, and I wish her well.

KIM WONG KELTNER

Rolf Keltner

When **KIM WONG KELTNER** isn't writing, she collects Chinese porcelain and plays Whack-a-Mole. She lives in San Francisco with her husband and daughter, whose first words were "capybara" and "museum quality."